ARKHAM HORROR

It is the height of the Roaring Twenties – a fresh enthusiasm for the arts, science, and exploration of the past have opened doors to a wider world, and beyond...

And yet, a dark shadow grows over the town of Arkham. Alien entities known as Ancient Ones lurk in the emptiness beyond space and time, writhing at the thresholds between worlds.

Occult rituals must be stopped and alien creatures destroyed before the Ancient Ones make our world their ruined dominion.

Only a handful of brave souls with inquisitive minds and the will to act stand against the horrors threatening to tear this world apart.

Will they prevail?

ALSO AVAILABLE

ARKHAM HORROR

Wrath of N'kai by Josh Reynolds
The Last Ritual by S A Sidor
Mask of Silver by Rosemary Jones
Litany of Dreams by Ari Marmell
The Devourer Below edited by Charlotte Llewelyn-Wells
Dark Origins: The Collected Novellas Vol 1
Cult of the Spider Queen by S A Sidor

DESCENT: LEGENDS OF THE DARK

The Doom of Fallowhearth by Robbie MacNiven
The Shield of Daqan by David Guymer
The Gates of Thelgrim by Robbie MacNiven

KEYFORGE

Tales From the Crucible edited by Charlotte Llewelyn-Wells
The Qubit Zirconium by M Darusha Wehm

LEGEND OF THE FIVE RINGS

Curse of Honor by David Annandale
Poison River by Josh Reynolds
The Night Parade of 100 Demons by Marie Brennan
Death's Kiss by Josh Reynolds
The Great Clans of Rokugan: The Collected Novellas Vol 1

PANDEMIC

Patient Zero by Amanda Bridgeman

TERRAFORMING MARS

In the Shadow of Deimos by Jane Killick

TWILIGHT IMPERIUM

The Fractured Void by Tim Pratt
The Necropolis Empire by Tim Pratt

ZOMBICIDE

Last Resort by Josh Reynolds

ARKHAM HORROR™

The
DEVOURER
BELOW

EDITED BY
CHARLOTTE LLEWELYN-WELLS

ACONYTE

First published by Aconyte Books in 2021

ISBN 978 1 83908 096 8

Ebook ISBN 978 1 83908 097 5

Cover art by John Coulthart

Distributed in North America by Simon & Schuster Inc, New York, USA

Printed in the United States of America

9 8 7 6 5 4 3 2

ACONYTE BOOKS

An imprint of Asmodee Entertainment Ltd

Mercury House, Shipstones Business Centre

North Gate, Nottingham NG7 7FN, UK

aconytebooks.com // twitter.com/aconytebooks

CONTENTS

Running the Night Whiskey by Evan Dicken   7

Shadows Dawning by Georgina Kamsika   47

The Hounds Below by Josh Reynolds   89

Labyrinth by Thomas Parrott   117

All My Friends Are Monsters by Davide Mana   157

The Darkling Woods by Cath Lauria   199

Professor Warren's Investiture by David Annandale   227

Sins In the Blood by Thomas Parrott   249

Litany of Dreams by Ari Marmell   293

Contributors   309

RUNNING THE NIGHT WHISKEY
Evan Dicken

They crept like rats in the night – two men Leo could see, and at least one he couldn't. Normally, they would've never gotten past the shabby brick wall separating Leo De Luca's apartment from the jumble of warehouses lining Arkham's River Street, but he'd been up all night losing his bankroll to a gaggle of shysters in a backroom of the Nightingale Club. Leo had been cheating, of course, they'd just been cheating better. Last call had found him red-eyed and stumbling, his pockets lighter by the roll of C-notes he'd planned on turning into Miskatonic County's newest still.

Now, Leo lay stretched out on the threadbare davenport, mouth tasting of whiskey and stale Chesterfields, moonlight streaming through his open window. He considered drawing the curtains, but the tepid breeze wafting off the Miskatonic River was the only thing that kept him from roasting in the late summer heat.

Boots scuffed on the alley outside. Leo was already up and moving before something heavy slammed against his door. Even in a fog of whiskey fumes, he had remembered to bar it – a habit left over from a childhood spent in the rougher outskirts of Biloxi. Unfortunately, Leo's riot shotgun was leaning against the icebox in the kitchen, and his nickel-plated Colt 1911 lay buried somewhere beneath the pile of castoff clothes near the door.

Leo snatched up the contents of the nearby coffee table and was moving before the next hit, gin bottle in one fist, a handful of loose change in the other. When the bar gave way, he flung the change at the man who stumbled through. The mug flinched as coins rattled off his face, earning a bottle to the skull for his hesitation. Gin and glass scattered across the floor.

Bloodied, but still moving, the man swung a length of iron pipe like he was fixing to round the bases. Leo had been in enough scraps to know he wasn't getting out of the way in time, so he stepped into the swing, letting the man's arms glance off his shoulder. He'd have a helluva bruise the next day, but it was better than a leaky skull.

Leo grabbed the man's coat collar, gently but firmly guiding his unwelcome visitor face-first into the wall.

There was a flicker of movement in the doorway.

Leo threw himself back to avoid the downward arc of a baseball bat. He had just enough time to register relief that neither of his attackers had guns before the bat's backswing clipped him in the jaw. The fact that whoever had sent these lugs to bum rush Leo didn't want him dead proved little consolation as he crashed through his second-favorite chair.

Boards creaked under heavy footsteps as the second attacker closed the distance.

Leo kicked blindly toward the noise. The momentary glimmer of satisfaction he felt as his heel connected with the man's shin was quickly eclipsed by dismay as the big mug fell on top of him. After that, it was all knees and elbows, the two of them rolling amidst clothes and broken glass. Leo did his best, but the guy on top was broad-shouldered as a longshoreman, with a face that looked like it had been hacked from bedrock.

Granite-Face got ahold of Leo's neck and gave his head a good wallop against the boards. It felt like the girls in the Nightingale's dubious "chorus line" were tap-tap-tapping on his skull.

Leo drove a finger into Granite-Face's eye, followed by a slap to the ear. He drew in a racking breath as the lug let up for a second, then twisted to feel around amidst the balled-up clothes. Something hard had dug into his ribs as they rolled across the floor, and Leo was willing to bet a case of uncut whiskey it wasn't one of his wingtips.

His fingers brushed metal, and he snatched up the Colt. When Granite-Face regained his bearings he found himself staring down the barrel of a pistol.

"That's enough." Leo kept his voice level as he could manage. It was always best to look like you were in control, especially when you were very much not.

The man raised his hands, leaning back nice and slow so Leo could scramble away. A glance to the door showed Granite-Face's colleague still ensconced in the loving embrace of Leo's front wall.

He got to his feet, pistol never wavering. Things had been dicey for a bit, but all in all, it seemed like Leo had the situation in hand.

Which made it all the more surprising when he felt the cold jab of a rifle muzzle between his shoulder blades.

"Drop the Colt." The man's tone was calm, his voice vaguely familiar.

"Mind if I set it on the table?" Leo asked. "Don't want to scuff the finish."

"Sure. Anything for a pal."

Leo laid the pistol on the table, slow and careful. The other two lugs looked to be straight bruisers, probably hired out of some Boston gin joint for a bottle of hooch and a few bucks off their tab. But the man with the rifle – the man Leo *would've* been looking for if he hadn't been working off a night of heavy drinking punctuated by a mild concussion – he felt like a professional.

"I know why you're here," Leo said.

"Do you?"

"Listen, you can tell Johnny V that I'll have his cash in a few–"

"Turn around."

Leo winced. It was never a good sign when a button man wanted to see your face.

"I said turn around."

Leo turned.

The man lowered his rifle to grab the front of Leo's shirt. Expecting the worst, Leo was startled when the man dragged him close to plant a kiss on each cheek.

"Corporal De Luca, you old booze hound, what the

hell are you doing in Massachusetts?"

"Donny?"

He offered a sloppy salute. "Private Donald Alighieri reporting for duty."

Donny Alighieri was paler than he'd been when the Germans had shelled them at Apremont. The years had hollowed dark circles under his eyes and left a scattering of gray in his black mustache, but Leo still recognized the smile, made crooked by the long scar a German trench knife had carved from cheek to chin.

"Christ, how'd you get mixed up with these goons?" Leo thrust his chin at GraniteFace, who was staring, open-mouthed, at the two of them.

Donny shrugged. "I could ask you the same question."

"Why you jawin' with this sap?" Granite-Face took a threatening step toward Leo. "He put Tony through a wall!"

Donny placed a hand on the big man's chest. "That's enough, Phil."

"But Johnny V said rough him up."

"He looks pretty rough to me," Donny said. "Why don't you help Tony outside while the big boys talk?"

Phil looked about to argue, but something in Donny's expression seemed to settle the large man. He stomped over to pull a half-conscious Tony from the wall, glaring at Leo the whole while.

Happy as he was to not have his face rearranged, Leo couldn't quite summon any gratitude. Especially since Donny was still the one with the rifle. Leo settled for a level stare as Donny waited for Phil to drag his moaning partner out onto the street.

"Sorry about all that." Donny waved an absent hand at the wreckage. "Gotta keep up appearances."

"I'd pour you a drink, but I spilled my last bottle over Tony's head." Leo gestured at the couch. "Mind if I sit? It's been a helluva night."

"Be my guest." Donny pulled up Leo's favorite chair and sat, rifle resting across his knees.

Leo looked around for a cigarette, and, finding none, settled back into the couch with a sad shake of his head.

"So you're working for Johnny V now?"

"Isn't everybody?"

"So why the talk?" Leo sighed. "Shouldn't you and the two gorillas outside be fitting me for new kneecaps?"

"Can't two old army chums catch up a bit?" Donny asked. "Couldn't believe when I heard you were into Johnny V for five large. What the hell happened?"

"Prohis confiscated a big load I had coming down from Montreal, then they knocked over two of my stills. Next thing I know there's G-men snooping around the Nightingale club."

"Golly, didn't you pay them off?"

"Course I did. Johnny V just paid them more. He's always been keen to put the squeeze on us independent operators." As it always did, mention of Johnny V made Leo want to bare his teeth. He'd had a real good thing going in Arkham until the self-styled "Baron of Boston" stretched his spirituous tentacles down the coast.

"That's what I wanted to talk to you about."

"I know we go back a long way, Donny, but I'll tell you the same as I told the last three fellas Johnny sent by:

this is just a setback."

Donny held up a hand. "I'm not here to shut you down, Leo – quite the opposite."

Leo blew out a long breath. "Is this the part where you rake me over the coals with some lowball offer to buy me out?"

"Nothing of the sort," Donny laughed. "I've got a friend, runs a still across the Canadian border out near Coaticook. Strange fella, but he can really cook. Calls his stuff 'night whiskey'. It's black as tar and thick as molasses, but it'll knock you down faster than Jack Dempsey's left hook."

"What are we talking?" Leo asked.

"A quick jaunt up to Canada for two cases of the stuff. I've already got a buyer lined up." Donny flashed his lopsided grin. "They're willing to pay through the nose, twenty large. I figure we split it fifty-fifty, which gets you out of Johnny V's pocket with some green to spare."

"What about Johnny V?" Leo leaned forward, interested despite himself. "What's his end?"

"That's the beauty of it, Johnny don't know nothing," Donny said. "That's why I came to you."

"So what's the catch?" Leo asked. He'd lived enough life to know offers that seemed too good to be true usually were.

"No catch." Donny spread his hands. "If things go well, we might even be able to make it a regular thing."

"This ain't some Chaplin movie, Donny." Leo shook his head. "Some old army chum I haven't seen for years shows up out of the blue to drop a golden egg in my lap? More like Johnny V wants me to save him the trouble of dragging my corpse into the sticks after he puts a bullet in my head."

"You wound me, corporal." Donny nodded at the broken door. "If I wanted you dead, those two lugs outside would be happy to oblige."

Leo chewed his lip, considering. Apart from the loan, he didn't owe Johnny V a red cent. And it wasn't like turning down this job would put him in the mob boss' good graces. At the end of the day, Leo had nothing but a fast car, a failing gin joint, and a mountain of debt to his name.

He blew out a deep breath. "When do we leave?"

"Soon as I can shake those two." Donny hooked a thumb toward the street.

"I'll have the car gassed and ready," Leo said. "Meet me at the Garrison Street bridge in two hours."

"There's the 'Louisiana Lion' I remember." Donny slapped Leo on the knee, then stood to leave. He made a half-hearted attempt to shut the door behind him, but only succeeded in pulling it further off its hinges.

Leo scrubbed a hand through his hair as he surveyed the wreckage of his front room. The scuffle had left him too juiced to sleep, and just the thought of cleaning up made his head throb. Besides, if things went south on the run, a clean apartment would be the least of Leo's worries.

He knelt to rummage through the tangle of clothes for his shoes and hat, then retrieved his pistol and headed into the kitchen for the shotgun. Better to have and not need, and all that malarkey.

Whistling, Leo stepped over the remains of his door. Despite the new bruises, he felt strangely pleased. Painful as the night had been, it seemed Leo's luck was about to change.

Speaking of luck – he wondered if there were any card games still running.

"She really does purr, doesn't she?" Donny gave the car's dashboard an affectionate pat.

"Studebaker EK Big Six, faster than any of those clunkers the bulls drive." Leo checked the side mirror, frowning at the car behind them. They had left Arkham just ahead of the sun and driven north most of the morning, stopping only for a bit of gas and runny eggs at a hash joint just outside of Ipswich. Roads had been mostly clear, until the green Model T had fallen in behind them.

"Whatcha staring at?" Donny started to turn, but Leo nudged him.

"Use the mirrors." Leo nodded at the side view. "That Model T has followed us for the last three turns."

"Think it's a copper?"

"Might be the prohis," Leo replied. "But they all drive black cars."

"What's the matter if it is?" Donny chuckled. "It's not like we're packing any hooch."

"We've got guns."

Donny shrugged. "No law against that."

Leo sucked air through his teeth. "Just rubs me the wrong way, is all."

"You're the expert." Donny held up his hands. "If you wanna lose 'em, let's lose 'em."

Grinning, Leo gave the car a bit more gas.

The Model T kept pace, never drawing too close, but always staying barely in sight. Despite his anxiety, Leo couldn't help but feel a bit of admiration for the driver. In the years since Prohibition, Leo had seen his share of tails, and this one was a pro. If he hadn't known exactly what to look for, the Model T would've skimmed just below notice.

He glanced at Donny, suddenly wary. "You sure you didn't tell no one about this run?"

"Scout's honor."

"Let's see how he likes a bit of flash." Leo shifted gears, opening up the throttle. Had they been on twisting backroads it would've been more of a contest, but although the county road wasn't paved, it was straight enough for Leo to really build up some speed. Within a few minutes they had left the Model T sputtering behind.

"At this rate, we'll be north of the border by sunset." Donny let out a low whistle as Leo let up on the gas. "This is the life, eh?"

"Ain't that the truth." Leo nodded, keeping an eye toward the scattered pine and dogwood trees lining the bumpy country road. In this heat, the county coppers were like as not to be sitting back on a porch somewhere with their feet up, but the Model T had made Leo jumpy. He knew the backwoods roads from Innsmouth to Montreal better than any two-bit prohis, but it always paid to keep an eye peeled.

"To think, just a few years ago we were squatting in that trench outside Epieds." Donny gave a tilt of his head. "Now look at us."

Leo returned a tepid smile. He'd come out of his time with the 104th unscathed apart from a fleck of German ordnance in his thigh, but that didn't mean he wanted to be reminded of those days.

"Jerries thought they had us pinned down, but we showed 'em, didn't we?"

Leo's nod was more of a wince, but Donny never could take a hint. Some men moved on, others dragged the past wherever they went.

They crossed the Vermont border and jogged east along an overgrown county road. Leo let Donny rattle on, the occasional nod enough to keep the other man happy. He'd forgotten how much Donny talked. Back in the war, nothing short of a gas attack had seemed able to shut the man up. Still, it was better than the alternative. Donny would go for hours, sometimes days. Then it would be like someone had shut off a spigot, and he'd turn all sharp and angry. The rest of the squad knew to leave well enough alone when Donny was in one of his "moods", and woe befall any German who crossed his path.

Leo focused on driving. The roads were clear as a summer sky, and a breeze cut the lingering humidity. A bit of off-roading took them over a pasture and onto an old logging road that snaked up into Canada. Although not the smoothest of rides, it had the benefit of avoiding border checkpoints. Apart from a brief stop to stretch their legs and answer nature's call, they made good time.

Coaticook was a town of a few hundred souls, settled by British loyalists fleeing New England in the decades after American independence. It was far enough off the beaten track for the locals to comment on strangers, so Leo gave it a wide berth, interrupting Donny's monologue to get directions.

The route led into low hills, the road tapering off into

little more than a rutted track as it wound around the edge of a marshy lake. Leo wasn't willing to risk bogging his car down in the mud, so they had to hoof the last mile.

There was something about the place that made the skin between Leo's shoulder blades prickle. Like when they had cleared the Jerry machine guns out of Epieds, but weren't quite sure they'd gotten the last of the snipers. Try as he might, Leo couldn't shake the suspicion someone lay hidden, just waiting for him to blunder into their field of fire.

"Leave the shotgun," Donny said. "Old Enoch can be a bit jumpy."

Heading into the woods with just his Colt left a sour taste in Leo's mouth, but it was better than catching a bullet from a nervous bootlegger.

"Harrow," Donny said, as they squelched along the edge of the lake.

"Come again?"

"It's what this town used to be called." Donny gestured at the water.

"I don't see any town."

"Whole place flooded just after the Revolution. Over a hundred settlers up from just north of Arkham." Donny snapped his fingers. "Gone just like that."

Leo whistled, looking out over the lake. Leaves rustled overhead, stirred by a gentle breeze. The lake's surface stayed flat as a sheet of tempered glass, undisturbed by even the smallest ripple.

"People say it was God's punishment on account of the settlers being witches or somesuch. Story goes they got up to all sort of strange malarkey – moonlight rituals, great pits dug into the earth. Some folks say they even snatched babies from the local Abenaki, if you can believe it."

"Sounds like a load of bunk to me."

"Can't say for sure, but I've been out with Enoch when the silt settles. If the water is clear enough you can even see the church steeple, and what's on top ain't a cross. Sometimes a body even comes loose and floats up from the muck." Donny's grin was almost predatory in the light of the setting sun.

Leo glanced at the lake, unsettled despite himself. He'd seen more than his share of corpses over in France, but the thought of a whole town of bodies bobbing up through the churning murk set the hair rising on the back of his neck.

A rifle shot echoed through the deepening shadows. Leo reached for his Colt, but Donny laid a hand on his arm.

"Don't mind that." He nodded at a ragged copse of pine down the bank. "Just Enoch saying hello."

Donny raised both hands, walking slowly forward. He glanced back when Leo didn't follow.

"Don't tell me the Louisiana Lion's afraid of some old coot with a .22."

"Biloxi, actually."

"What's that now?"

"I'm from Mississippi. Louisiana just sounded better," Leo muttered as he sloshed into ankle-deep mud. The muck seemed to swallow Leo's footfalls, the evening breeze cool on his sweat-streaked skin. Unease twisted in his gut. It was a feeling that had saved Leo's life more than once, and he found his hand creeping to his Colt despite Donny's smiling assurances.

They ducked beneath the spreading pines, limbs sketching long shadows in the last light of day. The sharp tang of sap filled Leo's nose, undercut by a strange sickly odor.

"Enoch must be cooking." Donny sniffed the air. "Smells like a million bucks, eh?"

Leo wrinkled his nose. He'd worked enough stills to recognize the syrupy tang of corn mash or the rich malty aroma of barley. This was more like stink that had wafted from the medical tents when the wind changed direction. Leo swallowed against the sudden tightness in his throat.

Whatever Enoch was cooking, it wasn't grain.

The pine cleared to reveal a ramshackle structure – old boards and bits of corrugated steel hammered into something approximately cabin-shaped. Behind it was the strangest still Leo had ever seen.

Low fires burned beneath half a dozen long copper boxes. About the size of a bathtub, they were each capped by a curving metal bowl, a nest of tangled piping above leading to an oddly shaped condenser. Roughly cylindrical, its outline rippled like frozen flame, eight fluted tubes curling out like tendrils from a hothouse vine. The condenser seemed almost to shift and roil in the shadows. Leo realized the whole thing was made of glass, the apparent movement caused by the steady drip, drip of the thick, tarlike distillation through its twining innards.

A high, rasping gurgle rose above the crackle of pine logs. Leo thought it was steam escaping the boilers until a tall figure rounded the still. Clad in a ragged work shirt and overalls, the man cradled a crate of empty bottles in his knobby arms. Donny had said Enoch was old, but the moonshiner's face was smooth as a boiled egg, nary a bit of stubble to be seen on his cheeks or head. His eyes were large and pale, almost luminous in the evening light, his nose little more than two black slashes. From Enoch's mouth came a sound like someone trying to talk through a slit throat.

Leo had his Colt halfway from its shoulder holster before he realized the man was singing.

"Enoch, old pal!" Donny swaggered into the clearing, arms spread wide.

Enoch turned his rheumy gaze upon the two of them, his song tapering into a low hiss.

"Brought some more of that jerky you like." Donny fished a wax-paper bag from his pocket.

Enoch set the crate down and took the bag, his eyes never leaving Leo.

"Oh, Leo? He's a peach," Donny chuckled. "We were over in France together."

Enoch slipped a ragged strip of jerky into his mouth, chewing loudly.

"Don't be like that," Donny said. "Everything's copacetic. We'll settle up later."

The moonshiner's eyes narrowed to slits, lips drawn back from teeth the yellow of old newsprint. He extended one long finger toward a ratty tarp tented against the cabin's side wall.

Donny grinned at Leo. "I think he likes you."

Leo followed Donny toward the cabin, taking care to give the old moonshiner a wide berth. There were two crates under the tarp, each big enough to hold a dozen bottles. Leo bent to heft one, and found it surprisingly heavy.

Donny nudged him. "Careful, this stuff's worth its weight in gold."

Enoch gnawed on his jerky, watching the two men stump back toward the treeline. Leo's shoe caught an exposed root, and he lurched forward with a rattle of glass, almost stumbling into one of the low fires.

"Watch the flames." Donny nodded at the crate of night whiskey. "One spark and that stuff goes up like a Molotov."

Leo steadied himself. He glanced back just before they entered the pines and found the old moonshiner still staring.

"Your friend doesn't say much," Leo said, as they squelched back toward the car.

"Give him time to warm up," Donny said. "He'll talk your ear off."

As if to echo Donny's reply, Enoch's rough warbling cut through the evening like a church bell, the whine of cicadas seeming to rise in tuneless accompaniment.

It might have been an echo, but Leo swore he heard an answering song from across the lake.

He squinted across the water, but the shadowed trees on the far side appeared empty. The lap of waves on Leo's shoes caused him to look down. Ripples spread across the lake as if something large had momentarily broken the dark surface to regard the two interlopers on the bank.

With a shiver, Leo quickened his step.

Donny matched his pace without a word.

They were just driving around a bend in the wood when the Model T hit them with the brights. It straddled the road ahead, trees rising on either side. The top was up, so Leo couldn't see inside.

"What do we do?" Donny asked.

With a tight smile, Leo dropped the Studebaker into second gear, flicking the wheel left before spinning it hard to the right. The rear wheels kicked up a shower of dirt as the car spun in a quick half-circle. A moment, and they were facing the opposite direction.

From behind, Leo heard gravel popping under tires as the strange car gave chase.

He flicked off the headlamps, driving by the light of the thin streamer of stars visible through the branches overhead. The car crested a hill and went airborne for a second. Leo relaxed, flexing like a leaf spring as they hit dirt. Donny had followed his instincts and gone rigid. The only thing that kept the impact from jouncing him from his seat was Leo's outflung arm.

Leo turned onto a side path, wending alongside some farmer's orchard before doubling back along an old tractor trail. Back on the main road Leo opened up the throttle, letting the car shoot the curves.

After twenty miles without seeing headlamps, Leo finally let up on the gas.

"That was some pretty slick driving," Donny said.

"No one outruns me on my roads." Leo shook his head. He'd mapped every track, trail, and country lane from

Arkham to Montreal; it would take more than slick driving to get the drop on him.

A hundred yards up the road, a pair of headlamps clicked on. The sudden brilliance made Leo squint, but not so much he couldn't catch the flash of green paint behind the light.

Donny swore.

Leo expected to feel anger at being outplayed, but instead a strange lightness filled his chest. It was the same feeling he got staring across the poker table at a canny player, a sense of jittery excitement as Leo decided whether to fold or double down.

His lips drew back in an expression that was part grin, part snarl. Leo wasn't folding, not when he held all the cards.

He sent them careening down the embankment into an old cattle field. Unbelievably, the Model T followed. They jounced across uneven grass for the better part of ten minutes, their pursuer's headlamps flickering in the side mirrors.

"What are you doing?" Donny shouted as they shot across a tiny stream and along a low ridge.

"I can't shake him on the backtrails, but the county road should be just beyond this field," Leo replied. "He'll never be able to catch us on the straightaway."

They crashed through a tangle of branches and out onto an expanse of paved road. Leo threw the car into high gear, smiling as their pursuer's headlamps grew distant.

He had just about started to breathe easy again when he saw the prohis.

They had pulled a truck across the road, two other cars idling off on the shoulder. Leo's first thought was that their pursuer had herded them into a trap, until he saw the Model T's lights flicker and head the other way.

"Of all the rotten luck." Scowling, Donny reached for his rifle, but Leo laid a hand on his arm.

"Wait."

Donny cocked his head. "Wait for what?"

"To see if they start shooting."

The crack of gunfire told him all he needed to know.

"They're in Johnny V's pocket." Leo switched gears, accelerating toward the blockade.

The prohis' shots kicked up plumes of dust. Leo kept the car straight, partly to make for a smaller target, and partly to shield the night whiskey. It was packed tight in hidden compartments below the back seat, but if the stuff was as flammable as Donny said, he didn't want a stray shot setting it off.

"How'd you know they're Johnny V's?" Donny hunched behind the dash.

"Only the crooked ones shoot first," Leo said, as they bore down on the roadblock. "See if you can return the favor."

"With pleasure." Donny snatched up his rifle. "Just keep her steady."

They took a couple more shots as Leo bore down on them, muzzle flashes bright as lightning against the darkened trees. One bullet clipped Leo's right mirror, showering him with broken glass.

Whooping, Donny fired back. One of the prohis

tumbled from the truck, clutching a bleeding hand. The others scrambled back, heads low.

Leo jerked the wheel to send the Studebaker skidding along the stony left shoulder. Branches shrieked across the car as they edged by the truck and back onto the road. Leo glanced back to see a prohis staring at them from where he crouched behind the hood, mouth open, pistol held in front of him like a shield.

Then Leo was off into the night. Brakes squealed farther back as the agents ran afoul of their own blockade.

The smell of scorched rubber thick in his nose, Leo straightened the car and sped down the road. Now the initial rush of nerves had faded, he was left with anger and questions. He'd known Johnny V's pet prohis were leaning on his operation, but he hadn't figured they'd copped to his routes.

Johnny must've given them everything. Suddenly, the reason for the missing whiskey shipment became clear. It was probably getting cut right now in some Boston warehouse.

Leo broke into a savage grin. These G-men might know this run, but he'd bet his Studebaker they didn't know *all* his routes.

"Stay low," he nodded to Donny. Dim light flickered in his remaining side mirror as the prohis got moving again. Leo kept up a good clip, fast enough to keep out of view, but not so quick he would spin out on a turn.

About three miles down the winding road they passed a row of jagged boulders, and Leo slowed down to scan the shadowed ridge.

"Geez, you want them to nab us?" Donny glanced back.

"Get out."

"What?"

"There's an old wagon trail here, mostly overgrown, but wide enough for a car if we're careful." Leo thrust his chin at the barest break in the tree cover. "When I pull in, I need you to move the brush back into place."

Donny regarded him for a moment, frowning.

"If I wanted to leave you for the G-men," Leo pointed out, "I'd have pushed you out as we drove by."

The rumble of engines from back up the road seemed to make up Donny's mind, and he slid out of the car with a nod.

Leo turned off the road, threading the Studebaker's long body through the tiny gap in the woods. Although he could hear the prohis coming up, he moved slow, careful not to break any of the hanging branches. Donny stepped in behind to straighten the crushed grass and move the limbs back into place.

The car rattled another dozen yards down the furrowed path, then Leo shut off the engine. Hunkering down in his seat, he felt around in the back for his shotgun. Leo had no qualms about getting pinched, but these weren't normal prohis. The only thing Leo could look forward to if they nabbed him was a bullet in the skull.

Leo sighted on the distant road. In the dim moonlight, he could see Donny crouched behind a rock outcrop a little way back, rifle in hand. He didn't worry the other man would give them away – these punk G-men were a far cry from German snipers.

Two cars shot by, leaves fluttering in the wind of their passing. The truck came behind, slower. Leo could see the shadow of three men inside, one driver and two in the flatbed with handheld spotlights. They scanned the forest to either side.

The truck pulled abreast of the trail entrance, and stopped.

Leo glanced toward Donny, who nodded at the man in the bed of the truck. Leo sighted on the other one with a lamp.

Searchlights stabbed amidst the trees. Leo shut his eyes against the glare, finger tight on the trigger of his shotgun.

One of the prohis muttered something.

Leo almost shot him right there, but a moment later the other two men laughed, and the truck rumbled on down the road.

Leo ran a hand through his sweat-slicked hair, daring to breathe again.

"That was a tight one." Donny hopped into the passenger seat. "Almost as bad as when those Jerries had us pinned down in that old barn north of Epieds."

Leo grinned despite himself. "This place smells better."

"So, where we headed?" Donny asked.

"Same as before." Leo started the car. "Only the ride is going to be far less comfortable."

Leo let out a sigh as his headlamps fell across a stretch of gravel road up ahead. They'd spent the better part of three hours jouncing over backcountry trails and his back felt like a chain gang had been hammering on it.

"Those prohis will never catch us now," Leo said as

they pulled onto the road. "Unless they can drive through mountains."

Donny nodded, mouth pressed into a tight line. He'd been mostly quiet during their cross-country jaunt.

"What's eating you?" The question came sharper than Leo had intended.

"Nothing." Donny glanced at his hands, then back at Leo. "You ever think about how it would've been? Y'know, if we hadn't shipped out to fight the Kaiser?"

"I'd probably be working in a cannery," Leo shrugged. "That, or drunk and dead like my daddy."

"I can't even remember before. And when I do, it's like I read it in a book or something."

"Everybody came back different."

"Those who came back." Donny's lips twitched. "I can't even talk to regular people anymore. All I can think about is how they'd look with a bullet in their gut, or scattered across a half mile of mud by a German mortar."

"Lotta guys have trouble adjusting to civvy life," Leo said. "That's nothing to be ashamed of."

"I ain't ashamed of nothing." Donny's lips drew back from teeth that flashed white in the moonlight. "I just get so mad when I see them laughing, or dancing, or drinking at a speakeasy. Where do they get off acting like that? Like there ain't thousands of us face down in France; and who knows how many more who'll never walk, or talk, or think straight ever again."

Leo gave a tight-lipped nod. When Donny was in one of his moods there was nothing for it but to let him play himself out.

"Animals, just tearing at each other." Donny's voice was a low growl, barely audible over the rumble of the motor. "We saw it – over in the Ardennes, at Epieds – didn't we, Leo?"

"I reckon we did."

"Sooner or later, they'll see it too." Donny's smile was ugly. "We're all of us nothing but meat."

They drove in silence after that.

Leo glanced over at the broken mirror, the bullet scars along the side of his car. It would all be worth it when he had that ten large – enough to get the prohis off his back and set up a few stills. Johnny V had crossed a line when he gave the feds the Canada route, and Leo knew more than a few bootleggers who might want to have a few hard words with the self-styled "Baron of Boston".

They crossed into Massachusetts just after midnight, stopping only to gas up at a little all-night place just outside of Amherst. Leo knew the owner from way back, and always tried to slip the man a few extra bills when he came through.

Donny stepped out for a smoke, dragging on the cigarette like he was about to face a firing squad.

"Not far now." His expression was unreadable as he got back into the car.

"I don't want to risk main roads with all these bullet holes." Leo started the car. "Still, we should make decent time."

Donny nodded, then went back to staring out into the night.

They were just rounding Providence when the Model T

caught up with them. It was concealed behind a stand of hemlock just off the road.

This time, it didn't bother with the headlamps.

The car rammed Leo's car just behind the passenger side door. Leo managed to get a hand up in time to stop his head rebounding from the dash. Donny slammed into his side, cursing and flailing.

Leo shoved him away, laying on the gas, but the Model T had forced his rear wheels into the loose dirt at the edge of the road, and they couldn't get enough traction.

Their attacker flicked on his headlamps. Leo heard a door slam, then boots on gravel.

"My rifle!" Donny fumbled around the seat. He'd hit his head on the dash – a nasty cut that oozed purple-black in the sudden light.

A man stood silhouetted in the glow.

"Think you could give me the slip again, Alighieri?" He dragged Donny from the car.

Leo reached for his Colt, only to have the cold barrel of a revolver pressed into his cheek.

"I'm not after you, but I won't hesitate if you try any funny business." The man was square-jawed and handsome, with close-cropped brown hair sticking out from under a tan fedora. He wore a dusty overcoat, pale red tie poking from the shirt beneath, but what Leo was most interested in were the revolvers he held in each hand.

Leo swallowed an exasperated sigh. He was getting awfully tired of having guns aimed at him.

"Where is it?" Fedora pointed the other pistol at Donny, who was struggling to rise.

Donny mumbled nonsense under his breath, a stream of harsh consonants that seemed nothing but sharp edges. Poor sap must have hit his head harder than Leo thought.

"I'll have none of that." Fedora kicked Donny in the ribs.

"You don't look like a prohis," Leo said. "You one of Johnny V's guys? Maybe we could work out a deal."

The man shot Leo a derisive glance. "There's only one thing I'm interested in."

"The night whiskey," Leo replied.

That got Fedora's attention.

Donny shifted with a groan. "Don't tell him anything!"

"I'm not about to get ventilated over some hooch." Leo raised his hands. You could always make more money, making more life was a harder proposition. "Listen, friend, you've chased us over the better part of three states. From what Donny tells me, this stuff is worth a pretty penny. Let's say we cut you in. Everybody walks away with plenty in their pockets."

The man's jaw pulsed. "You think I want to *sell* it?"

"What gives? You some temperance hack?" Leo blinked. No one but the straightest arrow would turn up their nose at a payday like that.

"My employer paid me to burn the night whiskey and bring Mr Alighieri back alive." The barrel of Fedora's revolver dug into Leo's cheek. "She didn't say anything about you."

"Easy," Leo said. "It's under the back seat. Hidden compartment."

Donny let out a sound that was half-moan, half-snarl,

and Fedora favored him with another kick.

"Get it." The man gestured with one revolver. "Slowly."

Leo turned in his seat and reached down to trip the hidden latch, careful to keep his hands in view. In the back seat, fallen just behind the shadow of the rear door, lay Donny's rifle. Despite the sudden flush of hope, Leo gave no indication he'd seen it. Being dealt a bad hand didn't mean you were out of the game, best to wait and see how things played out.

The back seat lifted, revealing the carefully packed crates.

"Christ." Something akin to fear flickered across Fedora's face. "There must be forty bottles there." He gestured with his pistol. "Unload it, and be care–"

Donny lunged up from the ground.

Fedora's revolver flashed, the shot going wide as Donny fell upon the man, eyes wild, his fingers hooked into claws. Fedora clubbed him with his other pistol, the heavy blow barely seeming to shake Donny.

Leo dove into the back seat to snatch up the rifle. The car rocked as Donny slammed Fedora into the rear door. Leo stood to see the man had almost brought his pistol to bear. Whatever wild rage animated Donny, Leo bet it wouldn't survive a bullet.

The rifle stock made a very satisfying noise against the back of Fedora's head. Leo reversed the rifle as the man stumbled away.

"Throw the pistols into the woods." He aimed at Fedora's chest. All things considered, Leo much preferred being on this side of a gun.

"Shoot him!" Donny shouted.

"I'm a bootlegger, not a button man." Leo didn't consider himself a religious man, but he'd seen enough killing for a lifetime. No need to add to the tally. "Drop the pistols, pal."

Fedora tossed his revolvers into the bushes. "You don't know what you're dealing with."

"Neither do you," Leo said.

"Kill him!" Donny's voice had risen to a maddened screech.

"Get in the car, Donny," Leo said.

"But–"

"I'm not gonna tell you twice." Although Leo kept his eyes on Fedora, he could see Donny practically shaking with fury. It didn't bother Leo one bit. Since last night he'd been beaten, chased, shot at, and run off the road. Let Donny stew, it wasn't *his* car sporting a double fistful of bullet holes.

Jaw tight, Donny slid into the passenger seat.

"You're making a mistake," Fedora said.

"Wouldn't be the first." Leo shot out the Model T's tires, then slipped back into the front. Scowling, he threw the engine into low gear and rocked his car out of the gravel pit.

"What the hell was that all about?" he asked, as they sped away.

"How should I know?"

"He sure seemed to know you." Leo glanced over, sure that Donny was holding something back. "Who was that man?"

"Meat." Donny crossed his arms.

Leo sighed. It really was no use talking to him when he got like this.

Leo's profession necessitated more than a few clandestine meetings out in the sticks. He liked fresh air and nature as much as the next man.

Arkham Woods was different.

Those few roads that meandered through the somber trees were thick with fallen branches and creeping brush. Even the lightest shower seemed to turn them to a boggy mess, and Leo had lost more than a few tires to sharp stones that seemed to constantly worm their way up through the earth.

"The cave is just up that hill." Donny leaned forward in his seat, eyes bright in the dappled shadows of the Studebaker's headlamps. The woods seemed to have restored Donny's good humor, although he still remained infuriatingly tight-lipped on the subject of their strange pursuer.

Leo glanced over his shoulder. For a heartbeat, he thought he saw distant light through the trees, but it was probably just his nerves. There was no way Fedora could still be on their tail. Then again, he had tracked them across a hundred miles of New England backwoods.

At Donny's direction, they turned onto a narrow switchback almost buried by elm and oak. The trees seemed to hunch close as Leo drove by, branches swaying in the stagnant air.

The road leveled as they crested the low rise, opening

into a wide clearing, bounded by sheer rock cliffs on either side.

Leo braked, but didn't turn off the engine. The car's headlamps revealed a carpet of moss and switchgrass broken by a scattering of broken stone. At first, Leo thought the rocks had fallen from the cliff above, but they looked too regular. As he looked, he realized the stones had words etched into them, weathered to faint shadows by age and the elements.

He squinted at the stones, trying to decipher the dates. Arkham was littered with graveyards and family crypts, but it seemed odd to find one so far from town. A sense of morbid unease tickled up the back of Leo's neck. Midnight meetings were the stock-in-trade of a bootlegger, but what kind of buyer chose to conduct business in a dilapidated graveyard?

Donny twisted to unlock the hidden compartment in the car's back seat. Glass clinked as he fished a bottle of night whiskey from the straw-packed crates.

"They're going to want to sample the goods." Donny got out of the car, ambling amidst the shadowed stones like he was taking the air on a country jaunt. He paused in the glare of the car's headlamps.

"You coming?"

This time, Leo brought his shotgun.

The headstones seemed scattered at random, many broken as if some drunken farmer had driven a herd of cows through the clearing. Even so, Leo could see the outline of graves, the soil loose and dark like they had only recently been filled in. The sight conjured an all-too familiar roil in his gut. He realized he was gripping his shotgun too tightly, and forced himself to relax.

Donny led him into the trees. There, almost completely hidden by bracken and twisted vines, was the cave.

In the dim glow of the car lights, Leo couldn't see more than a few feet inside. The walls didn't have the rough lines of a natural cave, nor did they bear the telltale marks of pick and shovel. Rather, they were striated by hundreds of meandering lines that reminded Leo of the trails wood beetles bored beneath tree bark – almost as if the cave had been gnawed from the mountain.

Donny walked into the entrance, and, cupping a hand to his mouth, gave voice to a keening wail. It echoed down the cave, distorted into a strange, shuddering howl by the snarled acoustics.

From deep inside the tangled dark, there came an answering cry.

Leo smelled them long before he saw them. It came as a musty reek, the sharp scent of ancient, creaking flesh overlaying a sickly sweet odor of putrefaction. Leo pressed a forearm across his mouth and nose to stifle the smell, and was immediately glad he had, for it served to muffle his gasp as the first of the things crawled into view.

Although roughly man-sized, it was human only in the broadest sense. Grub-pale skin stretched across an armature of knobby bone, its flesh seeming almost too thin to contain the wiry ropes of muscle that coiled around its emaciated frame. The creature's eyes were little more than hollow shadows beneath a heavy brow, thin lips stretched back to reveal teeth like broken glass. Its tongue wriggled, wormlike, in a mouth that seemed to stretch across the whole of its face, the beast's wide, underslung jaw like the muzzle of a vicious dog.

Leo had seen corpses in every stage of decomposition, carpets of broken men and horses littering no-man's land, torn bodies strung like marionettes across tangles of barbed wire. But none of it had prepared him for the abomination that now stood before him.

A low moan snaked its way through Leo's clenched jaw as he leveled his shotgun.

Donny stepped into his shot. "Easy there, corporal."

Leo didn't lower his gun. "What in the hell is that?"

"I know it's a lot to take in, but I'll explain everything."

More of the things scuttled from the cave, crouching behind bushes or scrabbling up the rock face like man-sized spiders.

A tremble ran up Leo's legs, his chest tight, his throat dry as old stone. It was the same feeling he got just before the brass ordered them up and over the trench; a sense of terrible anticipation that seemed almost to press down upon him like a physical weight.

Against his better judgment, Leo didn't open fire. He did, however, put his back to the nearest tree – more for something to lean against than to keep from being caught from behind.

"Remember the Ardennes?" Donny asked.

"I try not to." Leo swallowed against the thickness in his throat. It seemed impossible they could be trading war stories while those things crept through the shadows.

"The Jerries were dug in, and so were we – miles of

trenches, tunnels, holes burrowed deep into the earth."
Donny gave an ugly laugh. "I remember the boom of
German artillery, crouching in that pit we'd dug, hugging
the earth and stone like it was my mother, like it could
protect me. And it did."

One of the creatures shuffled closer to Donny, and he
reached down to stroke its wrinkled head.

"We winnowed them out, didn't we, Leo? Hundreds,
thousands dead on both sides, their bodies left to rot deep
down below." Donny cocked his head. "Surely you must
have seen them, surely you must have heard the whispers
at night."

Leo shuddered as memories of the war bubbled through
the cracks in his resolve – dark shapes crawling from the
earth to pick through the tangled dead, the sharp crack of
breaking bone, the wet rip of flesh, the smack of hungry
lips. They'd had a name for them – the corpse rippers, the
body snatchers, scuttling along the trenches at night.

Ghouls.

Leo tried to edge back around the tree, but several of the
ghouls moved to cut off his retreat.

Donny spread his arms. "It called to me: the hungry
dark, the skittering maw… Umôrdhoth."

The unnatural name seemed to blister the very air. Like
the screams of men dying in the field, it cut to the heart of
Leo's being – simultaneously unbearable, but impossible to
ignore. He flinched as if he'd heard the boom of a distant
mortar, unconsciously waiting for the deathly whistle of
falling ordinance.

"It saved me, Leo. It saved all of us." Donny's smile

was almost luminous in the moonlight. "Umôrdhoth is generous, kind. It asks only one thing in return – to be fed."

With effort, Leo managed to stop the shaking in his legs, sure that if he balked, even for a moment, the ghouls would be on him like a pack of wild dogs. He nodded at the bottle of night whiskey.

"This thing has a hankering for booze?"

"No, this is for us." Donny pulled the cork, then tipped the bottle into the mouth of the creature by his side. "Drink up, lad."

The night whiskey flowed over the ghoul's cracked lips, dark and thick as molasses. It gulped at the thick brew, sucking at the bottle like a drunk after Sunday mass.

Leo watched in horror as the thing began to change.

Jagged fangs lengthened as the creature's jaw stretched wide in a hideous shriek. Its claws became hooked talons, spiked bits of bone ripping through pale flesh. Bruise-purple flame seemed to ignite within its eyes even as its gaunt frame bulged with heavy, corded muscle.

"We'll be unstoppable." Donny raised his arms to the night sky. "Umôrdhoth shall feed!"

Leo shook his head. "Christ, Donny. This… This is…"

"Inevitable." Donny extended a hand to Leo, grinning like a country preacher mid-sermon. "No one could see what we saw, do what we did, and come away sane. I know you feel it. We don't belong to this world anymore, Leo. Come with me, and we'll make a better one."

Leo's shotgun blast sent the ghoul behind him tumbling off into the brush. He spun, dodging between the trees as the ghouls gave voice to snarling shrieks. One leapt from the shadows to Leo's left. He unloaded a round in its gut, then pumped the forestock before pivoting to fire blindly into the forest behind. His pursuers ducked behind trees and rocks, scattering through the forest.

Breathing hard, Leo staggered into the cemetery. He vaulted over a tumbled headstone, almost twisting his ankle on the churned earth beyond.

"Don't worry, Leo." Donny's mad laughter rose above the chorus of snarling shrieks. "You'll understand soon enough."

A ghoul charged from the shadows of a fallen cenotaph. Leo ducked the swipe of a clawed hand and smashed the butt of his gun into the creature's distended jaws, following up with a heavy kick.

The car was maybe twenty yards ahead, lamps bright, engine still running. Leo staggered toward it, only to have his hopes shrivel as the bulky form of Donny's pet ghoul lunged from the shadows behind the car.

Unable to bring his shotgun to bear, Leo tried to step into the blow. Although his quick advance kept the creature's hooked talons from doing anything more than shredding Leo's work shirt, the ghoul's terrible strength was enough to knock him from his feet.

He landed hard, somehow keeping hold of his shotgun. The ghoul's shadow fell over him. This close, there was no way he could miss.

He unloaded a round into the ghoul, but might as well have been firing at a brick wall. The impact barely staggered the massive creature.

It tore the shotgun from his hands.

Leo screamed as the ghoul's talons dug into the meat of his shoulder. White hot pain seared along his side, dark spots swimming along the edges of his vision as the ghoul lifted him from the ground. He tried to kick at the thing, only to have it shake him like a dog with a rat in its jaws.

"I forgive you." Donny walked into the circle of headlights. "We vets have to stick together."

"OK, you win." Leo forced the words through gritted teeth. When you'd been dealt a losing hand, all you could do was bluff. "I'll run your hooch, feed your pets, whatever."

"Oh, Leo." Donny regarded Leo with a sad frown. "I know you better than that."

Shaking his head, Donny glanced toward the ghoul holding Leo, but whatever order he was about to give the beast was cut off by the sound of a distant car.

Donny's face twisted into a rictus of fury. "He hunts me, even here."

Judging by Donny's reaction, it had to be Fedora. From the sound of tires on gravel, Leo figured he was passing just beyond the switchback – a half mile distant, maybe less. The noise seemed to agitate the ghouls. The one holding Leo let out a snuffling grunt, the charnel reek of its breath making him feel faint.

"He can't find us here." Donny raised a calming hand. "Umôrdhoth's power hides this place. That stupid gumshoe could drive right by the path and not see it."

Leo clenched his jaw against the urge to shout. Even if Fedora heard, Leo was likely to be ripped limb from limb before the cavalry could arrive. He needed something to keep them busy.

Although Leo's Colt was still in its shoulder holster, he doubted it would do much. Donny was an obvious target, but at the moment he seemed to be the only thing keeping the ghouls from devouring Leo. The car was idling nearby, keys in the ignition, two cases of night whiskey in the back seat.

And there it was.

Jaw clenched against the pain, Leo twisted to draw his Colt. It felt awkward in his off hand, but the cases were barely ten feet away.

Leo's first shot smashed through a half dozen bottles, spattering night whiskey over the Studebaker. His second shot struck sparks from the steel door, a glittering cascade that fell among spilled booze. There was a heartbeat of expectant silence, then flames blossomed in the back seat, casting Leo's beloved car in tones of red and orange.

There was no time for regret. The explosion snatched the breath from Leo's lungs. If the ghoul hadn't been between him and the car, the blast would've almost certainly shattered his ribs. Instead, it tore Leo from the creature's grip and set him rolling across the broken ground.

Flames crackled all around, the air full of acrid smoke and the shrieks of fleeing ghouls. Dimly, Leo heard another rattling boom as the Studebaker's gas tank went up, a hail of jagged metal pinging from the stones around him. The gouges in his shoulder burned like someone had pressed a hot coal to Leo's flesh, and it was all he could do to lay gasping like a consumption victim as the wave of heat and sound rolled over him.

For a moment, it was like being back in France.

Donny's aggrieved howl cut through the din. He staggered from the smoke, expression turning feral as he saw Leo crumpled on the ground before him.

Leo tried to move, but couldn't seem to find his breath.

Donny stepped toward him, fingers crooked into claws. Muttering, he reached for Leo, only to flinch back as a bullet ricocheted from a nearby headstone.

More gunfire sounded in the swirling smoke, and Donny staggered back, one hand clapped to his bleeding arm. Teeth bared, he shot Leo one last hateful glare, then staggered off into the smoke.

Boots crunched on broken stone.

"I suppose I have you to thank for all this?" Fedora stood above Leo, a revolver in each hand.

Leo braced himself against the remains of a tombstone and slowly pushed to his feet. "What the hell is all this?"

Fedora let out a low whistle. "The tip of the iceberg, pally."

Leo regarded the man. "You got a name?"

"Tony Morgan." He reached up to tip his hat.

"Leo De Luca." Leo glanced over his shoulder. The woods were quiet but for the crackle of flame. In the dim firelight, he could just make out the cliff beyond the clearing – its sheer face flat and unbroken, as if the cave had been some vast and terrible mouth, snapping shut behind Donny and the ghouls.

"You've done the world a real favor here," Tony nodded. "I won't forget it."

Leo looked back at the blackened remains of his car, throat tight with anger and loss. The wreckage sat like a smoldering punctuation to Leo's dreams of creating a bootlegging empire. With a grunt of pain, he straightened. Donny may have taken almost everything from him, but Leo De Luca *always* had cards to play.

"Mind giving me a ride back to town?"

"Sure." Tony holstered one of his revolvers to give Leo a hand limping back to the Model T, now sporting four new tires. "It'll give us time to talk about how you got mixed up in all this."

"I'll do more than that." Anger whetted Leo's words to razor sharpness. "I know where Donny is getting the hooch, and what it does. We can take apart his whole operation."

"We?" Tony cocked an eyebrow.

"The man owes me ten large, not to mention a new car." Leo fixed Tony with a steady look. "And I aim to collect."

SHADOWS DAWNING
Georgina Kamsika

Lita Chantler stumbled to her knees, bracing her hands on the rough ground. The sharp gravel dug into her palms, blood dripping from her many cuts. She took a breath, then another, before forcing herself upright. There was an ache in her knees, either from too much exertion or from falling onto them, Lita wasn't sure. She dragged freezing air into her lungs, focusing inward, readying herself to move.

There was a noise from the dark house behind her, low enough that she couldn't tell if it was from a human or not. She had only recently found out that there were other things besides humans. Other monsters.

That new reality pressed against her sense of consciousness; with it came a wave of numb panic. She swallowed it with the bile in her throat. She could panic later. Now, she had to run.

Lita scrubbed her hand over her jaw, leaning back onto her heels as she contemplated the sliver of moon above. A wisp of cloud passed in front of it on the cool spring breeze, but she heard no more noises from the house behind.

The last time John had kissed her with affection had been under a moon like this. It had been a day without an argument. Rare enough that they'd celebrated it, without acknowledging the reason with words, of course. They had a midnight picnic on the hill overlooking Easttown. Cold meats, some bread, a woolen blanket and soft starlight. They'd kissed in the moonlight, talking about their future, about trying for their first child. It had been a night she would never forget.

The next day John had left bloody butcher's clothes to stain their bedroom floor. Lita had snapped at him; he'd snapped back that the blood had been earned through his hard work. They sank into their usual routine of shouting. Not long after that, John was gone. Had been killed. And then there were no more chances for affection for Lita.

A misty rain began to fall. Lita shivered. Her blood soaked, sticky and uncomfortable, into her hemline. More blood earned from hard work. At least she wouldn't drop the dress to stain the bedroom floor.

She glanced behind her, the stranger's house silent and still. She had followed a clue to find a cultist cowering inside. He had been coerced into helping; a weak man addicted to alcohol, he'd told her everything he'd known. It wasn't much, a name, a profession, but it was enough for Lita to continue her search. Another link in the chain leading her to the people who had murdered her husband.

Now the place was of no more use to her, she began picking her way home. The route was quiet at this time, no people walking the streets, none of the few cars on the road. Lita swept past Velma's Diner, ducking away from the faint light by the front windows. Agnes peered out but didn't acknowledge her, the diner clearly closed despite the couple of people talking to the waitress. Lita expected no less; she barely talked to the server beyond polite greetings and ordering her food.

Lita was more careful about keeping to the shadows after that. She'd already managed to mess up her reputation over the last few weeks since John's murder, she didn't need anyone to see her wandering the town covered in blood.

John's murder. Tonight felt like the first time in a long time that she'd had a clue as to what happened. A glimpse into what had brought the horror into her home. After her husband's murder, her only goal had been to find the monsters that killed him. Not the ghouls – well, not just them – but the humans, the cult, that had killed him for refusing them.

Lita hadn't taken them seriously, not at first, the strangers harassing her husband at his butcher's store. What kind of customer wanted to take his shipments? These strange, pale men, what could they do with live meat? But when the same strangers had started to follow them around, harassing them at all hours, Lita had insisted they go to the police.

What a mistake. The police in Arkham refused to help, and then threatened to arrest her when Lita had raised her voice in frustration. The strangers had kept up their harassment until the day Lita found John murdered.

She rubbed at her brow, wincing at the sharp pain beginning to dig into her temples. Enough. She couldn't

think about the past. She was doing everything she could
to make them pay now.

Her house, a little older, a little more rundown than its
neighbors, stood brightly lit, a beacon calling to her. Lita
couldn't hear much over the soft chuckle of the Miskatonic
River nearby, but she knew the lights meant safety. Meant
that her friend who had a key was there waiting for her.

Lita forced her aching legs to limp up the high stone
steps to her narrow door, pushing her shoulder against the
frame to lift it enough that the key turned in the lock. Her
friend Priya stood behind it, one hand holding a cast-iron
poker above her head.

"Lita!" Priya lowered the poker, reaching to help her up
the last steep step into the house.

Priya Anand. A couple of years younger than Lita,
but almost as stubborn. They'd met a few years ago,
butting heads in the grocery store. What had begun as an
argument over produce quickly turned into laughter and
jokes. It was rare for Lita to find someone she related to so
well, especially someone who did not mind her occasional
flaring temper.

Priya was tall, like John, but with a softness and
sweetness he'd never had. They'd never been close, but
John had appreciated Lita having a good friend. Priya had
never married, instead choosing to share her home with
her longtime friend Emily. Lita didn't judge. They seemed
happier than she and John had ever managed.

"You're bleeding." Priya hooked an arm through hers
and pulled her toward the kitchen.

"Most of this isn't mine."

Priya glared over her shoulder, tugging harder. Her thick dark hair fluffed around her shoulders as she shoved Lita ungracefully toward the dining chair. Lita slumped back with a relieved grunt, some of the aches easing as she relaxed back into the wooden seat. She shook out her arms, trying to release the tension in her shoulders.

Priya moved around the old oak kitchen as if it was her own, heading straight for the first aid kit. The dark cabinets were cluttered, but Priya found it easily. Lita didn't think about why. About the number of times Priya had stayed up late waiting for her. About the cuts and bruises she'd helped treat.

Lita sat quiet, controlling her breathing as Priya cleaned her wounds. Her entire body ached from a mix of pain and adrenaline. She jerked as the medicine stung a particularly deep cut on her hand.

"These will get infected, stop fighting!"

"Stop fussing!" Lita snapped automatically.

Priya pushed her back into her seat. "You're too young to be this crotchety."

Lita's annoyance flared at the word, before she winced as another wound stung. "Ow!"

"Just sit still, then." Priya's grip got tighter, holding her firmly in her seat. Lita closed her eyes, zoning out at the gentle feeling of Priya's soft hands and the astringent smell of the medicine. She pushed down the feelings of pain, taking deep breaths that helped her to relax.

"There. Done. Don't do anything to tear these bandages."

Lita nodded her thanks, gathering the bloodied cotton to dump into the trash. She washed her hands, the rust-red water swirling down the sink. The combined smell of medicine and blood made her stomach shift. "C'mon."

Priya followed her into the sitting room, settling primly on the edge of the sofa, her hands clasped in her lap. Lita ignored the gas lamps, lighting the half-melted candles on the mantelpiece. The golden glow banished the dancing shadows to the corners of the room. Lita moved to the mahogany sideboard, then waggled the brandy bottle. Priya shook her head, wrinkling her nose. Lita poured herself a couple of fingers, then splashed some more on top.

Lita settled in John's old armchair, the cushion still compressed into his shape. The lumps dug into her back, while old springs tugged on her legs. It was the most uncomfortable piece of furniture in the room, but she never wanted to sit anywhere else. The room was mostly silent as Priya stared at the ticking grandmother clock, Lita swirling the brandy in her glass. The adrenaline was wearing off, and she felt shaky and cold. Her mood dipped and she slumped further back into the unpleasant chair.

"I didn't mean to get hurt. I just want justice for John." Lita spoke gruffly, making it clear she wasn't apologizing for anything.

Priya scoffed. "John wouldn't want you to hurt yourself."

"I don't know, after some of our fights, he might."

Priya glanced over, her mouth twitching. Lita couldn't help herself and let out a low chuckle. Then they were both laughing hard, tears leaking from Lita's eyes. Happiness bubbled up in her chest as her shoulders shook with amusement.

With some of the tension eased, Priya sank back against

the sofa cushions. "I understand why you're doing it, but you have to stop sometime. You have to move on with your life."

Lita's smile dropped. Priya's words were a harsh reminder that it felt wrong, somehow, to laugh, with everything she knew. With Priya asking her to stop. She missed John, his smile, his anger, everything good and bad. There was a hollow carved in her chest that would never be filled again.

Lita gulped down the brandy. Sweet and warm, it took the edge off her aches. "I've told you what happened to us. The harassment, the stalking, even John's murder and who did it and why. Could you move on from it? Can you now that you've found out there's more underneath this faked civilized veneer in Easttown?"

Priya shook her head. "I don't know anything, not really. And I don't want to."

Lita tried to stop the flare of annoyance at her friend's deliberate ignorance, but it was hard. She understood it was a form of defense, but it was a dangerous one. One Lita couldn't let her hide behind. Her breathing increased as her agitation rose. "What if it was Emily who had been harassed? What if Emily was scared and upset? Who one day you find bloodied and cold on the floor?"

Priya's face creased into a frown. The hands clasped on her lap started to twist. "That's not fair."

"It's not fair, no, but that's what happened to us. We didn't do anything to invite these people in. They chose to target us. Him. They wanted something so they took it. Just because they don't need anything from you or her now, doesn't mean they might not come back next week or

next month, demanding something from you." Her voice
rose in volume as she continued, the words bursting out of
her throat, scorching more than the brandy had. Her chest
ached with the hurt she'd bottled up. How could Priya not
understand?

Priya frowned. "I... I don't–"

There was a noise at the front door. Lita almost didn't
hear it, but she was already tense, tense enough to catch the
faint scratching. She stared at Priya, then wound her hand
in a "keep talking" motion. Priya raised her eyebrows, but
stuttered on further about how much she cared for Emily.

Lita glanced to the fireplace, but the poker wasn't there.
Still by the front door. She tamped down her worry and
stalked toward the hallway, Priya's voice covering any
other sound. There it was again. This time it sounded like
footsteps on the stoop, one person back and forth. One
person. Good. Lita knew from experience that she could
handle one. Lita dipped down to grab the poker propped
at the foot of the stairs. It was a solid cast iron piece, easily
the best weapon she had to hand.

There was the sound of running. The cracking of wood.
The door smashed open, splinters stabbing Lita's bare skin.

Lita had been in fights before. She'd been in one earlier.
But she was in her own home, relaxed, safe. She froze as
knuckles swished past her nose. It was a man, someone she
didn't know, half-hidden in the shadows. He was breathing
fast, his sallow cheeks flushed red.

He was older than her, though, and slow. It was easy to
avoid the sluggish swing of his fist. They ducked and swayed
until Lita arced her arm back, then up and around. The man

saw it coming. He raised his arm and deflected the blow. The poker crunched the delicate bones of his wrist. His face paled, his chest heaving. Lita almost missed him striking out with his left, just managing to dip the other way.

Lita didn't know the man, just assumed he was one of the cultists. But he wanted to hurt her, that much was certain. It didn't help that she was already tired. She had to finish this and quickly. The man was panting loudly now, sweat dripping down his forehead. He'd cradled his injured hand to his chest, flailing at her with what looked like his less dominant arm.

One swing went too wide. Lita waited a fraction of a second, then used his off-center balance to slam a shoulder into him, throwing him back against the splintered door. She wielded the poker, wincing as it cracked against the bones around his collarbone. The man didn't let out a word, just slumped backward with a harsh wheeze. He staggered back out the doorway, his body jerking with pain as he tried to run.

Lita took a step backward, her heart slamming in her chest. She pressed a hand to her throat as she gulped. She felt breathless, as if she hadn't taken in any air during the fight.

"Are you OK?" Priya asked from behind her.

"Yeah, he didn't touch me." Lita lowered her hand, controlling her gasps to slow down her panic. "Not sure what he thought he was doing, but–"

"What who was doing?" a new voice interrupted from outside the front door. Lita looked up as the silhouette moved into the light. A police uniform. Bill? Billy?

Something like that. One of the men who had failed to help her with John, who had done everything but call her a murderer herself.

"Someone attacked us!" Priya blurted out. Hot anger flared up at her friend telling this policeman anything, but Lita pushed it aside, not wanting to argue. She moved in front of the staircase, blocking entry to the house to keep him outside.

The policeman, Billy Cooper, Lita remembered, crossed his arms and eyed Lita. "Lotta blood on you."

Lita stayed still, ignoring him. He had the same attitude as before and it brought back painful memories.

"Another *animal attack*? They must smell the meat from your butcher shop."

Lita's eye twitched at how he stressed animal attack, but kept her silence, only shrugging one shoulder. It would do no good for this policeman to see her frustration.

"Keep it down, it's late." Billy tapped on the splintered doorframe and stepped back into the gloom. Lita waited until he'd disappeared into the darkness before pushing her damaged door closed.

"Why didn't you tell him?" Priya moved out of the way as Lita lifted the door back into the frame.

"He knew this wasn't an animal attack – what animal breaks into a house? He's one of them," Lita muttered as she popped the door back onto its hinges. The wood had never sat right and now it felt as though it might never open again.

"You're so lost in your paranoia, you think everything is one big conspiracy." Priya moved into the other room. Lita heard a clinking noise which sounded like she had begun tidying the glasses. Lita took a few seconds to breathe in deeply, holding it in her lungs before exhaling noisily. She felt some of the tension in her shoulders seep away with the air.

"Isn't everything a conspiracy, though?" Lita raised her voice a little over the sound of Priya's anxious tidying. She was too tired and in too much pain for this argument. She followed Priya into the sitting room, pausing by the old wooden cabinet. John's .41 sat inside. She'd taken it out with her now and again, but she wasn't confident with it. Not yet. With the way things seemed to be escalating, practicing her shooting was something she would need to work on soon.

"Leave it. Emily will be worried about you," Lita said, to stop Priya's anxious cleaning.

Priya glanced at the front door before heading toward the exit in the kitchen. "And I'm worried about *you*. What if they come back?"

"They won't." Lita unlocked the back door, letting Priya past her into the dim streetlight. "Stay safe, Pree."

"Night, Lita."

Lita watched her friend stroll toward her home a couple of streets away, the town quiet with no sign of any trouble. Priya got to her doorstep and waved, merely a tiny stick figure now, before disappearing inside. Safe. Lita closed her door, rolling her neck to loosen the muscles. A night like tonight required more brandy.

Lita had been too sore to sleep. She sat alone in the

Arkham Horror

dark room, staring at the barely visible pictures on the mantelpiece. They had a thin layer of dust on them now that she had more important things to think about, but she knew them all anyway. John, handsome and broad, unsmiling even on their wedding day. The next a picture of Lita in her white gown, her red hair piled on top of her head. She had never looked as happy or as beautiful as that day.

She'd never look that happy again. Not without John. Not knowing what she knew now. She snarled, throwing her tumbler against the wall. The glass shattered, golden brandy dripping down the faded wallpaper, smearing their wedding photograph. She collapsed back into her chair, her breathing heavy.

It was the chiming of the old wind-up grandmother clock that woke her. Six am – six bell clangs. Lita groaned, rubbing at her forehead. Her already sore body ached from sleeping slumped in the old armchair. She pushed her tangled hair out of her eyes, blinking blearily in the washed-out morning light. She dragged her gaze around the room. Despite Priya's visit, it looked cluttered and disorganized. Dirty, if she was honest, as if she'd barely cleaned properly in weeks.

She shuffled down the corridor, the walls overflowing with family pictures, each badly in need of dusting. They catalogued a short life with her husband, John, from their happy meeting to their later argument-fueled marriage. No children, that was something they'd just talked about when… Lita stopped that line of thought.

Lita put the kettle on the hob, then opened a cupboard,

rummaging for coffee. John was the one addicted to this new instant stuff, but she'd not finished the last jar. As the kettle began to bubble, Lita studied the pantry for a moment or two, before the pit in her stomach convinced her to abandon the thought of breakfast. She made herself a cup of coffee and sat at the table. She drank in silence for a long, dark, brooding moment, the loneliness unsettling.

She missed her husband. She missed the smiles and the laughter. The arguments and the pain. Everything they'd had that she'd taken for granted. People had told her that it got better, that the pain faded. But she still woke up with the full weight of her grief. The worst part was that sometimes she'd forget that he was gone and turn to tell him something, only to see an empty room. Or she'd see a tall man in the crowd and raise her hand, about to call his name before she froze, mouth hanging open uselessly. There was always a split second of joy and relief, before reality pulled her back to the depths.

Suddenly, the telephone rang. Lita lowered her cup, staring at the device, her eyes tired. It had been some time since anyone had any reason to call her. She stood, walking to the wall slowly to answer it.

"Lita Chantler," Lita said. There was no response, just the soft hum of an open phone line and the hint of someone breathing. Lita waited thirty seconds, more, then the other person hung up. One of the cultists, then, but there had been no clue in the background. Nothing she could use. No point trying to ask at the exchange who had made the call. The cultists protected each other. There would be no record of the call, of that she was convinced.

Lita hung up the handset and returned to the kitchen table, sinking slowly down into her chair. She didn't weep, despite her exhaustion, her hands trembling as she lowered her face in excruciating, utter, and complete sorrow. Once upon a time people had called on her with invites to dinner, or simply to chat. But after the rumor spread around town, and the police made sure to spread it far and wide, that John's death was suspicious and Lita was the number one suspect, those friends had stopped calling. One by one, they had withdrawn from her life until only Priya and Emily were left. She had no idea how lonely and isolated she felt until that call. The call wasn't even threatening, not really, just a reminder of her status as a loner and a victim.

She allowed herself to indulge in negative thoughts until her coffee had grown cold, at which point she made another and headed toward John's study.

Unlike the rest of the house, his space was pristine and clean. John used to do all his business paperwork in here, but that was long gone. The wall behind the desk was a map of information, everything Lita had found laid out, lines crisscrossing between clues.

She sat at the desk, a pencil in hand, a pad of paper before her, thinking. The person she'd found yesterday had given her a clue. Not much of one, just a name, but it was enough for her to follow. *Ida Smith.* She pulled out her map of the town, creased with an old coffee stain in the middle, then flipped through the telephone directory. There was no guarantee this Ida was in it, since not everyone had a telephone, but while Lita wasn't a trained investigator, she'd formed her own methods. Tapping down the Smiths, there were a few, until she got to the only Mrs I Smith. She made a note of the address and checked the map. Not too far.

Lita placed the pencil upon the pad before sliding them both aside. She unscrewed the cap off the bottle of scotch and poured herself a healthy dose. She opened John's desk drawer, reached into the back, and found an old pack of his cigarettes, half-empty. She tapped one, placed it between her lips, and lit it, taking a deep pull. She held it and exhaled, her body relaxing. Lita spun the chair, leaning back to peer up at the wall of clues.

From John's murder to the police cover up. Her discovery of ghouls, and the cultists that aided them.

Ghouls. Those weird, almost humanoid, monsters that had opened her eyes to the real world that coexisted with the safe reality most people lived in. Slumping monsters with red eyes and bony claws, they haunted her nightmares.

"That house, those people led me to the mechanic," she muttered to herself, barely aware she was doing so. "He was pressured into helping them build something, but he wouldn't say what. John refused them, but that fool didn't. Acting like he wasn't responsible because they threatened his worthless life."

Lita leaned forward, staring at a newspaper clipping, tracing the red thread to the person she'd talked to last night. She grabbed her scribbled note, "Ida Smith, librarian" and stuck it to the wall. She lowered her head with a sigh, lost in thought. This librarian, Ida Smith –

who knew if she was really involved, or if the cultist had been lying? She couldn't trust any of them. But she had no choice. This was the only clue she had.

Lita hadn't been to this side of Easttown for a while. The houses were lacking in variety, dismally standard white siding, paint flaking off the walls, dirty windows, entrance doors standing open, washing hanging in lines at the side of the house. The local library was small, barely more than a dingy room stacked with a few shelves, but clearly librarians got paid worse than Lita thought.

Lita peered into the leaded windows. It didn't look like anything special. A living room similar to hers, but with walls lined by floor to ceiling bookshelves. A small side table laden with candles and herbs and other strange things. A few weeks ago she'd have thought it nonsense, but now she knew better. The librarian, Ida, was one of them. Another link on the chain bringing Lita closer to the people running this whole thing.

There was no one inside, but despite the clearly unlocked front door, Lita folded her arms and waited. She had lost track of time, staring up at the scudding clouds, when a middle-aged black woman headed up the path. Most of her hair was tucked tidily under a scarf, but her temples were graying and her eyes carried more bags than the grocery stores. She held a shopping bag in both hands, slowing a little as she spotted Lita.

"I need to talk to you." Lita straightened up, still waiting beside the front door.

"I have done everything you asked." The woman's voice

was low and deep, with a resigned sadness tinged through it.

"Yeah, and that's why I need to talk to you. Why are you helping them?" Lita's annoyance seeped out. She couldn't help it, she could never control her temper.

Despite her clear anger, the woman, Ida, relaxed a little as she registered Lita's question. Her eyes lost their haunted look as she peered at Lita. "Who are you?"

"Someone who wants to stop them before they hurt anyone else."

Ida scoffed, moving past Lita to her front door. "By yourself? Ha."

Lita shrugged.

"Well, this shopping is heavy. I guess you'll follow me in whatever I say." Ida seemed unconcerned by Lita closing the door behind them.

Ida headed through the dim corridor into the kitchen. With faded pale green tiles and worn flooring, it was clearly old but loved. In contrast to Lita's disheveled home, everything was scrubbed sparkling clean. The old iron stove looked freshly tended. Ida placed her shopping on the counter and filled a kettle. She pointed to the tiny dining table and chairs.

Lita sat sideways on the chair, her legs free to stand quickly if need be. Ida handed her a steaming mug of dark tea. It smelled sweet. Not usually how Lita would drink it, but she took a polite sip.

"Want some eggs?" Ida had moved back to the cooker, taking down a frying pan.

Lita realized it was well past lunchtime. "I could eat. Need a hand, Ida?"

Ida threw a sharp glare over her shoulder. "You know my name, but you don't tell me yours."

Lita sipped her tea, staying silent. Ida started moving around the kitchen. Cracking eggs. The sizzle of butter. Her stomach growled. It felt like an age since she'd eaten warm, cooked food.

"I can't help you," Ida said as she moved about the kitchen.

"I'm not leaving here until I have somewhere to go to." Lita stretched out her leg, easing the kink in her sore knee.

"I don't know anything." Ida didn't even stop to consider Lita's words.

"Then I'll be here a while," Lita said placidly, sipping the too-sweet tea.

Ida brought over the plates. Fried eggs. Toast. Some fried white mushrooms. Lita didn't pretend to be polite. It had been a long time since anything had tasted so good.

"Better than Velma's Diner," Lita said.

Ida scoffed. She was eating more slowly. "Hardly a compliment."

That made Lita look up from her food. Both women laughed in acknowledgment of the truth.

"You seem too kind to help them," Lita muttered, as she finished her toast.

Ida didn't reply, just shook her head as she ate.

"When we met, you said you did everything they asked," Lita reminded her.

"Yeah, ask is the wrong word. *Demand.* Demand or they hurt my baby girl. She's happy, settled, her own baby on the way. I have to protect her from them."

Lita lowered her fork and leaned back. That changed things. Would the cultists hurt, maybe kill, Ida's daughter the way they'd killed John? They had never got the chance to have the kids they'd wanted. She couldn't imagine how she'd react if they were threatened. She stared at Ida with more understanding. Sympathy washed over her, reminding her that there was more to worry about than her revenge.

"I'll stop them," she promised.

Ida shook her head. "I want to believe you, but you're just one person."

"One person who has had enough. I'll stop them." Lita leaned her elbows on the table, wanting Ida to understand how earnest she was. She had come here to follow the truth, not to place another person in the firing line. Ida was already targeted; Lita did not need to make things worse for her. Not if she could help it.

Lita thought she heard a scrape outside – by the back kitchen window. Cold panic crept up the back of her neck.

"I didn't think they'd followed me here," Lita muttered, eyes wide, holding out her hands to shush Ida. Lita had accidently led her stalkers here. She had to make sure she kept Ida safe at least.

"They're dangerous people." Ida leaned across the table to grab her wrist. Her eyes were wide with fear.

"Aren't they always?" Lita patted her hand, extracting herself with an attempt at a comforting smile.

Ignoring the startled look on Ida's face, Lita grabbed her iron from on the side, then, padded softly out of the unlocked front door, carefully circling the house. There was a man peering in the kitchen window, his face pressed up to the glass. It wasn't the same guy who had attacked her home last night, but he looked similar enough to be a cousin, maybe.

Lita kicked at his legs, throwing her whole bodyweight to pin him down on his back, his arms twisted beneath him. He struggled, trying to buck her off, but one swift knee between his legs had him lying still, clutching at himself.

"I'll never say anything!" he spat out, his pale cheeks flushing red.

Lita cuffed him at the side of his head with the iron, smiling as he dropped back, unconscious. "I don't need you to."

She'd learned her lesson now. These people believed too strongly, they'd never knowingly give up their cult. But there were other ways to get information. She dug in his pants pockets, ignoring the loose coins until she felt a wallet. She brought it out. It was leather, had a picture of the man and his brother, perhaps, in the front window. There were a couple of dollar bills, and a cluster of receipts. Lita flipped through those, spotting the local hardware store, a nearby grocers, and then finally a bus ticket. She examined the details. The bus ran from town to the outskirts, somewhere Lita didn't recognize.

Lita glanced up to see Ida peering down at her. The woman smiled, her white teeth gleaming through the glass. Lita nodded an acknowledgment before grabbing the cultist under the armpits. She sucked in a huge breath, then dragged him away from the dilapidated house. He was heavy and it was a struggle, but there was no way she was leaving him near Ida. Let him wake up confused and alone. Safer that way.

The bus ticket was important, but she had no desire to arrive wherever the destination might be at nightfall. Rushing into anything would be what got her killed.

Once she had rid herself of the snooper, she headed to Priya's house, to see if they could catch up after their small disagreement the night before. Priya was only worried about her, she knew, and her own prickly response to that worry was to push back.

"Lita." Priya opened the door with a wide smile. Good. She didn't hold a grudge. "Come in! Emily is visiting her mother, but you're welcome to join me for dinner."

Lita patted her stomach. "Maybe a snack."

Priya scoffed. "How do you think I was raised? You think my mother would let a guest eat *just a snack?*"

They bantered back and forth, friendly jokes that calmed Lita after the adrenaline of her fight. It felt strange but relaxing to sit in the kitchen, listening to Priya talk of Emily's work, of their plans for the future. The mundane ritual was comforting, especially the smell of delicious spices and sizzling food.

As Lita nibbled on the tasty fried snacks, she stayed quiet and let Priya manage the conversation. Her friend lit up when she talked, her eyes bright, her smile luminous. Emily was just as smitten when she came home, kissing Priya on the cheek, taking her hand and leaning against her side in contentment.

It was good to sit here, safe and warm, after all Lita had

gone through. Not everything had to be about death and pain and fear. It was good to remind herself, sometimes, that life still had joy in it. Good food, kind friends, honest conversation. She could build her life around this.

The moon was high in the sky when Lita finally got home. She rubbed at her eyes, tired after a long day. The first part, the waiting, the fighting, had drained her. Seeing Priya and Emily's happiness had actually recharged her, just a little. Good company, friends who understood her. Perhaps Lita had made the wrong choice. Was revenge the right path for her future?

There were times, like today, when she wondered if she should just stop. Stop wondering what happened to John, stop chasing after ghosts. Putting down her anger and her frustration and her rage would be an immense relief. Kneel by John's grave and empty herself of all her negative feelings. She would never fall in love again, she had no illusions about that, but if she spent her time with her friends like the evening she'd just had, she could lead a contented life.

It was the dusty pictures that brought her back to reality. The reality where her husband had been murdered. Where his murderers walked free, still threatening others, as Ida had told her today. They told the sorry tale of her life. A marriage built on arguments, a nursery half-painted and abandoned, a husband cold in the ground, a house barely lived in. She should feel shame at the layer of dust obscuring John's half-smile, but it felt symbolic, somehow. The colors had leached out of everything, and there was nothing else left.

Lita dragged her gaze from the photographs to the bus ticket on the mantel, at the unfamiliar destination that held her hopes. Her resolve firmed. She had to do this.

The early morning sun hung low, the light gleaming off the road, as the bus huffed to a stop every few minutes. Not many people got on and off; it was clearly an unpopular route.

Now it was rattling up a long hill, empty bar Lita and one gentleman with a hat pulled low on his forehead. Lita studied his profile: tanned olive skin, full lips, wide dark eyes. Handsome, but hardworking. Nothing like most of the cultists she'd crossed paths with. She didn't completely dismiss him, but figured he probably wasn't following her.

Eventually the bus pulled up to the curb, pausing for a moment as the driver called out the town's name. Lita exited, standing still as it rattled away. The other passenger had not got off. In fact, the quiet street on the edge of town stood silent, almost eerily so.

Lita was ready, her gait steady, her shoulders relaxed, her hands loose at her sides. She was here. Wherever here was. The street headed off into the distance, turning from sparse shops into a thin scattering of trees. She was on the absolute edge of this town, so deserted there were few houses, even.

Most of the shops were shuttered, their windows soaped over, their doors boarded up. The only sign of life was a closed tavern, and even that looked to be on its last legs. There was only one building that might be of interest. An abandoned church, half-hidden. It didn't look too old, mostly just forgotten. A two-story wooden building with a tiny bell tower rising in the middle. A couple of fir trees stood at each corner, and overgrown bushes lined the path toward the door.

What had drawn Lita's attention to the place was the sturdy door with shiny looking locks. Why would an abandoned church need such security? She circled the building from a distance, scouring for a side entrance, but saw no alternate way inside. The back of the church was blocked by stacks of old wooden crates and flattened cardboard. It looked like they had been building, or perhaps had a lot of deliveries.

The front glass had been soaped opaque, but the side windows hadn't. Lita circled the white building again, then found an old pallet and dragged it closer so she could look within. It scraped against the gravel, the sound echoing across the open lots adjacent. Lita froze, her heart in her throat. She waited, breath locked in her chest as she watched the door. It didn't move. She saw no shadows in the windows. No one came from any of the houses. Time dripped by, and slowly she relaxed. She gently dropped the pallet, leaving it abandoned.

It was barely nine in the morning, and the only noise was of birdsong. She started to doubt her certainty. Why did she think an old bus ticket meant anything? Perhaps the guy had liked visiting that tavern? Perhaps he lived on this side of town?

The building seemed quiet enough for Lita to try the doors. Locked. The lock was new, as she'd suspected, and solid. Nothing she could pick with her recently learned skills. Now she was beside it, she noticed another oddity –

a symbol carved into the main door. She didn't recognize it: a strange mass of vines or roots, or tendrils, perhaps? There were other shapes carved around it, words perhaps, in a language unknown to her. She might not have recognized it for sure, but this was the sign of the people she was hunting, she had no doubt about it.

The symbol reinforced her belief that there was something wrong here, despite the lack of any other evidence. She resumed her investigation of the area.

It was on her second circuit that she spotted a guy, the first person she'd seen since her arrival. There was something about the cultists she'd met, the true believers. They had this blankness in their eyes, a slackness to their mouths. This man was one of them. He was facing away from the church, and had probably arrived there while she was around the other side of the building.

It was easy for Lita to incapacitate him. He was barely guarding anything, squinting into the sun-lit street smoking a cigarette. She picked up a piece of pallet, approached him as quietly as she could from behind, and whacked him hard on the side of the head.

She'd been right. Somehow, this church was important to them. A local base? Perhaps. It was quiet enough that Lita felt emboldened to explore further.

Quickly she searched through his pockets. The man didn't have any keys on him, only his cigarettes and some matches. Lita looked at the matches and smiled, a better idea forming. She headed to the back of the church where all the wood had been stacked. It took some effort to get the fire burning. The wood was pretty dry, but the stacks of cardboard had soaked in the morning dew. Lita lit it in a few different places, fanning the tiny flames until it roared into life. As soon as the flames had licked up the white siding and caught, Lita dropped the matches and headed away.

She looped around the side of the church, when she heard the sharp snap of a branch. She froze. The man she'd knocked out couldn't be awake yet, so this had to be someone else. Perhaps someone had been inside the building. Had she underestimated the cultists? Were they gathered already? She kept quiet, but didn't hear any more. Her blood rushed through her ears, loud enough that she couldn't trust her hearing. She stayed still, but heard nothing more.

Lita was about to move forward when she noticed the shadows shift. No noise, nothing else, but the shadows beside the church changed. Someone was there. No, more than one person was standing just around the corner, waiting for her. Her instincts kicked in, her body reacting before her brain had fully registered the information. She bolted.

By rights, Lita should have been caught the first time she fell, sprawling to her knees in the loose gravel. Except somehow she managed to clamber to her feet and start running again before her pursuers closed the gap. Slamming through lopsided fencing into the dim sunlight, she crossed the tavern's empty parking lot as they trailed her. She dodged the few cars scattered along the road, where tall weeds had broken the surface into little chunks. Her pursuers were closing in, the crunch of their boots mere seconds behind. Panting hard, lungs straining, the copper flavor was so strong Lita could hardly taste the dust layering her mouth.

"Got her!" one of the men shouted.

"Do you require help?" a fainter voice called back.

"For one girl?" Lita heard him snort. "Almost run her into the ground."

Lita drew closer to the dilapidated buildings sprawled like a labyrinth at the bottom of the hill. Every step forced her oxygen-deprived muscles to push that bit more. Then her left knee popped as she hit a rough patch, and she fell forward on all fours. Her palms stung from the cement chips scattered throughout the rubble. Hot tears and fear choked her throat. She couldn't fail now.

She struggled to pull herself upright using some rusty spikes that dug metal into her grazed hands. Her bloodied knee stuck to her dress as she stood up, and the joint made a grating sound. She had been abusing her body for days now, and she had little gas left in the tank.

The men's footsteps sounded closer, two men moving with seemingly boundless energy. Dodging around the rubble to put distance between them, Lita hobbled down the hill, her legs aching. Her vision blurred, her heart pounded, but adrenaline numbed everything to a fine point. She bound her terror, holding it at bay with her will to live. She darted into a maze of row homes, listening as her pursuers missed the turn. She grinned wryly; it had turned out exactly how she'd hoped. Their greater mass and momentum clearly made them less agile than her, even with her injured knee.

Lita navigated the network of buildings carefully,

conscious her pursuers knew the terrain much better than she did. She stuck to the shadows, listening out for the men following her. She wandered the twisting roads, unsure that she'd lost them, but soon the only sounds were of a lonely bird. Peering around a doorway, Lita spotted an exit – a narrow alleyway that looked like it led far from the main street. She should be able to disappear into it. Heading into the weak sunlight, she allowed her stride to lengthen. Seconds later, there was a shout, then the sound of shoes thudding after her resumed.

Lita veered toward the alleyway. Another left, then only about six hundred yards along before–

"No, no, no!" A sturdy wire fence blocked the route she'd planned, piles of old wooden boxes and stacks of bricks making passage impossible.

With one hand pressed against the stitch forming on her right side, she peered at the alleyway, her chest heaving. There was no quick way out – she was cornered. Lita pushed down the panic fluttering in her stomach and reassessed the area, her brain humming along on overload.

Stepping behind one of the mounds of bricks, she faced the two men as they approached the alleyway entrance. Her lungs screamed at her, causing her to pant like a bulldog in the summer sun. Her hand drifted slowly down, so as to not attract attention, but encountered an empty space.

She glanced down in horror. She wasn't wearing her holster. In her panic she'd forgotten that she'd decided not to carry her gun because she was travelling on the bus. However, strapping a .41 to herself would not have been inconspicuous the way she had wanted to be. For the first time that day, cold fingers of fear slid down her spine. She shivered, despite the sunshine.

The men had noticed her hesitation, moving to either side of her. The alley wasn't wide, but she couldn't keep both of them in view at the same time. She tried to turn her attention from one to the other, but her aching body moved slowly, so slowly that she didn't notice the fist from behind until it connected with her temple. Her teeth snapped on her tongue. Blood spattered her attacker's face.

Her vision flashed white, then Lita found herself on one knee, her head ringing. The shorter of the two men kicked her stomach and flipped her flat on her back. She tried to punch, but the other man grabbed her hands.

Her head was ringing so badly she barely cared as they hauled her to her feet and dragged her back toward the church. The smell of smoke helped pull her back to her senses as they drew closer. And now there was a crowd milling around outside. A crowd of people she'd not seen the whole time she'd been there, but who were now trying to put the fire out themselves. But the church was taking significant damage. It was clear the people hadn't wanted help from the fire department, instead trying to quell the flames alone.

Lita blinked hard, trying to clear the tears from her eyes. No, she realized, her tears had dried, this was her vision doubling. Twenty, no, maybe more, people were scattered around the building. Had they been inside the church? Were they all cultists?

She was being dragged toward an old shed, maybe a garage, a few feet away from the burning church which she'd not taken much note of during her snooping. The air was thick with smoke, sparks spinning in the air. She didn't get a chance to stare as she was taken off into a dark corner away from the fire. The place was mostly empty, a few tools on the wall, a bolted door at the far end.

The men tied her to a chair, a solid wooden one, using ropes with zero give. She tried to flex her arms as they tied her, but one of them punched her in the stomach again. Winded, she couldn't fight back.

"Tell him we have her."

The shorter of the men, the one fond of winding her, scurried away. Lita tried to swallow and still her head to stave off the nausea, dizziness, and double vision, but her head throbbed and her ears rang. She blinked again, struggling to stay awake despite the darkness trying to take her vision. Her thoughts sped, memories, pain, and panic whirling through her brain in a way that only made the nausea worse. She realized distantly she was injured. Concussion, maybe.

Not that knowing about the injury helped. She was struggling to focus while tied tightly to a chair. There were twenty or so people nearby and someone – presumably a leader of some sort – was coming to deal with her. It was now, unhelpfully, that cold determination gave way to grief and pain. She started to shake, tears spilling from her eyes unbidden. Her vision blurred worse, and pain lanced her throat as she tried to swallow. She needed to be strong now more than ever, but all she wanted was relief.

Her shorter attacker returned with another man. The newcomer was taller, with broader shoulders and pale skin, and piercing dark eyes. Thick dark hair flowed loose over his shoulder, peppered with gray, as was his small beard. He had a few creases on his face – on anyone else Lita would call them smile lines – and as he walked closer, he did break out into a friendly smile which widened like a shark. Perhaps being tied to a chair before meeting him hadn't helped, but the man radiated an energy that made Lita's stomach turn. He reminded her of a car salesman trying to upsell her a clunker for the cost of a Cadillac.

"Look who we have here! I've heard you've been looking for me."

Lita didn't respond, trying desperately to swallow and keep her face blank.

"Lita, right? The poor lady who lost her husband and then went crazy. Yeah, the whole town knows about you." His scent was strange, none of the woodsy outdoor smells of the other men, but a citrus cologne that smelled expensive.

"And I have no idea who you are." Her voice wavered, despite herself.

The man didn't seem offended, placing his hands on his hips and laughing loudly. "Little lady like you got no business knowing about me. But sure, I can tell you. It'll make no difference anyway."

Though desperation had taken her only moments before, with every word that came out of his mouth it started to ease away, drowned out by anger that made her blood boil. Did he think she'd found him by luck? That it hadn't taken her hours of work and investigation to trace their corrupt network?

"I'm Sean Bateman. That'd be Mister Bateman to you.

Why are you harassing us? We're simple church folk who have done no harm to you."

Her dizziness was lifting slightly, her eyes able to focus more as the man paced back and forth in front of her. Behind him, the shorter attacker pulled out a knife, flipping it between his hands. Clearly a threat – as if she'd have a chance to run anywhere while tied like this.

"You killed my husband. Whatever lies you fed the police, I know it was you."

His smile tilted then, from friendliness into more of a sneer.

"The police know what's good for them. They work with us, so nothing gets past me."

Lita audibly scoffed, making her derision clear. His delusions were just that, and she wanted him to know that, despite their relative positions, she wasn't scared.

"You think we needed your husband's little shop for meat? We were being kind. You soon learned your place."

"You weren't being kind," Lita spat out. She thought of her husband, of how she'd found him. What they'd done to him. "I have no hope now. This is how I must grieve him."

"You have no hope because I took it. I ordered his death like I will order yours." Sean continued speaking over the top of her but she didn't listen anymore. This was the man who had killed John? He'd ordered his death, he said, as if it was nothing? Blood roared through her ears, her throbbing head inciting her temper to greater heights.

"However much you–"

Sean was interrupted as someone ran into the room.

"The church is beyond saving. Will this affect our worship of Umôrdhoth–"

"Silence!" Sean's beatific smile cracked as he whirled around to see what was happening. "We do not talk of Him in front of unbelievers." He ran from the shed.

As her head started to clear further, Lita thought about what she'd just heard. Umor, something? She tried to keep the name in mind. Umôrdhoth. She hadn't come across that name in her research so far, but there was something about it that resonated. Perhaps this was her next step? The name was obviously important to them; it must mean something. If, no– *when*, she got out of this, she would find out. She would find out and make them pay.

She strained to see what she could of what was happening outside. The discussion was clearly urgent, Sean Bateman calling over others to join in. In the distance she could hear the shouting getting louder, the splashing of water never ending as buckets were thrown in vain. The fire roared as it devoured the wooden structure.

Lita tried to catch their voices over the racket. They were talking about how it was vital to save the church. Lita's breath caught. That was good. This place needed to be destroyed. That gave Lita direction. Anything that would disrupt the cultists' plans.

Her own planning was disrupted as a blast ripped through the open door. Lita winced, despite the fact that the scattered wood chips didn't make it far into the little shed. Her heart pounded as dust and smoke choked the doorway. She couldn't see anything, only hear hurried movement, screams, flames, and smoke. A single figure pushed through the smoke, Sean Bateman glowering at her. He turned, heading off toward the town, tailed by her guards. They weren't gone far, so she couldn't move yet, but at least she had some breathing room.

Lita flexed her arms, testing the ropes. No give. Nothing. She fought exhausted discouragement. Next she tried pushing against the chair to see how flimsy it was. Solid oak. Not fragile in the slightest. Even if she tipped it, she doubted it would crack. Her legs weren't tied, though; at worst she could stand and try to smash the chair off her back. Anything to get out of here. Her simmering rage would give her the strength.

The fire flared, another blast shaking the ground and echoing. Smoke billowed in through the doorway. Sean staggered back in, bowing over and coughing and looking concerned for the first time. His bodyguard was gone, probably helping with the blaze. Lita's heart thundered. This was her chance.

She braced her feet, ready to stand, when a slender shadow fell across the floor. She froze. The shadow resolved into a familiar shape. Priya.

A hundred thoughts and feelings flooded Lita's chest. Happiness and relief at the sight of a familiar face, someone come to her aid in her darkest hour. But with it, guilt, terror, and the need to scream. Sweet, kind, careful Priya could not be here. Emily needed her. She needed Emily. Lita refused to destroy their lives over her plans for revenge. She ground her teeth, trying not to cry out for her friend or show her emotions, lest she endanger her.

Priya stood behind Sean Bateman in the door, her left

hand holding a gun, her right pressing her finger to her lips in a shushing gesture. Lita swallowed acid in her throat. Priya padded forward, the panicked cultists, Sean's hacking, and the burning inferno of a church covering the noise, and although her hand shook, she steadied the gun, her eyes wide. "Untie her," she told Sean, bluntly.

"What?"

That was all Sean managed to say before Priya shoved the gun in his face.

"Untie her," Priya repeated. She sounded angry, very unlike her usual soft and calm self. She wasn't quite as tall as the cult leader, but she still looked intimidating with her gun aimed at his cheek.

Sean flinched as though he'd been hit, glaring down at her with gritted teeth. His dark eyes flickered to the doorway. All it revealed was a wall of smoke and vague shadows, the sound of coughing and strained voices distant now. The mild concern in his face shifted to panic, the kind of panic you see in a cornered wolf. His hands shot up, a low jovial chuckle bursting from his chest as he tried to act in control. Priya stepped back, making sure she was out of his reach.

"I can do that, don't you worry, sweetheart," he said, but Lita could hear his insincerity. He was sizing Priya up, trying to determine if he could take her. Priya was smart. She kept her distance, herding him back toward Lita.

He slowly maneuvered around the chair, his eyes darting away from Lita toward the wall of tools, then back to her. Priya didn't seem to notice him sidling closer to the wall as he ostensibly headed to free her friend, but Lita did. Sean reached out, slow and casual, toward a huge wrench. Lita didn't have time to think, just react. She pushed up with her feet, hard, while leaning back. The wooden chair was heavy, her legs strained to move while tied, but she clenched her fists and pushed herself beyond all endurance. The chair slammed up, smashing into Sean's torso with a nauseating crunch. He huffed, then slid to the floor, wheezing.

"Lita!" Priya ran closer, steadying her as she settled back down.

Lita's legs screamed at her, the muscles tight and hot. She had to get up, try and stretch them, do something to ease the pain. Priya seemed to understand, grabbing a tool from the wall and cutting through the rope binding her. Lita stood, staggering a little as she fought for balance. The pain was intense, throbbing along her thighs, her calves screaming. She'd done too much for too long and her body was forcing her to stop.

"Not yet," she murmured to herself. She still felt more than a little dizzy, but her vision had cleared and her balance had stabilized. She shook out her hands and wrists, the blood flowing again. Lita gathered up the rope and knelt by Sean Bateman's prone body. He glared at her, his cheeks a rich purple as he gasped for breath. Maybe she'd hurt him too much to fight back, but she had to be sure. She used the rope to tie his arms and legs, twisting them uncomfortably until there was no way for him to move. Then she reached for an old greasy tool rag, ripping the stiff fabric open.

"What are you doing?" Priya asked.

"Gagging him." Lita slid the cloth underneath his head, readying it to twist into his mouth.

"Lita, the smoke in the air, the grease on that cloth. He's

going to suffocate." Priya sounded distraught.

Lita held back her initial response of "good," knowing that Priya deserved to escape this mess as innocently as she'd entered it. Lita might have no inhibitions about killing the man who killed her husband, but she refused to taint her friend in the process. She put the cloth down.

"We know where you live," Sean sullenly reminded her from where he lay.

"You have enough to worry about with your own house," Lita pointed out, as the heat and smoke thickened around them.

"We have time," Sean threatened. "You'll end up like your husband."

"One more remark like that and I'll put a bullet in you," Lita snarled. She took the gun from Priya, gently squeezing her friend's shoulder with her other hand. "Now we're leaving. Come after us and I will shoot you."

Sean scoffed but didn't try to move as Lita and Priya crossed the shed. The bolt on the back door creaked open, but the noise was insignificant compared to the blaze. No one would hear them. Lita let Priya go first, keeping an eye on Sean as Priya scoped out the road. When she motioned that it was clear, Lita started edging out the door.

"Help me! They're getting away!" Sean instantly bellowed from the floor, as a shadow darkened the smoke-filled main entrance.

Lita didn't want to wait, but she also knew how to shoot. She controlled her breathing, lowering it as she felt her blood beat through her neck, arms, and eyes. Focusing on that feeling, she shot between heartbeats.

Sean's body shuddered. Blood sprayed across the concrete floor in an arc.

Calm quiet flooded Lita's brain for a blissful moment. She let out a breath, her hand steadying. Then Priya's gasp echoed in her ears. Nausea roiled in her stomach. Priya couldn't see this.

Lita slammed the door shut to block the sight. The smoke was overtaking this side of the shed now, which helped. She didn't want to see the look on her friend's face. She grabbed Priya's wrist and bolted. She had no plan now, nothing but the need to get far away. To get to safety. She was in too much pain to run fast, but she had to get Priya away from them.

They stumbled away, hips bumping into each other, hands clutching together. Whenever Lita felt like she might stumble, Priya seemed to know, pulling on her arm to support her. They were in the middle of nowhere, the end of a long road out of Arkham, with no easy way back home.

There was a shout behind her. The sound of panting. Lita pulled on Priya's hand before dropping it, skidding to a stop in the center of the deserted main street. She raised her .41, holding it steady as the people pursuing them rounded the corner. Two men, cultists, both middle-aged and flushed from the exertion. They slowed down, mouths hanging open in surprise when faced with the gun.

"You might like to know that I'm a good shot," Lita lied. "I recommend you turn the hell around right now before I lose my patience."

The men glanced at each other, then headed toward her again, their faces the usual chilling blank. Lita only wanted to escape, but she had no choice. She aimed her gun and fired, clipping one of them in the shoulder. Red blossomed over his white shirt as he stumbled, grabbing at the wound.

"Any closer and I'll aim for your heart. That was your last chance." Lita aimed the gun toward the uninjured man. "One... two..."

Lita had barely started counting before both men had turned on their heels, throwing fearful glances over their shoulders. She waited for a moment or two, surprised it had been so easy.

She only realized that the gunshots had damaged her hearing when a large fire truck pulled up beside her. She lowered the gun, tucking it out of sight in her clothes.

A square man of middling height jumped down from the cab. He was dressed in the recognizable long blue-black coat of the Arkham fire company. Lines creased his face with age, though he had a thin beard that dusted a soft chin. He peered around warily and rushed to them, placing himself between them, the fire and the cultists in a protective, pointed way.

"Priya?" His voice was scratchy from smoke and young sounding. He let out a breath, reaching out to touch her friend's arm. "I thought that was you. You alright?" He scanned them both eagerly with big, concerned eyes.

Lita had never met this man, but it was clear Priya knew him well. That made him safe. Lita relaxed, but only marginally, her gun held tight under her clothes.

"Dean," Priya sounded relieved, taking a moment to cough some of the smoke from her lungs. "I'm not sure. There's a huge fire just up the road, and these crazy men are running around shooting guns."

"Did you hear that? We better get some help out here. Someone go call the State Police." Dean tapped on the cab door before turning back to Priya, grabbing her by the shoulders. "Do you want to sit in the truck? What can I do?"

"We need to leave. It's not safe," Lita butted into the conversation. She pointed to some nearby bicycles thrown to the floor. "We can cycle out of here."

Dean eyed her, taking in the blood on her clothes, the soot darkening her skin, before nodding. "Yeah, OK. Well, we're here now, we won't let anyone past us. You two get home safe, alright, Priya?"

Priya nodded, patting his hands on her shoulders until he dropped them. "I'll call you later. You stay safe too, it's dangerous up there."

"Dean's got us," a new voice called from inside the truck. The man leaned out of the open door, a huge fire axe in his hands. "We'll be fine. If we get a move on."

Dean nodded, taking a step back. "Right, stay safe. We'll speak soon."

Lita grabbed Priya's hand, leaving Dean to head back to his firefighting buddies. Lita moved toward the bikes, glancing behind her to see the fire truck driving toward the burning church.

"They'll be OK," Lita reassured her friend. "It's too public for the cultists to do anything."

They had almost made it back to town when Lita dropped off the bicycle, blood dripping from her head wound, her knees trembling. She took a breath, then another, gulping the fresh air into her lungs. Her head really hurt now, and she figured a doctor's visit was her next step. Once she could get her legs to work again.

There was a noise beside her. Priya had dropped her bike and lay sprawled on her back, staring up into the midday sky. Her soft breathing turned into a laugh. Soft and low. Relieved. Perhaps a little shocked. Her eyes were wide, but there was a curve to her lips.

"We made it. Thanks for finding me," Lita grated out.

"Idiot." Priya punched her lightly. "If I hadn't gone to check on you and found your note I wouldn't have. What would have happened to you? Huh?"

Lita sat back on her haunches, gazing up at the bright sun. It warmed her, helping her to feel good despite all her aches and pains. "Honestly, I don't know. Maybe I could've broken that chair. Maybe we'd have all burned together. But we're here now. That's good enough."

"It's not good enough. I worry about you and your obsession." Priya frowned. "At least make sure you're fully healed before you go back out there. You've got weeks-old bruises still."

"Fine. I'll heal," Lita nodded, smiling as Priya lit up at her agreement. "I don't want this to happen again."

Lita thought of John, of how she'd brought him some small measure of vengeance in killing Sean, the man who had ordered his murder. But what she didn't mention was the name Umôrdhoth. That the cultists worshipped him.

Perhaps she didn't know anything about him or how to stop him. But Ida Smith the local librarian might. And, if not, Lita would access the Miskatonic University library. She might have won one small victory today, but her war was far from over.

THE HOUNDS BELOW
Josh Reynolds

... infra canes videte quoniam tu ululabitis...
LUDVIG PRINN, DE VERMIS MYSTERIIS

Holsten navigated the long, sterile corridors of the administration wing of Arkham Sanatorium, his shoes squeaking on the ugly linoleum. The writer walked briskly, with what he hoped was an air of purpose and determination. He shifted his bag from one hand to the other, comforted by the weight of his life's work.

Despite appearances, he was nervous. There was no denying that he'd begun to lose hope of ever speaking to Philip Drew. Mintz and a few of the other doctors seemed to regard the man as private property, and it had taken months of glad-handing and outright begging to even be allowed see him – let alone speak to him for any length of time. Even then, he'd had to agree to having a chaperone, as he wasn't a doctor or even an academic – just a layman, writing a book. Unfortunate, but insurmountable.

When he found the office he was looking for, the door was already open. "Is that you, Mr Holsten?" a woman's voice called out from within as he made to knock.

Holsten, surprised, nodded then, shaking his head at his own idiocy – of course she'd heard him coming – said, "Yes... Doctor Fern, wasn't it?"

"That's me. I heard your shoes squeaking on the linoleum. Thought it must be you." A prim red-headed woman, dressed in dark clothes and wearing glasses, stepped out of the office and shut the door behind her. She gave him a chilly smile. "I want you to know up front that I argued against this."

Momentarily taken aback, Holsten had no reply. Fern continued, "Philip's mental state is fragile at best – one wrong word, and he could very likely plunge into an abyss of personality so deep that we would never recover him."

"The papers called him feral," Holsten said.

"The papers said a lot of things. Most of it was hogwash."

"Then he's not a cannibal?"

Fern paused. "I don't care for that term. If you're asking whether he's gripped by anthropophagic compulsion, the answer is, unfortunately, yes. But to my knowledge, he has never eaten anyone."

"Didn't he bite off that police officer's ear?"

Fern grimaced. "Yes, but he didn't eat it." She looked him up and down. "I mean it, Mr Holsten. If I think your questions are out of bounds, I'll haul you out of his room myself. It's taken months to even get him temporarily lucid. I won't have you sensationalizing him like he's some freak in a travelling circus."

Holsten shook his head. "I assure you, I have no intention of hurting him – quite the contrary, in fact. I think the book I'm working on will be of great use in understanding Mr Drew, and those like him."

Fern gave a grunt of what Holsten judged to be either disagreement, or disbelief. As if in an attempt to change the subject, she said, "Philip is housed in the secure wing. That's another reason you need a chaperone – no one without proper credentials gets into the secure wing unescorted."

Holsten nodded. He'd found out that much himself in his previous attempts to gain access to Drew. "I thought you said he wasn't dangerous."

Fern's face was expressionless. "I never said that."

Holsten frowned, but didn't protest. If she thought she was going to scare him, she was wrong. He'd once trailed a madman through a snowstorm; this was nothing. She led him away from her office and down the corridor.

Fern kept up a tour guide's commentary as they walked. "The secure wing houses around fifteen patients at any one time. Drew has been here the longest. Due to his compulsions, we can't let him interact with the rest of the patients – even supervised, he's a danger to himself and others."

"Has he tried to escape?"

Fern glanced at him. "Once or twice. Along with his compulsion to eat human flesh, he seems to be gripped by an irregular mania – usually brought on by emotional distress. At that point there's nothing much you can do with him, save sedate him."

Holsten, despite wanting to ask more about the mania, simply said, "I'm surprised anyone's brave enough to get that close." He'd decided to keep his questions to a minimum. It wouldn't do for Fern to think him too eager.

Fern sighed. "Philip is not a monster, Mr Holsten. He is not a boogeyman to be feared, but rather someone to be pitied. Despite the moniker the newspapers hung on him, he's no more a wolf-man than you are."

Holsten nodded. "I never claimed he was. I've been studying anthropophagic compulsions for years – mostly out west and up north. I've found that cannibalism is often the result of environmental stressors – not just hunger, mind, but also isolation, weather, and even the pull of the moon on the waters of the brain – which are then filtered through cultural and religious perceptions. Cannibalism is a relatively rare occurrence, but our perception of it lends it a weight that is far out of proportion."

Fern glanced at him again, more appraisingly this time. "An interesting theory."

"Hopefully my publishers will agree," Holsten said, with a laugh. Fern didn't join in. She seemed a humorless woman. Then, in his experience, working in a place like this often sucked the joy right out of a person. He'd learned swiftly that such places were not for him. He much preferred being a writer.

The walk was an uneventful one. Despite all the stories he'd heard, the sanatorium was no ancient asylum, full of gibbering prisoners or brutal treatments. It was a modern facility, run by a modern staff. Fern's presence alone proved that. Patients wandered freely, but always under careful observation by the orderlies who seemed to stand sentinel everywhere he looked. He clutched his bag more tightly.

Each wing of the sanatorium was separated from the others by a set of heavy doors, as well as a desk. Orderlies were stationed at each desk, in order to check IDs and paperwork. Fern ushered him past the desk guarding the path to the secure wing with little difficulty. The orderly barely looked at them, being more intent on his copy of the *Arkham Advertiser*.

Finally, Fern gave a discreet cough. Startled, the orderly looked up. "Oh, hiya, doc. I didn't have you on the roster for today."

Fern glanced at Holsten. "Schedule change, Rodney. Not my idea."

"Who you here for?"

"Drew," Fern said. Rodney took a key off the board and handed it to her. Holsten set his bag down on the desk.

"Do you need to check me over?" he asked. "Make sure I'm not hiding a file in a cake or something?"

"Did you bring a cake?" Rodney asked.

"Well, no."

"Then why would I care what you hid in it?" Rodney grinned, to show he was joking. "You're with the doc, that's good enough for me. Abandon all hope and such."

Holsten blinked. "What?"

"Ignore him. Rodney read a book once and he never lets us forget it." Fern had a slight smile on her face as she spoke, and Rodney guffawed. Holsten got the sense the two knew each other well. "Come on."

She led Holsten through the doors and into the secure

wing. It was quieter here than in the rest of the building, presumably because none of the inmates were allowed to roam about. That was not to say it was silent.

There were sobs and shrieks, the pounding of fists and bellowed protests. A cacophony of the lost and the damned. All of it muffled by the thick cell doors that lined either wall, each one a matte black rectangle with a single viewing slot set into it at eye level.

Only one door was silent. Holsten knew who was behind it before Fern said anything. She indicated the door. "This is his."

Holsten nodded, clutching his bag to his chest. He wondered if Drew knew they were there – maybe he could hear them, or smell them. If so, there was no indication. Fern unlocked the door and stepped back as it swung open. "Philip? It's Dr Fern. I've come to speak with you again, if you're up to it."

Silence. The interior of the cell was dark, and the smell – it reminded Holsten of a wolf's den he'd once had the bad fortune to stumble on. Noticing his discomfiture, Fern said, "We have electricity rigged up throughout the building, but Philip has asked that we keep the lights off in his cell. They hurt his eyes, or so he claims." She cleared her throat, as she had with the orderly. "Philip?"

Inside the cell, someone grunted, and springs squeaked. Squinting, Holsten perceived a lanky, pale shape unfolding off a cot. The man had been laying with his face pressed to the wall. He was naked, his lean frame pockmarked by scars, and his face resembled a waxen mask beneath a shaggy salt and pepper mane.

"He's naked," Holsten said.

"He doesn't like clothes. Tears them to ribbons. Easier just to avert your eyes."

Drew set his bare feet on the floor, but did not rise. "Dr Fern?" he croaked, in a voice rusty from disuse. "Is it time for our appointment?"

"No, Philip. This visit is unscheduled."

Yellow eyes rolled in deep sockets until they settled on Holsten. He felt a flicker of fear as he met that placid, yet somehow malign, gaze. It was like meeting the eye of a tiger at the zoo. The animal appeared content, but that contentment was merely a mask.

Drew rose; he was taller than Holsten had thought. His nudity made him seem only more of an animal. There was nothing lewd about it, the way there might have been with another patient. "Who are you?" he asked.

"Philip, this is Mr Holsten. He wants to talk with you, if you're up to it."

"About what?" Drew continued to stare. Holsten wondered whether it was simple curiosity, or something else. He shifted his weight, trying to hide his sudden nervousness.

He screwed up his courage and spoke. "Your story, Mr Drew – Philip. May I call you Philip? I'd like to ask you about your troubles, if I might."

Drew blinked. He looked at Fern. "I'm hungry, doctor." He said it almost plaintively. As if it were an affliction, rather than a simple fact of biology.

"It's in your mind, Philip. You've eaten today, I'm told. Whatever you're feeling – this craving – it isn't physical."

Fern spoke quickly, the words rote. Holsten wondered how often this conversation had played out between them.

Drew nodded. "I know. I know it's in my head. Unfortunately, it's my stomach you need to convince." He gave a sorrowful chuckle at his own joke, and his attentions swung back to Holsten. "Why?" he asked.

Startled, Holsten said, "Why what?"

"Why do you want to know my story?"

"I – ah – a book. I'm writing a book."

"About me?"

"People like you."

Drew smiled, showing his teeth. They were long and seemed not altogether right for the shape of his mouth. "Cannibals, you mean."

"Yes, if you like."

Drew studied him for a moment, and then sat back down on his cot. He stared at his hands for a moment, then stiffened. Head tilted, he seemed to listen intently to something for a moment, then gave a resigned nod. "Very well. Where would you like me to begin?"

"The beginning, if you would."

Drew's expression became positively saturnine. "The beginning? If you like." And, hesitantly, he began to speak.

How to start? I will not bore you with how I came to join the army, or why. Suffice to say, I was motivated by the usual foolishness that a man my age ought to know better than to succumb to, but so rarely does. I wasn't the only alumnus of Miskatonic to precede our nation into the war – there was that tow-headed devil, West, for instance. Like him, I joined a Canadian regiment, and was a first lieutenant by 1915.

Nor will I waste breath on describing those first fear-fraught months at the front. The noise, the smell – it was an alien world, far removed from the gambrel roofs and narrow lanes of Arkham. I may as well have been on Mars. Despite it all, I am told I was an exemplary soldier. My parents own – owned – a farm out near Aylesbury Pike, halfway to Dunwich, and I grew up knowing how to pot what I aimed at. Though it must be said that rabbits are not known for shooting back.

We – us and the Germans both – made a charnel house of Flanders. I toughed out gas attacks and raids. I could swing a mattock with the best of them, and when the enemy came over the lip, I met them with whatever was to hand. I learned the fine art of cooking rats and shoe leather. I learned to relieve myself where I hunkered, so as to better keep warm.

In a word, I survived. That is all any man can do in such awful conditions. I survived assaults and counterassaults, sickness and bombardment. More, I survived the stupidity of my superiors, and their superiors. I survived it all. Though sometimes I wish I had not.

No, forgive me – I am fine. I will continue. My story – the part of it you wish to hear – begins in 1915, in Flanders. Specifically, Chateau Wood, near Hooge. I was part of a detachment ordered to... Well. It does not matter now, I suppose. The war is done, and my part in it is of little importance. Suffice it to say, we did not succeed in our mission, and none of us made it back to the safety of our lines.

I alone survived the disastrous affair, though I was left with a bullet in my leg – you can see the scar here – and an accompanying infection. Injured and delirious, I found myself wandering in the emptiness between our lines and those of the enemy – a wasteland of shattered trees, burned out houses and mud.

The mud is what I remember most. An odd thing, I know, but some days it seemed the whole of our world was a purgatory of mud and smoke. Worse were the great boreholes that had been gouged in the earth by incessant bombardment. They reminded me of graves waiting to be filled, and, more than once, I fancied I saw maggots of immense size squirming in these craterous wounds – but it was only ever smoke and shadows.

I do not know how long I wandered. It is trite to say time had no meaning, and yet for me it did not. The days bled into one another, and it seemed that the whole world had been emptied of life, save the dogs. I never saw them, but I knew they were there, for I heard them howling in the distance or even, in my less lucid moments, beneath my feet, and I often saw where they had been at the dead.

Indeed, they were my constant companions. However far I travelled, wherever I hid, their howls reached me. In my growing delirium, I fancied that they were guiding me somewhere. When their cries grew faint, I found my path altered until they became loud once more. I did not mean to follow them – I simply did.

I stumbled on and on, day into night. The guns thundered and the war progressed, but I noticed none of it, even as I took cover from rolling banks of poisonous fog, or buried myself in mud to escape the attentions of distant passersby. Ally or enemy, I could not tell, and I had not the heart to risk it. Fear was my armor.

I had no destination in mind, no desire, save to go where the dogs wished. They led me a merry trek, along shattered roads and through burnt-out fields, and in my delirious state I was only too happy to follow. At night, when I allowed myself rest, I tried to dig the bullet from my leg – though with no success.

Finally, I could walk no farther. My injured leg ceased to bear my weight at an inopportune moment, tumbling me into an abandoned section of trench line. Racked by pain, I crawled across splintered duck boards. I could hear something moving around me, within the very walls of the trench, just out of sight – rats, I thought then. I know better now.

I called out, I think, but received no reply save a distant howling. The dogs were abandoning me, or so I feared. Survival of the fittest. I howled for them, clawing at the mud and dragging my useless leg. I was wholly mad by then. Feverish and starving, having drunk no water save what I had gleaned from filthy craters.

But my delirium was not so great that I could not recognize death when it was rolling towards me. Every soldier grew to fear the tang on the air that heralded the yellow cloud. It crept down the trench behind me, filling every nook and cranny with lethal inevitability.

Frantic, I turned and spied a body, half-sunk into the muddy wall of the trench. I could not tell his nationality, nor did I care – all that concerned me was the battered gas mask in his stiffened, claw-like hands.

I scrambled to the body and wrestled with it, trying to tear the mask from the corpse's grip. The closer the cloud drew, the angrier I became – as if the dead man intended to spite me. I cursed and wept, pleading and screaming.

Finally, I seized upon a rock and hammered at his hands, reducing them to pulp. I tore the mask free even as the first tendrils of yellow caressed the trench wall. I dragged on the mask just in time. The world turned a sickly shade of jaundice, and where the cloud touched my bare skin, I burned. But better burning than drowning. I huddled against the corpse, seeking shelter in the mud, waiting for the fog to pass over or disperse.

Then, through the befouled lenses of the mask, I saw black shapes emerge from the cloud and prowl down the trench line. My first thought was that it was an offensive, by one side or the other. But as they drew close, and I saw the mishmash of gear and uniforms, I recognized them for what they were – scavengers.

There had been rumors, of course. And deserters were common enough. But to see them, to witness their desecration of the dead for myself – I could scarcely believe it. The sight of them shocked me into lucidity, and my first instinct was to look for a weapon. As I said, I'd heard the rumors, and I knew what such men would do if they caught me.

But as I searched for something to defend myself with, I heard a metallic *shink* and the barrel of a pistol dug into the base of my skull. "Hello. What's this, then?" a muffled voice murmured. An English accent, though I couldn't be sure.

A strong hand gripped my shoulder and flung me onto my back, jostling my injured leg in the process. I'm afraid I screamed in pain – and passed out.

I still recall something of my dreams – they haunt me even now. Of squirming, pallid bodies and tumbling earth. Of mountains of corpses, and the sound of teeth. Of eating and eating and eating–

Forgive me. Sometimes all of it gets the best of me. The hunger is a weight, sitting in my stomach, dragging me down into darkness. The more I struggle against it, the heavier it becomes. I am always so hungry – oh so hungry... No. No. Thank you, Dr Fern. I... I am capable of continuing. I want to continue.

When I awoke, I found myself laying on a bed of sacking in a gloomy redoubt, lit by lanterns and candles. There were maybe a dozen other men crammed into the shelter. They spoke to one another in low voices, or played cards. Some were eating, and my stomach gave a treacherous rumble as I smelled the heady scent of trench stew. None of them paid me any mind, not even when I issued a hoarse greeting.

Then, one turned and came to my side. He crouched beside me, forcing me to lay back. "Easy there. You've had a time of it, and you're not shipshape just yet." It was the same voice I'd heard in the trench. The Englishman was short and broad, with a heavy growth of bramble-like beard. He introduced himself as Ramsden – a former general practitioner from Hartlepool, I came to learn.

He was also the closest thing the scavengers had to a leader. He was more solicitous than one might have thought, though in a rough sort of way. The war had that effect on some men, wearing away any sheen of respectability they might once have possessed.

"It would have done for you, soon enough," he said, showing me the offending bullet as if it were a trophy. "Tried to get it out yourself, didn't you?"

I nodded mutely, and he chuckled. "I figured that's why your leg looked like it had been near as gnawed off. You're lucky. Fever broke almost as soon as I had it out, and the wound clean. You're a tough lad, right enough."

"Thank you for saving me," I said. "I thought…" I hesitated, not wanting to offend my rescuer. He smiled.

"Thought you were for the stewpot, eh?"

I laughed. "In a manner of speaking."

Ramsden made himself comfortable. "I won't lie, if I'd thought you weren't liable to survive, I might have put you out of your misery there and then. Only the strong survive here – the rest are naught but meat." He said it solemnly, as if it were nothing more than plain truth, but the words made me shudder.

We spoke at length, though I cannot now recall the substance of that conversation. At some point he went and procured a cup of stew for me, as well as water. Though the stew tasted strange, I tucked in. As I greedily ate, Ramsden told me about him and his fellows. Like me, it seemed, they were largely victims of circumstance. Or so Ramsden insisted.

They were men with no loyalty save to one another. The relentless grind of battle had worn away all nationalism, making patriots into survivors. They endured a twilight existence in the cartographic gaps between the lines, scavenging what they needed but otherwise taking no part in the greater conflict. They could not return to their fellows, for they would be shot as deserters – or worse.

And, for better or worse, I was now one of them. As you might imagine, I was somewhat taken aback by this – but I am ashamed to say I saw the appeal. My experiences had, if not quite broken me, then surely battered my youthful certainties. All that I had seen, all that I had endured – there seemed no point to any of it. Ramsden spoke quietly of all that he had experienced, and I found myself in agreement with his weary philosophy.

Why? Fear, Mr Holsten. Earlier, I said that fear was my armor. So it was, and I clung to it. I feared to return to the meat grinder that had almost claimed me. And, too, a part of me saw the hand of fate in my new berth. Had I not been guided to safety, after all?

The dogs – yes, Mr Holsten. Yes, indeed. Their howling continued to haunt me, at the edges of my hearing. I never spoke aloud of them to Ramsden or any of the others. I could not believe that they did not hear it, but I did not wish to reveal it, if it was simply a trick my mind was playing on me.

No – no, Mr Holsten. Save your questions, please. My tale is almost finished.

Slowly, but surely, I fell into their routine. By day, we would crouch in our hole, listening to the thunder overhead. And at night, we would slither out and salvage what we could. I don't know how Ramsden found our bounty. Luck, perhaps. He claimed it was God, looking out for his flock. Later, I wondered – but no. We are not there, not yet. We scavenged weapons and ammunition, clothes… food. We were always short of food. That is my most vivid recollection of those shadowy days.

I became a shrunken ghost of the man I had been. But no matter how often the specter of starvation haunted us, Ramsden always seemed to find food, just as we needed it most. Whenever I thought I might faint from hunger, there Ramsden was, with a bowl of trench stew and the occasional bolt of rancid protein – rat, I thought. Maybe horse, or dog.

I began to wonder about that, however, for the howling of the dogs never seemed to lessen. Indeed, it swelled, and often I awoke to hear the sound of frantic digging from somewhere on the other side of the dirt walls that sheltered us. I feared that at any moment an invading horde of starving animals would pour into our lair and devour us all.

Finally, unable to bear it any longer, I spoke to Ramsden of it, and he laughed. "Nothing to fear there, my lad. We're all of us dogs here, and they know their own kind. Besides, there's a world of corpses out there – plenty for everyone." His words comforted me, though I found them confusing at the time.

What? Oh yes, the corpses. We collected them as well. No, no; not for the reasons you think, Mr Holden – though perhaps that might have been preferable.

If I am to be a monster, let me be an honest one. Someone famous said that, I think. I am a monster, but an honest one. My fangs are bared to the world, and I do not clothe my wolfishness in sheepskin. Eh? Yes, yes, forgive me. Where was I? Oh yes. The dead.

Ramsden, you see, insisted on giving them a proper burial, whatever their country of origin. He was, it seemed, something of a religious man. His argument against the war was as much theological as it was philosophical, and I spent many hours in friendly debate with him. He believed that our situation was akin to a holy calling – that we were pilgrims of a new way of peace and brotherhood. Men united in their hatred of the war, and their reverence for the wronged dead.

I could not find it in me to argue with him on that point, for the evidence was unmistakable. The men he had gathered to him spoke more than English or French; Dutch, German, Flemish – even a few Russians, though God alone knew how they'd wound up so far west. Regardless, all of them believed as Ramsden did – and fervently, with a devotion that was frightening at times. Perhaps it was simply that Ramsden fed them – fed us.

When we found the dead, we buried them in communal graves – artillery craters, often – using whatever tools were to hand. Ramsden said words over them, as kindly as any country vicar, as we heaped mud and dirt over them. At the time, I thought these homilies to be Latin – a sign of Papist leanings in the good doctor. It was only later that I realized… Well. I'm getting somewhat ahead of myself.

But for every one we buried, two more would be found the next day. I suspected that at times we were burying the same men over and over again, so similar did they look – then, all dead men resemble each other. Yet I was certain of it, save that the bodies were often more mangled on their subsequent interments. The others ignored my suspicions, though from the looks that passed between them, I knew that I was not the first to take note of it.

At first, I thought the dogs had been at them. That as we hunted, so too did they. And yet, as before, I never saw them. Not once. I could not imagine such a large pack of animals hiding anywhere in the wasteland without leaving some sign – but I never saw so much as a paw print. Nor were any of my new compatriots helpful in that regard. They did not admit to it, but I knew that they heard them nonetheless.

How? Ah. The looks on their faces. The way some of them flinched, or turned – as if listening to the howlers in the dark. Whenever we found a twice-buried body, they murmured to one another in quiet voices, always excluding me.

Finally, I decided to satisfy my own curiosity. I told Ramsden of my suspicions, and my intention to wait beside one of the recent graves to see what came, if anything. To his credit, he did not try to talk me out of it. Somewhat to my surprise, he offered to join me.

I armed myself with a rifle, and as night fell and the rest of our merry band dispersed to scavenge, I settled myself to wait near the most recent grave. It was a deep crater – deeper than most – and we'd rolled at least a dozen bodies down into it the previous night. Then we'd heaped mud and dirt onto them as best we could. I could still just make out the vague suggestion of bodies, but had no interest in looking any closer.

We sat at the edge of the crater, in the lee of a lonely wall – the last remaining vestige of a farmhouse, perhaps. I felt a curious sense of anticipation. Not fear, but eagerness. As if I were on the cusp of solving some great mystery. I said as much to Ramsden.

"And what mystery might that be, my lad?"

"The dogs, Ramsden. I will find where they go – where they hide." I could not tell you now why such a thing mattered to me then. I knew only that I must.

"Dogs?" Ramsden chuckled. "Yes, I suppose they are dogs of a sort. Us too." He settled himself against the wall and scratched his bearded chin. "All of us dogs together. But not street curs, no – prize hunting dogs, we are."

"What do you mean?"

"How many have we buried, lad?"

I had no answer for him. I had not even considered it, through all our weeks together. Ramsden smiled and something in his expression made me shiver. He went on. "In all this time, we've never seen another living soul." He gestured vaguely. "The war continues, but we are untouched. God's hand."

I shook my head, not understanding.

"Don't you see? We're protected," Ramsden insisted. "They led you here, lad, the way they led all of us. They saved you, so that you might do our Lord's work and serve him up the banquet he desires."

"The…" Words briefly failed me as I at last grasped his meaning. "The dead?"

"The dead, yes. They belong to him. Always have, always will. That is why we bury them in this ravaged earth –

so that they might join him, in Heaven."

I made to speak, but was interrupted by a sudden noise – a bark. I rose and hurried to the edge of the crater, rifle at the ready. I saw movement. Ramsden followed me. "Keep quiet," he murmured. "They startle easy." I paid little attention to his words, being more intent on what I saw below.

They were not dogs. Not unless they were the very hounds of Hell, loosed to feast on the detritus of man's murderous hubris. Spindle-legged and raggedy, they squirmed up out of the mud and slithered among the dead, barking to one another with what I took to be guttural amusement. They were grotesque creatures, like some horrid jumble of man, animal and corpse, with pale, piebald flesh and fangs and claws.

Ah. I see by the look on your face that you recognize my description, Mr Holden. Perhaps in your research you have read of the ghul of the Arabian Peninsula, or the giaour of the Turk. The Romans knew them too, as canes ad infernis – the hounds below.

Yes, I have learned much of them since that night, though I wish that I knew nothing at all. I wish… I wish I was ignorant, or dead, or anything but oh so hungry.

I am hungry, Dr Fern. I know you say it is nothing, but I feel it gnawing away at me. I… No. No. I will finish my story. To do otherwise would be rude.

My breath caught in my throat, and before I knew it, I had the rifle up, and I sighted down the barrel. But before I could fire, Ramsden's hand fell on my shoulder. "I wouldn't. You'll only go making them angry, lad."

I glanced at him, and saw that he had a pistol in his hand. Though it was not aimed at me, I knew it would be, if I did not lower my rifle. "What... What are they?"

"Dogs, lad. Just like us. Our master's hounds."

"I am nothing like those... those things down there," I hissed, hoping they would not hear us. But, to my horror, those closest to us turned and looked up, their eyes gleaming in the gloom of the pit. Then, slowly, a handful began to creep towards us.

I made to back away, but Ramsden shook his head. "No, lad. It's time you saw this – time you took part, the way the others have. We've all done it." He turned and gestured to the creeping things. One gave a gurgling chortle, reached down and tore a red strip of meat from the nearest body. It tossed this gory prize to Ramsden, who caught it easily, as if he had done so a thousand times before.

He turned back to me, and I am sad to say I flinched back. Ramsden shook his head, disappointed. "It's not like you haven't had it before, lad. Just a bit fresh, is all."

I stared at him in incomprehension. His smile was almost fatherly as he said, "The stew, lad. Where did you think the meat came from?"

It is obvious, in retrospect. After all, dogs are often fed from their master's table, are they not? And like any spoiled dog, I have grown to long for the taste of my master's food – a longing which has only grown in the years since.

Ramsden extended the chunk of meat. "This is different, though. It requires witnesses. Eat, and you will truly know the glory of he who waits below."

At his words, the creatures howled as one, and I knew then that it was their voices I had been hearing, their voices that had guided me to Ramsden and the others. I saw it all in that instant – the terrible scope of it. I was damned, and had been damned the moment I had survived where the others had died.

"Eat – or be eaten, that is the way of it." Ramsden held out that gory hunk of meat, and for a moment I was tempted. Something about it, about the smell of it – my stomach growled, and Ramsden smiled, and it was that smile that shook me loose from my horror. For it was not a sinister smile, or a cruel one.

It was a smile of contentment. Of satisfaction.

The smile of a well-fed hound.

I fired the rifle without consciously choosing to do so. A reflex, prompted by sudden revulsion. Ramsden fell back, slowly – so slowly. He tumbled down into the charnel pit, there to join the rest of the meat. And I – I turned and ran.

I ran so long and hard that I thought my lungs might burst. I do not know whether they followed me. I do not think so. After all, what need had they to chase me down, when I was already theirs?

I do not recall the events of my flight, or how I managed to stumble back through Allied lines. I remember only the quiet murmur of a nurse's voice, and the harsh lights of a hospital tent. And the howling, of course. Distant, but ever-present.

Malnourished and sick – I could keep no food down – they invalided me home. My tribulations continued as I searched in vain for some way to cure my affliction. I could not sleep, could not eat. I dreamed of dead men, and bestial maggot-shapes barking in joy. I dreamt of Ramsden, falling back, a single word on his lips.

No. I cannot dwell on it. Not when my stomach clenches, and I dream of great feasts. But what sort of feasts? And who are these others in attendance?

I do not wish to think about it.

And yet, I cannot stop.

Drew completed his tale and sagged back on his haunches, head bowed. His hands gripped at the air. Holsten and Fern were silent. From the look on her face, Holsten thought she might have heard the story before. But even so, it still repulsed her.

Witless fool.

Holsten cleared his throat. "Very... interesting." He fought to keep the glee from his voice. Drew's tale was exactly what he'd hoped it would be.

Drew's head snapped up, eyes narrowed. For a moment, Holsten thought he might lunge – and felt something like a thrill of anticipation. But instead he shook his head and looked away. "You think I am deluded."

Fern spoke up quickly. "No, Philip, he doesn't. None of us do. Confused, maybe."

Drew laughed, a raspy, rusty sound. "Confused. Yes. Maybe I am." He looked at Holsten again. "Are you still going to write about me?"

"I... Yes. Yes, obviously. The... The name. What was it?" He regretted the question even as he asked it. It was something better asked in private, without the disapproving presence of Fern to put Drew off. Even so, he could not stop himself.

He needed to know. Had to know. Else what was it all for?

"What name?"

"The one Ramsden spoke. What was it?"

Drew stared at his hands. "I do not recall," he said, slyly. "Some nonsense. He was mad, as I am now mad."

Holsten frowned and made to press the issue when he heard a sudden, sharp clangor – as of a fire alarm. He turned to Fern. "What is that?"

"The general alarm," Fern said, her face going pale. "Something is going on."

"Go check it out. We'll be fine – won't we, Mr Drew?"

Drew nodded his shaggy head. "I shall be on my best behavior."

Fern hesitated. "Are you certain? He's not violent, usually, but…"

"I have a few more questions, and the orderly is right down the hall. We'll be fine." Holsten lifted his bag and opened it. He took out a leather notebook with a golden clasp, and a pen. He tried to appear nonchalant even as he prayed she would take the hint. Just a few minutes alone – that was all he needed.

Fern paused for a moment longer, then nodded and left the cell. She closed the door behind her, but did not shoot the bar, leaving it unlocked. Holsten listened to the tap of her heels on the linoleum, a staccato counterpoint to the alarm. When he raised his eyes, Drew was staring at him.

"You asked me the name," Drew said. "I did not say that it was a name."

Holsten froze. Then, with a sigh, he popped the clasp on his notebook. Inside, the pages had been cut to provide a hollow cavity. Inside was nestled a snub-nosed revolver. "No. You didn't. A slip on my part." Holsten drew the revolver from the book and cast the latter aside. "They didn't even check. Standards are not what they were."

"Have you come to kill me, then?" Drew straightened. He seemed almost relieved.

Holsten smiled. "No, Mr Drew – quite the opposite. I intend to free you from this place. You will be my Virgil."

Drew cocked his head, yellow eyes narrowed. "Virgil?"

"My guide into the underworld. You see, I too hear them howling. Though in my case, it is but dimly." Holsten paused. "I have heard them all my life, though for the longest time I did not know what it was I was hearing. But then I learned, and I began my search... looking for the one who might lead me to my destiny. The one who might know the name of that which I seek."

"Your book..."

"A convenient fiction." He turned towards the door. "Fern will be back soon. She will be our ticket out – a hostage always comes in handy. I didn't count on the disturbance, but it was timely nonetheless. It gave me a few moments to explain things to you."

"I've tried to escape before," Drew murmured.

"But this time you'll have help. They'll follow us, of course, but I think between us we can come up with a good hiding place, don't you?"

Holsten turned back to Drew, still smiling. Faintly now, he could hear the howls, as they shivered up from far below. Even muted and distant as they were, they promised him such delights as no man had ever known. Delights that had been denied him for so long. If he would but free their long-lost brother and bring him home.

"We'll have to kill her, of course..." He bared his teeth. "Then, I expect we'll have worked up quite the appetite in the interim." The thought filled him with incalculable joy. He had tasted human flesh before, but only hurriedly. Less a meal than a snack. But to savor, to feast – that would be a true pleasure. He was practically salivating at the thought.

Drew pushed himself to his feet. "I knew it from the first," he said, wearily. "I could see the beast in your eyes as you introduced yourself. You are not so far along as I, but you walk the same path nonetheless."

"Yes, yes," Holsten said, intently. "We are members of the same brotherhood, you and I – the servants of blessed Umôrdhoth." As he spoke the name, the howls increased in volume. The room seemed to echo with them, and Holsten closed his eyes, glorying in their raucous thunder. Drew clapped his hands to his ears.

"Do not say that name," he growled.

"Forgive me," Holsten said. "It is only that I am excited by the prospect of it." He paused. "They have forgiven you, you know – for your fear and weakness. I was weak too, once. I did not understand. But now I see. I hear the glory of it in their cries. So shall you, in time. And soon, we shall join our voices to theirs and howl our joy forever beneath the welcoming earth."

Drew smiled, but there was no mirth in it – no joy. "No."
Holsten paused. "What?"

"No. No, I think not." Drew shook his head. "What
makes you think I would go with you – or let you harm Dr
Fern?" His yellow eyes widened. His smile stretched into a
snarl even as he spoke. "But you were right about one thing,
Holsten – I have worked up something of an appetite."

With that, he leapt on Holsten, bearing him to the floor.
The pistol clattered away, out of reach. Holsten was big and
strong, and Drew was little more than a scarecrow of flesh
and bone. But his teeth were sharp, oh yes, and his nails
were thick, and he was hungry.

Oh so hungry.

LABYRINTH
Thomas Parrott

It was half past five when Joe Diamond heard the package come through the mail slot on his office door. Way too late for normal delivery. It hit the ground with a light smack, not much weight to it. For a moment, a shadow lingered against the frosted glass of the inset window, then it was gone.

The private eye came to his feet slowly. He already had one of the Colts in his hand. The metal of the grip was warm from where the shoulder holster kept it close to his body. Some people might have called that level of readiness paranoia. Those people hadn't seen the things that Joe had seen.

Joe made his way to the door. He unlocked it with a click and pushed it open. The hallway was empty. Whoever had dropped the package off had left in a hurry. The other offices were dark. Sensible people had gone home for the day.

He shut the door and locked it again. Only then did he return the 1911 to its holster. The package was in a manila folder. It rustled as he picked it up, a collection of paper inside. He carried it over to the desk and spilled the contents across the stained wooden surface.

The sun was sinking below the horizon. The last few rays were divided by the blinds on the window, scattering them across the items. Pictures and documents. Joe nudged through them with a frown. The photos were sharply divided. Most of them were of a young woman. She was olive skinned and dark haired. It was the expression that caught him, a mix of fear and exhaustion. She'd been scared for a long time.

The papers were police reports. Most of them were about the woman. She was an exchange student at Miskatonic University, named Nadia Leandros. She'd come to the city police multiple times begging for help. Something was harassing her, she said.

Something. Not someone.

Joe poured himself a finger of bourbon into a glass that hadn't been washed in too long. He sat down at the desk and set to absorbing all of this with his full attention. The police hadn't listened. How could they? The reports read like madness. Shadowy figures at night that dissolved when confronted. The sound of wings beating at her windows. Whispers from the drain of her sink. They dismissed her as a kook.

Someone had obviously thought otherwise. They'd brought it to the right place. Joe had seen a lot in his time. Too much to dismiss such things out of hand. There were things that went bump at night, and they were getting bolder by the day.

He turned his attention to the rest of the file. The difference was like night and day. The picture this time was of a stiff on a slab at the morgue. A man in his mid-fifties, if Joe was any judge. The body's skin was mottled strangely, but there was nothing conclusive to indicate how he'd died. The coroner's report called it natural causes.

Joe snorted as he read the rest of the notes. He didn't know of many natural things that made a man rot from the heart outward. There were pictures backing that up too. As if the insides had been dead and exposed for a month longer than the body itself. Joe knocked back the bourbon and sighed.

Something was circled on the picture: a birthmark on the back of the man's neck. A circle surrounded by dark tendrils, like a black sun. Joe flipped back to the pictures of the woman. Sure enough, she had the same mark. It was on her collarbone, only visible in one shot.

Joe drummed his fingers on the desk. There was only one sheet of paper left, a cursory police report on the man's death. The victim hadn't lived in Arkham for very long. He'd moved here only a few months before his death. The document included notes from conversations with his coworkers and neighbors. They spoke of paranoid behavior, of isolation, and of the impression of inescapable fear.

It wasn't as obvious as a one for one, but whoever had sent him this information was trying to paint a picture. That much was clear. A haunted person with a mark who ended up in the graveyard down by French Hill. Another person with the same mark, plagued by dark visitations. Do nothing, and she might end up in another cheap coffin.

Joe had never been good at doing nothing. He had a nose for trouble and a collection of scars to prove he never learned. That said, he was no one's fool. If one of the horrors that plagued the Arkham countryside was rearing its ugly head, he was better off knowing what he was up against.

There was no more information to be had from the file. If he wanted to find out more, he was going to have to hit the streets, and he thought he knew just where to look. The files at City Hall wouldn't be of any help. He needed sources more esoteric. Sources like the books in the library up at Miskatonic U.

Joe stood and pulled his trench coat on. It was getting on towards the end of fall and there was a chill to the night air. He propped his fedora on his head and swept out the door with purpose. If Nadia was in danger, time was of the essence.

He hurried through the streets of Arkham. The colorful splendor of sunset had given way to the gray of evening. A few especially enterprising bats swooped through the twilight for an early meal. Lights were coming on throughout the city. Many in the city had adopted electric lighting, but a few still made use of candles or gas lamps. All of them shone warmly through their windows, comforting reminders that he was not alone in the world.

Soon Joe reached Orne Library on the university campus. It was three stories of weathered granite. The silhouette of gargoyles stood out against the windows overhead. It was an architectural oddity, reminding Joe of nothing so much as the bastard child of a bunker and a cathedral. A lamp shone above the doorway, as if to guide late readers on their way in. Joe had only recently started coming here for research. It was usually restricted to students and faculty, but he had a friend on the inside.

He stopped in the foyer to hang his hat but kept his coat. The interior of the library was a drafty maze of bookshelves. It struggled to stay heated at the best of times. Besides, it was better to not go flashing his guns at people for no reason. It had a way of spooking folks.

"Detective," a familiar voice said behind him. "What an unexpected pleasure."

Joe turned with a genuine smile. "Miss Walker. How are you feeling?"

Daisy Walker returned the smile. The blonde librarian tugged her sleeve down to better conceal the bandages that swathed one arm. "I'd feel a lot worse if you hadn't been there that night."

The memory surged up. Ghoulish claws tearing at the barricaded door. Unearthly shrieks echoing on the night air. His smile died as quickly as it had risen. "We got lucky. That's all."

"People like us have to make our own luck, detective." Her green eyes searched his face. "This isn't a social call, is it?"

Joe shook his head. "No. I need information."

Daisy glanced around. "That kind of information?"

"Yeah."

She motioned for him to follow with a tilt of her head. They headed over past dusty shelves to where a table sat.

An electric lamp was nearby but it was dark. In its place a single candle in the center cast a dim glow.

"Atmospheric," Joe remarked dryly.

Daisy gave him a look. "We have a hard time keeping the lights on after dark. Candles are more reliable for some reason." The librarian looked around one more time. Satisfied no one was nearby, she motioned to him. "What is it?"

Joe produced the pictures from his coat pocket. The girl and the body. Anyone else, he might worry about their reaction. He knew Daisy had seen worse.

She leaned forward and took the pictures in with a keen eye. "The birthmark."

"Got it in one," Joe said. "Seen anything like it?"

Daisy frowned. "I saw something similar all too recently." She clenched the hand on her wounded arm, as though the ache had redoubled.

"Damn," Joe whispered. "The same cult? The same… thing?" He stopped short of saying the name, but it itched in his brain just the same.

"Same entity? Maybe. Same cult? No… I don't think so. The symbols aren't quite the same. Besides, those aren't brands or tattoos. These people aren't cultists. They've been marked since before they were even born, somehow." She locked eyes with him, expression dark. "Claimed."

Joe tapped his finger on Nadia's picture. "The girl is still alive, so far as I know. Is there anything else you can tell me?"

Daisy plucked at her lip thoughtfully. "You know, that birthmark is familiar for another reason now that I think about it. It'd be a heck of a connection, but…"

"My credulity strains a lot further than it used to," Joe noted wryly.

She arched an eyebrow. "Is that so? Wait here."

Daisy turned and disappeared into the stacks. When she returned it was with a sizable leather-bound tome. She heaved it onto the table. Joe leaned forward and blew the dust off the cover. He flipped it open to the first page. The title was printed in an older style, elaborate and decorative.

"*The Labyrinth: The True Tale of the Darkness Below Crete*," he read aloud.

Joe looked up at her with a frown. There was a twinkle of mischief in her eyes now.

"Tell me, detective. Did you pay attention when they covered mythology in school?"

Sebastianos vomited over the side of the ship for the umpteenth time. There was no relief in the act. It did nothing to ease his nausea or make the world stand still. All it did was wring out every muscle in his body and leave him a sweating, gasping mess. It was pointless misery.

In that way it was a microcosm of this entire voyage. The Athenian sank against the side of the railing with a helpless wheeze. It brought Sebastianos around to face the source of all his troubles: the man standing at the very bow of the ship. He could have been a figurehead on the ship, so stoic and so beautiful. As though a statue had come to life, as though a god had stepped down from Mount Olympus.

Theseus, son of King Aegeus and heir to the throne of Athens.

That prime specimen deigned to drop his eyes from the horizon to look at Sebastianos instead. "You would think you would run out of things to throw up at some point."

Sebastianos managed a sour smile. "It is truly a miracle of the ages, your highness."

Theseus stepped over and offered his servant a hand up. "Come, on your feet, man. We will pull into the port at Crete before you know it, and this trial will be over."

Sebastianos accepted the grip and let himself be pulled back up. "That is less comforting than it might be."

Theseus clapped him on the shoulder. "Cheer up. You are not part of the tribute. You should have nothing to fear."

"Nothing save bringing a father word that his son is dead," Sebastianos said. "Nothing save losing a friend. And for what?"

Theseus turned back to the horizon with a frown. "I do only what must be done."

"That's not true, and you know it. You don't have to be here. They would have chosen someone else."

The prince glanced at him. "Someone like you?"

Sebastianos paused. "Perhaps."

"And how is that fair?" Theseus asked.

"Lots are drawn. Every young person in the city shares the risk–"

"Everyone except for me. What is so different? Anyone they choose is someone's friend. Someone's son. For twenty-seven years our people have mourned their lost loved ones." Theseus took a deep breath. "It has to stop. I know I can stop it."

"How?" Sebastianos demanded. It was a frustrated blurt

as much as anything. None of this conversation was new. They'd had it a dozen times or more. Theseus had shown irregular patience for Sebastianos' directness, born of long years of service long since turned to true friendship. It helped that Sebastianos was of noble birth himself, honored to be placed at the prince's right hand.

"I will talk to them." Theseus gave him a sad smile. "King Minos was furious, and perhaps he had a right to be. But he has had decades for his anger to cool. Surely he can see this for the madness it is now."

Sebastianos sighed. There was nothing more to say.

They watched together as the hills and beaches of the island of Crete grew ahead of them. It had been a sunny day out on the open sea. That light gave way to overcast skies as they came closer. Cold rain misted down, joining the sea spray in a cheerless drizzle.

Sebastianos pulled his cloak closer about himself. "This island is a cursed place."

Theseus laughed at that, a burst of genuine mirth. "Zeus be merciful. A little rain does not a curse make, old friend."

There was something more to it, though. Sebastianos could not shake the feeling. Twenty-eight Athenian youths had already been surrendered to Minos' demands, never to return. The enigma of their fate had haunted his dreams ever since he had learned of Theseus' plan to volunteer. Nightmares of darkness and terrible hungers beneath the earth.

If anyone else had such premonitions, they did not share them with him. He was not the only one unsettled, though. A glance back at the rest of the ship showed him plenty of fear. The trembling and paleness of the rest of the youths sent in tribute was one thing, understandable enough. The wariness in the eyes of the rowers and other crew was another.

They had arrived in the city of Knossos. Grand buildings loomed all around them, stone towers decorated with elaborate frescoes. Sebastianos could not help a disloyal thought: this place was grander by far than his home of Athens. Then the silence seeped in.

Sebastianos would have expected a city of this size to be host to several trading vessels at any one time. Goods should be coming and going from their holds. Crowds could be expected; crews and merchants and city officials to tax the lot of them. Instead, everything was still. The only sound was the wash of the waves against their ship. Nothing moved.

"Perhaps they cleared the harbor in anticipation of our arrival," Sebastianos said uneasily.

"Perhaps," Theseus said. "One would think they would have sent someone to greet us in that case."

The Athenian ship pulled up to the dock to be moored. The crew hurried about their tasks, eager to be done and gone. Theseus glanced over the gathered people. None of the crew would look at him, Sebastianos noted. The other tributes, however, couldn't take their eyes off him. He was their one slender hope.

Sebastianos could see that settle onto his friend like an invisible weight.

Theseus stepped forward. "All of you remain here. Sebastianos and I will see if we can locate our kindly hosts."

"Delighted to volunteer," muttered Sebastianos as they climbed over the side of the ship. "Need I remind you that we're unarmed? No weapons on the tribute voyages?"

"Fortunately, we are not looking for a fight. Besides, nothing dangerous has happened," Theseus pointed out. He flashed a grin. "Yet."

"You are exceptionally bad at comforting people," Sebastianos said.

"Not people. Just you."

They headed up the pier towards the city. The first few steps were difficult; it felt like the world was unsteady beneath Sebastianos' feet. It took several seconds for solid ground to feel right again. Wood creaked beneath their feet. It was common for even a well-maintained port to show weathering. The sea was not kind to structures. This was worse. Entire planks had rotted through, forcing them to choose their steps with care.

"Something bad happened to this city," Sebastianos said.

"I'm starting to believe you're right," Theseus said. "But what? We've received no word of disaster. There's no sign of war."

Sebastianos shook his head. He had no easy answers.

They walked among desolate buildings. The doors they passed were shut. Some were boarded over. A window hung open. Sebastianos stepped up to glance inside. All was dark within the house. Dust layered the sill. He thought he glimpsed broken furniture. There was something truly desolate about the sight. His already abused stomach twisted with unease.

"Perhaps I could climb inside, see–"

"No need," Theseus said

A tension in his friend's voice made Sebastianos turn his head. The prince was staring down the street, expression grim. Sebastianos followed his gaze to a collection of dark figures gathered ahead of them. Had they been there before? It was hard to know. They were so still that he could easily imagine his eye skipping over them.

They were garbed completely in black, no hint of other color to be found among them. Each stood like a blot of shadow against the gray light of the day. Their leader drew the eye. They were taller than both men anyway, and their headgear added to that. Black horns swept forward from an ebon mask that hid their face completely. The front of the mask bulged outward into a false snout. It reminded Sebastianos of nothing so much as a great bull, of the kind often sacrificed to the gods.

"What in Olympus' name…" Sebastianos whispered.

Theseus stepped forward and raised a hand.

"Hail," he called.

Silence was the only response.

The prince cleared his throat. "We come from Athens with the tribute, as promised! I wish to speak to King Minos, however. I am Prince Theseus, and I hoped–"

"Minos has gone below."

It was a sepulchral voice, deep and gravelly. It must have been the leader speaking, but if it was then the mask scarcely seemed to muffle them. Their words echoed down the empty street like rocks falling at the end of a mine shaft.

Sebastianos' mouth was dry as the desert. His hand reflexively dropped to where a sword would normally have been belted at his waist. He cursed again the rule that barred anyone from traveling this voyage armed.

Theseus seemed much calmer. "I am sorry to hear it. Perhaps I could speak with his successor instead?"

The leader paced forward a few steps. There was something unsettling about its gait. It struck Sebastianos as somehow inhuman. He wondered, then, what lay under those layers of dark fabric, even as another part of him dreaded to know.

"You are tribute. You will come with us."

"In due time," Theseus replied. "If I must. But first I will speak with the ruler of this island. Surely that is not too much to ask? A final meal and a word with my captor?"

"Such needs are passing. The dead require nothing. All is still below."

Sebastianos took a step back uneasily. The only thing that belied Theseus' continued steadiness was his hands tightening into fists.

"I am not dead yet," the prince said.

"You are," the leader rasped. "You simply do not know it yet." It motioned with a black-wrapped hand, fingers unsettlingly long. "Take them."

The dark shapes rushed forward. They came on with dreadful celerity and silence. There were no shouts or war cries, just a terrible sense of purpose. There were more than a dozen of them, easily enough to overwhelm the two unarmed men.

"Run!" shouted Theseus.

The pair set off, sprinting up the street back towards the docks.

"Still feeling good about this plan?" gasped Sebastianos.

"Save your breath for running," Theseus replied.

It was good advice. The seasickness that had plagued Sebastianos the entire way here was catching up to him now. His endurance was badly drained, and he was soon wheezing. He clamped a hand to his side, where each desperate intake felt like a spike. His legs felt increasingly like rubber, a struggle to put one foot in front of the other.

Theseus dared a glance back. Whatever he saw did nothing to cheer his expression.

"They are gaining on us," he said.

"You must leave me, my prince," coughed Sebastianos.

"The gods scorn me if I let you pay the price for my choices," snapped Theseus. "Go. I will slow them."

"I cannot leave–"

"You will do as you are told!" barked Theseus. His tone softened instantly. "Go, Sebastianos. Get to the ship. Get everyone else out of here. Tell my father what has happened, that some madness has taken Crete."

Theseus pulled up and turned to face their pursuers. Sebastianos skidded to a halt a short way on.

"Theseus–!"

The prince had never looked more beautiful. Rage knitted his sweat-sheened brow. His fists were clenched, ready for a battle he could not win.

"Go!" roared the prince.

Sebastianos' last glance back revealed the cloaked figures swarming about his friend, pulling him down like wolves upon a bear. Tears clouded his vision as he fled. He raced on through the streets, panting desperately against the pain.

Whatever the weakness of his body, he could no longer allow it to interfere. To do otherwise was to let Theseus' sacrifice go to waste.

The sound of screams up ahead robbed him of that sense of purpose. Sebastianos darted into a side alley as he approached the docks and peered around the corner. Their dark-swathed foes had already come for the ship in their absence. Dozens of them rushed the Athenian vessel. Those who had tried to fight were being carried off, unconscious or dead. The rest were being led on chains.

Sebastianos eased back, mind racing. The situation had gone from bad to worse. There was no way he could sail out of here alone to get help. Even if he could have, it was hard to imagine retrieving aid in time to do any good.

Alone, unarmed, in a hostile place. There were a considerable number of things that he could not do, and very little he could think of that he could. He scrubbed his hands over his face in frustration.

Something grabbed hold of him and snatched him backwards into the shadows of the alley.

A hand was clamped over his mouth, stifling his instinctive yelp. Sebastianos bit down on that hand, drawing a very human curse from his assailant. He struggled fiercely and was shoved up against the wall for his efforts. The impact drew a pained grunt from him.

"Shhh!" rasped his attacker.

Sebastianos blinked as he got his first good look at them. It was a woman, with dark skin and hair. She had the look of the lands south of the Mediterranean. She was dressed in simple homespun clothing, the kind suited to hard work.

Furthermore, she was glaring at him fit to strike him dead.

Not, as he had feared, a monster of any kind.

"Who—"

She pressed an insistent finger to his lips to silence him and shook her head.

"Somewhere else," she mouthed.

At least, that's what it looked like. Sebastianos nodded in response and motioned for her to lead the way. Trusting her might have been a fool's choice, but he did not have many other options open to him.

She hurried off through the alleys with him trailing in her wake. Unlike Sebastianos, she clearly knew her way around the city. The path she chose avoided main thoroughfares. She was cautious the entire journey. Her obvious fear did nothing to soothe his own. Guilt layered onto it, his mind full of bitter self-recrimination for having left Theseus at all. When they did have to cross one of the main roads she pulled up long enough to carefully check in both directions before hastening onwards. At last, they stopped at an abandoned building.

It looked much like any of the others they'd passed along the way, but here she seemed somewhat more relaxed. There was dusty furniture in the room, and she wiped off a chair before settling into it with a sigh. She motioned for him to sit across the table from her.

Once he had, she leaned forward. "You are Athenian, yes?" Her voice was a steady contralto, even now kept quiet.

He nodded and responded as softly, "Yes. My name is Sebastianos. I came accompanying the tribute. You are a Cretan?"

She gave a wry smile, teeth flashing in the gloom. "Not by birth, though I have lived here for many years. I came here to serve the lady Ariadne. My name is Chrysanthe."

"Well met." Sebastianos took a deep breath. "Forgive me, but what in the depths of Tartarus has happened to this city?"

She looked down. "You are closer than you think."

"What does that mean?"

She rubbed the bridge of her nose and collected her thoughts. "It all started with the war with Athens, or so I am told."

"That was twenty-seven years ago," Sebastianos said.

Chrysanthe nodded. "The war was not going as King Minos wished. In the depths of his despair, he was contacted by... a group. A cult. Dedicated not to the gods of Olympus, but to some ancient chthonic power that we had never even heard of. They told him that by propitiating this power, he could turn the tides of battle."

"And what exactly did they want?"

"At first, just the dead. They took them into deep catacombs, paths into the earth that even those who had lived here their whole lives had never heard of. It seemed little enough, especially when the power they promised proved to be a real thing."

"Proved how?" asked Sebastianos. His mouth was dry as sawdust. "Do you have any water?"

Chrysanthe nodded and pulled a waterskin from her belt and tossed it to him. He took a deep drink. It was warm and tasted of the leather of the skin. It was divine. It also bought him a chance to think. The tale was a wild one, but something had shattered the peace of this island. She did not seem the lying sort, her eyes too full of real sorrow.

"I don't know all the details. The *thing* could shake earth and rack the sea. Miracles I would have thought the domain of Poseidon alone. It was enough to turn things around. Then that horrible hunger began to grow."

Sebastianos thought back to the masked leader telling them they were dead and didn't know it. "They turned on the living as well."

Chrysanthe nodded. They sat in silence for a few moments before she mustered the will to continue. "Small numbers, at first. That was the reason the tribute was applied to Athens in the first place."

Sebastianos had suspected, but the confirmation made him feel nauseous. "My countrymen were taken and fed to some…" He shook his head.

She gestured abortively, as if in some helpless attempt at apology. "Even here the idea was met with disquiet. Still, it seemed little enough. Harsher indemnity had been applied to those defeated in other wars."

He swept his arm out to encompass the whole of the desolate city. "It seems like at some point they lost all restraint."

"Yes, and Crete has paid the price for turning from the gods. Knossos is all but emptied. When Minos at last protested, he too was taken. Since, his daughter has ruled in name but not in fact."

"How can she stand to see this happen to her home?"

Chrysanthe's head snapped towards him, eyes blazing. "She did not choose this!"

The exclamation was like thunder in the quiet. They both froze in terror and listened. The city remained still, and they breathed simultaneous sighs of relief.

"My apologies," she whispered. "Ariadne did not approve of all that has happened. Here, at the end, she even set about trying to make things right. She crafted a plan to destroy the Labyrinth once and for all."

"The Labyrinth?"

"That is the name given to the tunnels where all tribute and sacrifices are taken. They lead down into the dark of the earth, turning in on themselves in intricate ways. It is said that only the cultists can find their way in and out."

"Ariadne..." Sebastianos realized. "You were speaking of her in the past tense."

Chrysanthe lowered her head. "I do not know if they caught wind of her plot or have simply abandoned all idea of restraint. A few days ago they came for her as well."

"What was her plan?"

The maidservant gave a bitter laugh. "She was counting on all of you, actually. When the tribute arrived she planned to solicit your help in destroying the wooden pillars that hold the Labyrinth up."

"Doubly ironic," Sebastianos said. There was no real humor to the thought. Their situation was many things, but it was not funny.

Chrysanthe raised an eyebrow.

"Theseus, prince of Athens, came this time. He hoped to treat with the royal family and convince them to bring an end to the tribute."

"Ah," she said. "And he is...?"

Sebastianos nodded wearily. "They took him." The image of his friend being overwhelmed welled up once more. He swallowed hard, fighting the knot in his throat.

"Then we are all that's left."

"It seems that way," he said. He could not keep the bitterness from his voice. To think they could simply have never come to Crete. There was no one left to be angered by it.

Chrysanthe picked the waterskin up and took a swig herself. She put it down with force, as if deciding. "Then we must do it."

Sebastianos studied her with some consternation. "Do what?"

"We cannot abandon them all to suffering beyond death. If you and I are the only ones who can try to end all of this, then that is what we must do."

Sebastianos' mind raced. He sat forward. "Do you think we could still save them?"

Chrysanthe bit her lip thoughtfully. "There is a chance. The way the cultists speak of it, they collect souls for sacrifice over time. Gather them down there in the dark, until the numbers are sufficient to please their master. If they were waiting for the tribute to arrive, we might still be able to get there in time."

"They say all is predetermined, that the Fates have already measured the span of our lives. If that is so, we cannot change what is to come. But it also means there is nothing to be gained by not trying." Sebastianos stood. "There is no time to waste. Is there somewhere I can get a sword? We were allowed no weapons."

She studied him and frowned. "A sword might be difficult, but a knife?" She patted the blade sheathed at her own hip. "That can be arranged."

Chrysanthe hurried off into the house. She returned with the promised item and held it out to him. Sebastianos pulled the blade and contemplated the razor edge. It caught the fading light of the gray day with a dull gleam. It would do. It would have to.

"Thank you." He motioned around. "You know this home well. Was it yours?"

"No. I lived with my lady at the palace and fled the night she was taken. This belonged to my cousin." Chrysanthe looked around slowly. "I used to visit him and his family on festival days."

Sebastianos mustered a smile. "We will save those we can, and avenge those we cannot."

She took a deep breath and nodded. They crept out of the house back into the streets of Knossos. The day was coming to an end, and the already gray sky was edging towards black. It would be night by the time they reached the entrance to the Labyrinth. Sebastianos tried not to dwell on that thought.

A light flamed to life down the road from them. Chrysanthe pulled him into a side alley. Both pressed up against the wall and tried to stay as still as possible. Sebastianos kept a hand on the hilt of the knife. He could hear his heart pounding. If it was half as loud to anyone around, they'd be found out in a moment.

Footsteps announced an approach. To his ears they sounded more like the click of hooves on the cobblestones.

Again, he was forced to wonder as to the true nature of their foe. Were they human? Had they been once? He did not know, and he was afraid to ask.

Four black-swathed figures walked past the alley. They did not speak among themselves as normal people would have. One carried a torch, but even that was strange: it burned too bright and pure, with an actinic white light. Still, Sebastianos gave thanks to Olympus for it. They might have come upon the cultists unawares had it not been for the light.

The rearmost one of the four paused. It turned its hooded head this way and that. Sebastianos could hear it snuffling, a wet noise that recalled a hound. He held his breath and counted the seconds, trying not to tremble as the thing searched around. The urge to retreat deeper into the alley was powerful, but he resisted. It made a sound, somewhere between a snort and a cough, and continued on its way.

They waited several more seconds before both sighed with relief. Chrysanthe slipped over to the wall on the other side of the alley and glanced after the cultists. She nodded and motioned him on; they had indeed left the pair behind. The two of them hurried on their way, eager to be out of the city.

The palace grew before them, a daunting construction of stone. The many windows were dark. It created an unsettling effect with the onset of night, as though they were great empty eye sockets watching them approach. Sebastianos shuddered.

"Is there anyone left in Knossos at all?" he whispered.

"Other than us?" she asked. She shrugged expressively. "If they are out there, they know better than to draw attention to themselves."

"A city emptied," he mused. "What is a traveler even to make of such a thing, should they find it? Just another mystery, never to be answered."

"Just another reason to not let it happen," Chrysanthe said.

Sebastianos nodded. They crept into the echoing hall of the palace. Tapestries showed many aspects of Cretan life, often accompanied by the great bulls the locals held sacred. It made him wonder about the mask. Was it mere camouflage? A mockery of what they had once held holy?

Only lush rugs kept their footsteps from announcing their presence to the whole building. Even so, he was surprised at how few signs there were of the cultists here.

"They did not take the palace for themselves," Sebastianos said.

Chrysanthe shook her head. "They dislike the great open spaces. They find the wind and the sun on their face abhorrent. They keep to themselves, down there in the dark of the tunnels, when they are not searching for tribute to feed their hungry god."

He could no longer resist. "Are they human?"

She glanced back at him and paused in her steps. "I... don't know. Some of them are, I think. Some of them seem like they're something else. Especially their leader."

"The bull," he said.

"Yes," Chrysanthe said and shuddered. "If that one is human, it gives us all a bad name."

She led the way down into the palace cellars. It became necessary to light a torch as they moved below ground. She plucked one from a wall sconce and lit it with flint and steel from her belt pouch. Rats scattered at the sudden light, squeaking in alarm. Part of Sebastianos longed to recoil the same way. If their foes saw the light… It did not bear thinking of. They would never find their way in the dark. Some risks had to be taken.

They passed among great amphorae of wine, covered with dust. Barrels of other supplies were stacked elsewhere. Some had sat unused so long the wood had rotted through. Spilled contents were what had drawn all the vermin. They glared at the passing humans with red eyes shining in the dark, returning to their feast once the intruders were gone.

At last the pair came to the entrance of a yet deeper passage. Gusts of chill air poured from it like icy breath. The darkness of the tunnel mouth seemed tactile. It resisted the light of the torch, retreating only reluctantly as Chrysanthe stepped forward. It slid back like oil, waiting just beyond the reach of the flame. All it needed was for them to step inside, and it could swallow them whole.

"It's not real. It's all in your head," whispered Sebastianos to himself. He shivered and tried to tell himself it was the cold and not the fear.

"What?" asked Chrysanthe.

"Nothing," he replied. He rubbed his eyes and shook his head. "We have come this far. There's no turning back now."

"First things first," she said.

She handed him the torch to hold, then reached once

more into her belt pouches. She came out this time with a skein of thread. She tied one end to a great heavy container of wine that sat nearby. Sebastianos raised an eyebrow when she looked around to him once more.

"An idea of my own. So we can find our way back out."

"If one of the cultists finds it, won't it lead them straight to us?"

Chrysanthe shrugged helplessly. "They rarely use this path. It was made to collect tribute from King Minos. Ariadne had me follow some of them when she was forming her plan. They have their own secret ways to come and go. There is at least a chance they won't find the thread." She looked back to the darkness. "I do not give us such good odds should we try to brave the dark unaided."

"As you say," Sebastianos allowed. "It is in the hands of the gods, as are we."

The maidservant lingered there in the arch. Perhaps she knew her own fears and hesitations. If so, she mastered them swiftly before plunging into the tunnel mouth. Sebastianos followed just behind. The torch guttered as he stepped across the threshold, pulled at by the cold wind from the depths.

The route was simple at first. It led them in great loops down into the earth. The construction here was of the same style as the city above, stone blocks decorated by intricate frescoes. These commemorated victories over the Athenian fleet in the war. The height of their dark alliance, mused Sebastianos.

Soon the passage forked, and the architecture changed. It became simpler and rougher. Old writing, divots and marks, was etched into the walls. Whatever meaning it contained was lost on Sebastianos. He could not help but imagine. Warnings, perhaps? "Go no deeper, you fools"? They could not afford to listen if that was the case.

They encountered their first dead end and were forced to retrace their steps. Soon there was a second, and a third, each one lost time. Both were shivering. It was increasingly cold the deeper they went, unnaturally so. Sebastianos could see the fog of their breath in front of each of them. He was ever more tired. The exertions of the day were catching up to him. He had slept poorly on the journey here, sick and tormented by nightmares. Chrysanthe glanced at him, her face drawn with fear and worry, and he mustered a smile for her.

Down and down they went. Sometimes there were short flights of stairs, but it was usually just a gradual slope. It was easy to lose track of how far they had come, though the ache of Sebastianos' legs suggested it had been a good distance.

"At this rate we shall stumble into Tartarus first and be forced to apologize to the Titans for our discourtesy," he said.

"Whatever it is the cultists worship, I fear it is even older than they. Something of the primordial Kaos, perhaps," she replied. The joke had clearly fallen flat. She was shaking, whether from cold or fear.

"You are brave to come so far for Ariadne," Sebastianos said. "She is lucky to inspire such loyalty."

"She is a good person, wise for her age. She will make a better ruler than Minos did." To continue talking was foolish, but neither of them seemed to be able to help it. The icy silence was unbearable. "What drives you, Sebastianos?"

He thought of Theseus, captured and taken down this way in the hands of monsters. Of the grim fate that awaited the prince. It steeled him, and he squared his shoulders. "Love," he said simply.

Chrysanthe smiled at that, and the expression was the warmest thing in the Labyrinth. "Then your prince is lucky as well."

The structure was changing again. Artifice gave way to natural rock. At first, there were still traces of humanity. They were simplistic russet paintings. Some were cattle, goats, and pigs. Others showed things far more strange and terrible, which Sebastianos had no name for. Living floods covered with eyes. Rugose, corpulent things with tentacle faces and bat wings.

Then even those were gone. As unsettling as they had been, Sebastianos soon missed them. All that was left was the stone and the darkness and the cold. Was this some natural cave system now, which the cult had claimed as a home? Or had this place been shaped by hands that predated any human civilization? His mind retreated from the thought. There was no solace in it, and he could not afford to challenge his courage here and now.

There was a sound up ahead. It came to them on one of the gusts of icy wind. At first Sebastianos took it for nothing more than the wind groaning through some outlet. It proved too constant to believe that for long. It rose and fell steadily, a sonorous pulse. As they drew closer to the source it became clear there were words, of a sort, though he did not recognize the language.

"The ritual?" he asked, daring to voice nothing above a whisper now.

Chrysanthe nodded slowly. "I saw such a rite once..."

She motioned for him to douse the torch. Sebastianos hesitated. His thoughts flicked to that oily darkness he had seen – imagined? – at the entrance. The flame was all that stood between them. Was this the chance it was waiting for to devour them?

He dashed the thought with impatience at himself. This madness was getting to him, and his fears would not save Theseus. He ground the torch out against the rock of the wall with a sudden violent movement. It plunged them into a black deep enough to make Nyx herself stumble.

The sounds were still there. The endless, alien chant of the cult ahead of them. Sebastianos could hear his own breath and heart too, fast and frightened. He willed them slower. It was something to focus on if nothing else. Easy, he told himself. There is still the thread. There is still Chrysanthe. You are not alone.

Something caught Sebastianos' eye. A single speck of light against the darkness, like a lone star in a blank night sky. It was so subtle that at first he judged it an illusion. Only when it did not go away did he look more closely. He held up a hand and waved it about, the light vanishing as he passed over it.

"Chrysanthe," he whispered.

"What?"

He could hear her rustle around in the darkness, trying

to find him. They fumbled and managed to catch hands finally. He took the chance to take her shoulders and point her towards the light.

"Do you see it?"

Chrysanthe took a low breath. "Yes. That's where we need to go."

"Are you certain?"

A pause. A low laugh. "I nodded as if you could see me. Yes. Hold on to me."

Hand in hand they proceeded down the tunnel towards that pinprick glow. It grew as they approached, and the chanting grew louder in proportion. There was a musical accompaniment, he realized. It was a hideous tuneless piping, a high-pitched whine that set his teeth on edge. The ground rumbled beneath their feet. He could feel a cloud of dust settle on him from the cavern roof.

"Their master hears," Chrysanthe whispered. "The Devourer Below stirs. We're running out of time."

Sebastianos could tell now that the light was the actinic brightness of the strange torches the cultists carried. A gust of hot air, startling after the chill, caught them as they approached. It was humid and heavy, laden with promise like the air before a storm.

The scent of death and rot came with it, sickly sweet and repugnant. He fought down a burst of nausea and pressed on. The light had grown bright enough he could make out his companion in the murk. Chrysanthe pressed the back of her hand to her mouth for a moment and convulsively swallowed. Then she followed. The fact that the pair had doused their own torch allowed them to creep right up to the entrance to the chamber where the ritual was taking place.

Sebastianos leaned around for his first glimpse of the ritual. If the space was natural, then it was a cathedral born of natural forces. It was a massive area, and the roof arched far overhead to be lost in darkness. The great wooden pillars Chrysanthe had spoken of were found here, holding up that vaulting height.

Filling this arena were biers that sprang directly from the rocky ground. Bodies were laid out on each, swathed in cloth and bound in cords. Each was surrounded by the accouterments of a burial: oils and sacred incense and more. Many were pallid and still, but a few were visibly struggling against their restraints. Standing among them were the funereal creatures of the cult, wrapped in their all-encompassing black garb. Some held the blazing white torches, raised high as if to illuminate as much as possible. Their attention was focused on a single point at the center of the chamber. Sebastianos followed their gazes and...

His mind reeled. He wrenched his gaze away.

It was like a pit, a hole into some greater abyss beyond. The bull-priest stood at the very edge, too-long arms raised high in macabre exultation. Within, the darkness reached a zenith. It transcended mere shadow and night and became something more. A gap in the fabric of the world itself, and beyond...

Sebastianos could only piece together fragments of what he'd seen there in the heart of the room. Charnel expressed unto infinity; that was the impression that remained. Bleached bones and rotting meat. Death on a scale beyond human comprehension, beyond possibility. A universe of elemental putrefaction.

There was something more in that other-place. Something approaching across desert plains of bone mulch and mountains of offal. A shape of pure shadow, a writhing mass of inchoate nothingness. There was a core and a corona… like a star turned inside out. The Devourer. It was coming, and soon.

Blood ran from Sebastianos' nose and the corner of his left eye. He wiped it away furiously. His hand was shaking like a leaf in the wind. It was hard to even think in the wake of such a thing. The reaction went beyond fear. It spoke to something primal in him, that begged him to quit this place.

"Sebastianos," rasped Chrysanthe.

He turned his head to look at her. Her own eyes were completely bloodshot, the irises ovals of brown in a sea of red. She must have looked too. Now, however, she was pointing to somewhere else in the chamber.

He followed the direction of her finger. She was pointing to one of the biers, and on it… His heart leapt into his throat. Theseus was laid out there. The prince stared at the ceiling with glassy eyes. Dead? Sebastianos refused to believe it. He ground his teeth in sudden rage. It was welcome, a hot spring within him that drove away the fear of this place.

"Do you see Ariadne?" he asked.

Chrysanthe nodded.

"Alright." He took a deep breath and wiped away a fresh trickle of blood. "We'll split up. Work around the edges in opposite directions and free as many people as we can."

She nodded again, but caught his arm as he turned away. Her eyes were intense. "If they spot you – if they spot either of us – then we start burning pillars. This has to stop here and now, one way or another."

"Agreed." Sebastianos placed his hand over hers for a moment and squeezed. "May the gods of Olympus smile on you."

Chrysanthe managed a smile at that. "May Isis watch over us both, my friend."

They separated. Sebastianos resisted the urge to make straight for Theseus. Instead, he worked his way along the edge as planned. He focused on the people who were still moving. Some were Cretan, some were Athenian. It did not matter. Each one he came to he held a silencing finger to his lips before cutting them free. By pantomime, he guided them towards the tunnel and the thread that would lead them back to the surface.

In this way he reached Theseus at last. A small blessing, the cultists were so focused on their rite they still had not noticed what was happening. Sebastianos could only hold his breath as he crept over towards the prince, staying low. His friend stared upwards sightlessly, unmoving. This close, he could see the blood in his eyes; there was no telling what terrible sights Theseus had gazed upon. Sebastianos cut the cords that bound him nonetheless.

He caught the prince's hand up in both of his own and chafed the flesh. Breathe, he willed Theseus. Smile. Live.

"Theseus, please," he whispered. "Do not let this all have been for nothing."

The prince blinked. He inhaled shakily. Slowly his head turned to the side, and his eyes focused again. His mind came back from whatever terrible void had held it.

"Sebastianos?" he rasped.

"Yes," Sebastianos said. It was difficult to speak around the weight of emotion in his chest. Tears welled up in his eyes. "Yes, my prince. I am here."

"What–"

An awful howl cut the reunion short. It sliced through the sonorous chant of the cultists and left a void of silence in its wake. Sebastianos turned his head with terrible certainty. The bull-priest had turned from the pit-void and was pointing. It wasn't towards them, however. The accusing finger was aimed directly across the chamber towards where Chrysanthe stood.

Everything hung in a tableau for a split second. Then dark-clad cultists began to rush towards her.

"Blood of Zeus," cursed Sebastianos. He gripped Theseus' hand tight for one more precious moment. "You must go, my prince. Run for the corridor. There is a line that will take you back to the world above."

"But–"

"There is no time, Theseus! Go!"

Sebastianos could afford him no more attention. He turned away and charged the nearest cultist carrying a torch. The creature's attention was across the room with the battle erupting there. He caught it unawares with a low tackle, lifting it up off the ground and smashing it into one of the biers. There was a crunch as hidden flesh met naked stone, and the thing went limp.

He snatched up the torch that had fallen from its hand. The strange white flame at the end had a garlicky stench to it, unlike anything he had encountered. It burned with a terrible heat. Sebastianos held it away from himself and grabbed an amphora of burial oils that lay nearby. He hurled it against the nearest wooden pillar with all his might, and the pottery shattered. He thrust the torch into the spatter it left.

The oil ignited with a sputtering hiss. Such oils burned reluctantly, but once lit the fire was hard to kill. Sebastianos felt a deep satisfaction in watching that blaze spread, but he could only savor it for a moment. His actions had drawn attention, and his advantage of surprise was gone.

Another of the cultists rushed him. Sebastianos greeted it with a thrust of the torch. Black cloth ignited instantly. Within a matter of seconds the creature had been turned into a humanoid bonfire. It staggered away with a keening howl that made his already aching head even worse.

That seemed to teach the rest of them some fear. A few other close ones shied away as he waved the torch at them threateningly. They were not driven off, merely circling for a better avenue to attack him from. Sebastianos did not care. He seized the opening to sprint further towards where Chrysanthe was fighting for her life. If they had to make a last stand, they would do it tog–

There was a sound like thunder. Something hurled Sebastianos from his feet. The whole world went white, then red. He smashed into a bier topped with a dead body. The whole thing collapsed under the impact, sending him and the corpse skidding to the ground. The torch tumbled from his nerveless hand and skittered away across the floor.

All Sebastianos could do was wheeze, the air knocked from his lungs. He tried to get his hands underneath himself to rise, but they were struggling to respond. A shadow loomed above him. He blinked against blurry vision. The shape was capped by the sweep of great horns.

It caught hold of his ankle with its elongated fingers and began to drag him towards the center of the room. The thought of the pit welled up in Sebastianos' dazed mind, and the terror of it set him to fighting as much as he could. He grasped at passing objects to try to stop his progress, to no avail. The priest was possessed of a strength beyond that of a man.

It spoke. "You have disrupted something you have no understanding of. You will learn. Sooner or later all will learn. If you had run for your life, you might have been last. Instead, you will go first."

The edge of the pit was mere feet away. Someone bounded in from the side. Chrysanthe. She was bleeding from several scrapes, and one arm appeared dislocated, but she was still fighting. She lunged at the priest, knife outstretched. It raised its free arm to ward her off. It wasn't enough. The blade sank home multiple times, and the priest screamed, an inhuman wail.

It released Sebastianos to better confront its assailant. It caught hold of her, and she was hurled bodily away. For one blessed moment, however, he was free. He staggered up to his feet and threw his entire bodyweight at the priest. He hit it in the side, and both toppled towards the horrid depths.

A hand caught hold of the back of Sebastianos' tunic. The priest seized him by the front. He dared a glance back. Theseus had him, muscles straining. They hung precariously at the edge, caught between the Labyrinth and something even worse. Something reached forth from the void-gate, snatching at the priest. Shadows, come to life. The limbs of a ravening god.

The priest's mask fell away, tumbling into the abyss. If it had ever been human, it wasn't anymore. The head was canine in shape, but hairless and pale, parchment skin pulled tight over monstrous bone structures. The sight burned into Sebastianos, a nightmare made real. He was sure it would haunt him if he lived.

Sebastianos pulled the knife from his belt and slashed it across both of its grasping hands. It screeched and let go. He met its eyes in a brief instant, and saw a terror there. Not of the unknown, but of a fate it suspected all too well. Then it tumbled back and it was gone.

Theseus and Sebastianos fell back the other way. Both scrambled to their feet as fast as they could. More of the columns were burning now, some of the freed peoples having turned to joining the fight rather than merely escaping. The ground shook beneath their feet and dust rained down. The ritual had been disrupted but not prevented. The Devourer Below was still coming.

"We have to go!" shouted Sebastianos.

Theseus nodded, and leaning on each other they staggered towards the exit. Sebastianos searched around desperately for Chrysanthe and found her nearby. She was being helped to her feet by a well-dressed young woman of

Cretan descent. The four of them fled to the doorway that led from the chamber to the tunnel upwards.

The mysterious woman pressed Chrysanthe to them. "Take her, please!"

The maidservant was in bad shape, but she stirred. "My queen," she slurred.

Ariadne smiled and touched her cheek. "Thank you, Chrysanthe. I cannot tell you how much I appreciate you seeing this through. But I cannot go."

"Why?" Sebastianos asked. He did not bother to hide his incredulity. This was poor timing for a jest, but surely no sane person would speak of staying in this vile catacomb.

The woman shifted her gaze to him. "The pact with Umôrdhoth is bound to my bloodline." She pulled her dark hair aside and showed them a mark. A black orb, circled with dark rays. Sebastianos thought at once of the thing beyond the pit. "As long as Minos' line continues, it will seek its due. If this is to end here, truly end, it must end with me."

The ground shook again, and something howled from the direction of the pit. Even the cultists were fleeing now, scattering towards all the exits.

"Take her and go!" said Ariadne.

"No," whispered Chrysanthe.

She lunged towards Ariadne, arms outstretched. Her wounds made the movement unsteady. Tears were streaming down her face. Ariadne stepped back and shook her head. She looked to Sebastianos with a plea in her eyes.

Sebastianos caught hold of Chrysanthe. "I'm sorry," he said. To Ariadne and Chrysanthe both.

Chrysanthe pounded at him in anguish. Theseus took her by the other arm, his face solemn with grief. They pulled her away, but Sebastianos could not bear to look at her. His heart broke for her already. The three of them fled that dark place deep beneath the earth. His last glimpse of Ariadne was her turning, face resolute, to confront the vile darkness her father had made a pact with.

Daisy closed the old book carefully. Joe sat back and whistled low.

"That is a hell of a story," he said.

It seemed a powerful understatement. On the face of it, it was unbelievable. Just another myth. But if monsters were real – and he knew they were – then why not heroes? If he and his friends could fight back now, why couldn't the people of the past?

There was something warming to the thought, as sad as the story was. A human kinship stretching down through the ages. They might fall, they might fail, but they were never alone as long as someone else took up the fight.

"Handed down, retold and reshaped. Even this version may not be the full tale," Daisy said. "But the mark…"

"Yeah," Joe said. He set aside grand thoughts of the past to focus on the demands of the present. He rubbed a chin that was bristling with five o'clock shadow. "Sounds an awful lot like the one on our girl here. A descendant of Minos, huh?"

"Perhaps," Daisy said. "Or connected to something else similar. There is no way to be sure."

"The Devourer Below," Joe said distastefully. "We've heard that name before."

Daisy nodded. "Too much to hope that night saw it done away with for good. What will you do now?"

Joe blew out a heavy breath. "What I can. Ancient curses are beyond me, but I still have to try." He drummed his fingers thoughtfully. "Maybe I'll stop by the diner."

"Ah," Daisy nodded. "Agnes. That's a good thought. I'll come with–"

"Nope," Joe said and shook his head. "Any other time I'd be glad to have you along for the ride, but you still have a bum arm. You've done enough. You gave me a place to start."

The librarian glared at her arm briefly as though it was doing this on purpose. Joe stood from the table, and she walked him to the exit from the library. Full night had fallen beyond, the sky dark and full of stars.

"Be careful, detective."

Joe grinned as he perched his fedora back onto his head. "I've never been anything less, ma'am."

There was a lot of work still to do if Nadia was to be saved. He set off into the night.

To Be Continued…

ALL MY FRIENDS ARE MONSTERS
Davide Mana

Later, Ruth Turner would tell herself that it all started on the night the cops raided the Southside Speakeasy. When things twisted out of shape and the nightmares began, she needed to find a starting point to give her story a direction and make sense of it. And the hectic run in the alleys, feet slipping on the wet paving, her breath short, was as good a beginning as any other.

Hidden in the arch of a doorway, panting, she had tried to catch a glimpse of whoever was coming after her, unseen steps echoing in the dark. Her heart pounded in her chest not just from the strain of the long run. Running in men's shoes was a lot easier than running in half heels. But being caught in a bootlegger's place? And wearing male clothing?

She shuddered. Everybody knew what cops did to people like her. So when the shout had sounded, "Raid!" she had followed a few of the other patrons through the back door behind the bandstand, in the small courtyard where the privy was, and then through the iron door into the alley, and into the night, each man and woman for themselves, running.

Trying to slow down her breathing, she leaned out of her hideaway, and a body smelling of rose and tobacco slammed into her, knocking her back against the closed door with a bump. A brief cry, and Ruth pulled the newcomer into an awkward embrace, and placed a hand on her mouth. She could feel the heartbeat of the woman, a frantic pulse against her chest.

"Hush," she whispered in the other woman's ear.

More steps approached. Slowed down. Ruth and her companion retreated further into the shadows, and held their breath.

"I'm sure she came this way–" a man's voice said.

Another man coughed, like a dog barking. "I'm too old for this rubbish," he gasped, and coughed again.

The first man came closer. A streetlight at the head of the alley cast his long shadow on the pavement. A cop. He wore a beret, he carried a bludgeon.

With a screeching mewl, a cat shot out from behind a dustbin and ran to the end of the shadows.

Ruth's companion pressed hard into her, just as the out of breath cop let out a rattling laugh. "There goes your mystery dame," he said. "Let's get back."

"I tell you I saw her run this way."

"If she did, she was faster than us. Let's go back."

The silence seemed to last forever. Then the first cop grunted. "Yeah, fine."

Ruth and her companion remained still for a while, after

the steps had died away. Then they finally let go of each other. "Are you alright?" Ruth asked, in a hushed voice.

The other woman nodded. She was about two inches shorter than Ruth, and wore a soft dress, the color impossible to tell in the yellow glow of the distant streetlight. Short, bobbed hair, and a sharp face, pointed chin and high cheekbones, her eyes and lips underscored by dark makeup.

"We're safe now," Ruth said, slowly.

The girl was staring at her. Taking in the double-breasted jacket, the fedora.

"I saw you in there," she said. Her voice was pleasantly husky. "I like your style."

Ruth was speechless for a moment. "Thanks."

The woman just ran a hand through her short hair, and sighed. "I lost my hat." Then she grinned mischievously. "I'm Charlie," she said, offering her hand.

"I am Ruth."

They were still standing real close, half in shadow. Ruth could smell Charlie's perfume.

"Have you got a cigarette, Ruth?" Charlie asked suddenly.

Ruth's hand went to her pocket, and then she froze.

Charlie smirked. "Worried we might get arrested? For smoking in public?"

Ruth chuckled and pulled out her pack of Lucky Strikes. She shook two cigarettes out of it. The click of her lighter illuminated Charlie's fine features, highlighting her bright eyes and the copper in her hair. Finally, Charlie stepped back and leaned against the frame of the door. She took a long drag and exhaled slowly. "I needed this," she said.

Ruth nodded and tipped the ash off her cigarette. She was not a heavy smoker, not really, but the Luckies were part of her persona when she went out at night, just like the jacket, the tie, the hat.

They smoked in silence, enjoying the sudden peace, the noises of the night city faint in the distance. Finally Charlie dropped the butt of her smoke on the ground and squashed it with the tip of her foot. "So, Ruth," she said, turning to stare at her, "are you into girls?"

Ruth's eyes widened, and she felt her cheeks burn.

Charlie came closer. "Because I am."

Her boldness was like a slap. Ruth retreated, and Charlie smiled at her. "Let me see your hair." She took Ruth's hat away. Ruth's long black hair fell on her shoulders, brushing the curve of her jaw. "Beautiful," Charlie whispered.

Later Ruth would tell herself it was there it all started.

In the following days, Ruth felt like she was walking two feet over the ground, and was so happy she was sure she was giving off light. She worried for a while her colleagues in Pickman Street would notice and ask her questions. It didn't happen.

To all around her, she remained the black-haired, silent woman working in the morgue, barely visible to the other employees, and a silent shadow to the people that would come and cry for their dead friends, or stare silently, unbelieving, at the still bodies of their relatives.

And yet, for Ruth the smell of disinfectant could not wash away the smell of roses, and her eyes sparkled with joy. She strove to set her features to a somber demeanor when she walked visitors to the icebox drawers where the bodies were preserved. She felt their pain, but her heart was singing.

Grief, like her, haunted these rooms, and she had managed to find a way to live with it so far, slowly retreating into a solitary existence, pushed into a corner by the leaden weight of the world's pain. Eat alone, sleep alone, her nights at home spent with a book, or a radio serial.

Of her youthful dreams, she had a distant, almost impersonal memory, like the ghost limb of a trench war survivor. Like the distant echo of a toothache: there, but not really anymore.

That had been Ruth's existence for years. Until the day the pale blonde girl arrived at the morgue.

They had fished her out of the Miskatonic, her hair intertwined with river grasses, her fingernails broken as she had tried to claw her way back onto the banks, and failed. "Accidents happen," the man from the ambulance said, handing Ruth his report.

No name, no history. She had been so young. So beautiful.

Moving like a machine, Ruth arranged the body on the slab and then sat down to fill out the forms describing the conditions of the remains. It was only when a single tear drew a black smear on the paper, washing away the ink, that Ruth realized her heart was broken.

She cried then, giving in to the emotion. She only managed to compose herself when one of the detectives from the precinct came and collected the report. The man had looked at Ruth in a strange way, maybe sensing something Ruth herself could not name.

No one claimed the body. A column appeared in the *Gazette*, but no one came forward. After the prescribed time, the men from Christchurch Cemetery came and took the blonde girl away, leaving behind a signed, stamped paper. A solitary ceremony, a cheap coffin and a shallow grave, paid for by the city. Ruth had accompanied the body and stood as the gravediggers shoveled dirt on the pine box, and the priest turned and walked away, his head down. As the men put a white wood cross in place, hammering it down with a shovel, the last of Ruth's heart crumbled.

She was standing on the brink of a precipice, and she decided to take a plunge.

Two days later, on her morning off, Ruth visited a shop selling secondhand clothes, in the old neighborhood where the Italians and Spaniards lived. She bought a man's suit, blue, three shirts, three ties. A pair of comfortable two-tone loafers, their soles worn, the leather scuffed. A wide-brimmed hat.

The following night, at home, she watched herself as though in a dream as she dressed in front of her mirror. The clothes felt so right. The jacket made her shoulders wider, her waist thinner. The hat hid her hair, cast her eyes in shadow.

Then, her head spinning and her heart racing, she went out in the night. As another person. Like Fantòmas, like the Scarlet Pimpernel. Looking for life.

It did not take long for her to find the steps down to the Southside, where there was music, and booze, and freedom. She had been patronizing the speakeasy for about a month when the cops raided the premises, and she met Charlie, and fell in love.

"They raid us once a month," Levon said. He placed the teacups down in front of them, filled with the dark amber of bootleg whiskey. He winked. "The cops want to make sure the boss keeps paying his dues."

Ruth took a sip of her liquor, the alcohol burning on her tongue.

"Damn nuisance," Charlie said. She was a little tipsy already, this being her third "tea" of the evening.

"They usually come on the Saturday, when the place's packed," the waiter said. "So tonight we're easy."

Ruth looked at the people crammed in the smoky room. To her, the place seemed packed enough. On the bandstand, the guys were warming up. The noise of a thousand voices went down a notch as the bass and drum picked up the rhythm. Jungle Blues. Levon nodded and moved on to the next table. Ruth sighed and relaxed against the back of her chair.

"Feeling good, love?" Charlie asked.

She did that thing she did, caressing Ruth's hand, running her long nail around Ruth's ring. Ruth had started wearing it two weeks before, on their first anniversary celebration. Three months, and a silver ring. Charlie had one just like hers.

Ruth drank some more and nodded. "Always, when we're together."

The music was jumping in time with the butterflies in her chest. She'd never get used to it, she knew. And she liked the feeling. A woman at a nearby table, her man's hand on her knee, looked at them and grinned. She gave Ruth a thumbs-up, like they were aviators in a film.

"We could go to the movies one of these nights," she said, suddenly.

Charlie shrugged. "If you like."

Ruth arched an eyebrow, and Charlie seemed to sober up suddenly. "I like it here," she said. "I like being with you in the bright lights. Where everybody can see us, and nobody cares."

Ruth chuckled and lit a cigarette. "You're drunk."

But she felt like it too. She ran a hand down the lapel of her double-breasted jacket, touched the lilac silk *pochette* Charlie had given her on their first date.

"Let's order one more tea," Charlie said, raising a hand to call Levon. "Then we go home."

Ruth gave her a look. "What do you have in mind, you minx?"

Charlie smiled like a happy, tipsy cat. "Wait and see."

"Some people were here to see you," Lumley said.

Morgue assistant, he was the sort of guy that carried a black leather bag like a doctor's, containing just his sandwiches. His shift over, he stood and picked his coat from the hanger behind the door.

"What people?" Ruth asked. It was not like she ever had any visitors.

Lumley shrugged. "People. A man and a woman. Nice clothes, the dame. He looked like a bum. I told them you'd be in tonight."

He picked up his hat and his bag and wished her goodnight.

Despite her seniority, Ruth still got nights, two weeks a month.

"It's because you're a dame," Charlie usually said. "We girls always get the short end."

Charlie worked at a milliner's shop on Church Street, and when Ruth was doing nights, they barely saw each other.

With a sigh, Ruth worked her silver ring around her finger.

"Nice bauble you have there, Miss Turner."

A man's voice. Rough. She started and turned. At the office door, a man and a woman stood, looking at her.

"Can we have a word?" the man said.

Ruth took a step back. They came in and closed the door behind them.

They were a strange couple. The woman was tall, aristocratic, her black hair pleated in an expensive do. Everything about her spoke of money. She pulled her fur cape closer as she looked with bored curiosity at the desks, the filing cabinets. Like a tourist. The man, on the other hand, looked a lot cheaper in a well-worn gray suit. He badly needed a shave, and kept staring at Ruth with a hungry, predatory look on his face. He had short stubby hands, his fingernails stained brown.

They were not the sort of people that usually visited these rooms. "How can I help you?" Ruth asked, warily.

The woman turned to her, like she had just noticed Ruth was there, and arched an aristocratic eyebrow. "Yes," she said.

Ruth frowned. The man nodded. "You certainly can, miss. Help us, that is."

His grin revealed big yellow teeth. Ruth looked at him, and then at the woman.

"We are seeking an arrangement of reciprocal benefit," the woman said.

"You know how they say," the man said. "One hand washes the other, and together they wash the face."

"I don't–"

"Do you have many unclaimed bodies?" the woman asked suddenly, with the same tone one might use to inquire about groceries.

"Sure they do," the man nodded. He was rifling through the papers Lumley had left on his desk. "John Doe, they call 'em."

"Don't touch–!"

He turned sharply, his mellifluous smile gone. "Don't you snap at me, woman."

His companion took a step forward. "Excuse my… partner," she said. The man scoffed. "He has some authority issues."

"Who are you?" Ruth asked. "What do you want?"

The woman sighed. The fur slid down from her shoulders. She had a long neck. A gold medallion rested on her chest. "Let us talk about what you want, first," she said, her voice dripping poisoned honey. "And what you don't want."

"We hear you like a bit of the night life," the man said, and winked. "One wouldn't say it, from the looks of you."

Ruth felt a chill. "What do you mean?"

"It is alright," the woman said. She came closer. She was wearing an intensely sweet perfume. "We can appreciate your... little indiscretions. We all have our weaknesses. But not many share our enlightened point of view, do they?"

Fear and anger bubbled in Ruth's chest. "Get out of my office," she hissed.

"And go where? To your boss? Or should we go to the police? Do you think they'd go easy on you and your ginger girlfriend? No, wait – maybe we should pay a little visit to your family." His evil smirk widened into a sickening grin. "Imagine finding one of them here on the slab, one of these days."

Ruth opened her mouth, but no sound came out of it. This couldn't be true.

The woman smiled. "Breathe, darling."

She pulled out one of the chairs, inspected the seat critically, and sat down. Crossed her legs. She smiled again. The man moved behind her and crossed his arms.

"What do you want from me?" Ruth asked.

The woman's smile did not reach up to her eyes. "We want your unclaimed bodies."

They had everything figured out already. The man's name was Collins. He worked as a gravedigger and general handyman in the graveyard on Hangman's Hill. He would provide the burial papers. Ruth was to take care of the paperwork on the morgue side and, when needed, just leave the service door open. Ruth would only need to call them when there was an unclaimed body in the morgue.

Doctor the papers and turn the other way. The friends of Collins and the woman would do the rest. Everything would look fine.

"Nobody cares about that dead meat anyway," Collins said.

"It's better than being forgotten in some common grave," the woman said.

"It's against the law," Ruth said. But her voice was uncertain.

"So is imbibing the bootleggers' booze," Collins said with a chuckle.

"And dressing up as a man," the woman said. "And a few other of your... shall we say, pastimes?"

Ruth was squeezing her hands together to stop them from shaking. "What are you going to do with... with these people?"

"That's none of your concern," Collins said.

"At least for the moment," the woman added. Collins gave her a weird look. "And you should stop considering them people. They are bodies. There's nothing to them but that. Dead meat."

"And if I do as you ask–?"

"You'll go on havin' a wild time, and no one will be any the wiser," Collins winked. "And all your loved ones will be safe."

"Indeed, you'll be much safer with us," the woman said, "than on your own. We are very good at keeping our secrets. And our friends.'"

Ruth's hands ached from the way in which she was pressing them together. She looked from the woman to

Collins and back. "If I were caught–"

"You won't be," Collins said. "People like you are good at keeping secrets, aren't you? But sure, we could rat on you alright."

He leaned closer, a cruel smirk on his face. "After all, we are law-abiding citizens. We have a moral duty to report your... indiscretions? I am sure they would like to have a talk with you, and your ginger-headed friend."

The woman gave him a hard look. "Enough."

She stood and took a step towards Ruth. She placed a nicely manicured hand on her shoulder. "You should think of this as an opportunity," she said.

Ruth remained silent, but she already knew what her answer would be.

"Nice girl," the woman said, like she was reading Ruth's mind. She squeezed her shoulder gently. "You won't regret it."

The first one was a man in his late seventies, dead of a stroke, alone in his two-room apartment on East Street. A widower, all of his family dead of the Spanish Flu ten years before. Ruth called the number they had given her, and started filling out the forms.

Ruth was working afternoons.

Early in the morning, someone dropped an envelope in her mailbox. She found it on her way out to work. Hangman Hill Cemetery papers, burial permits, general authorizations. She faked the missing signatures and got them stamped during the lunch break. Nobody locked their offices. Why should they?

Then, the following night, she left the door of the service corridor unlocked, and went home.

She tossed and turned in her bed through the night. Late in the morning, her head splitting with a headache, she made herself up and dressed and went to see Charlie for lunch.

They sat in one of the students cafés on College Street, just two friends having lunch together. But Ruth was distant, distracted. Charlie leaned across the table and placed a hand on her forehead. "Are you coming down with something?" she asked.

Ruth jumped, startled. She pulled back and looked around. "What are you doing?" she hissed.

Charlie grinned and picked up her sandwich again. "You're no fun today."

Ruth took a deep breath and shook her head. "I am sorry."

"What for? It's not your fault if you caught a bug."

They walked together after lunch, just two friends having a stroll. A few college students stared at Charlie, and Ruth felt a pang of jealousy that distracted her briefly from her mounting panic.

Then they parted ways, and Ruth went to her office, ready to face disaster.

The body was gone, the icebox drawer empty.

And nothing happened. Nobody came to inquire about the old man, no one checked or made any fuss about the records. As long as the papers were in order, nobody seemed to care.

Not a person, Ruth thought. Just a dead body.

That night, when she got home, she found a plain envelope in her mailbox. Inside were five five-dollar bills, and a card of fine ivory-colored paper. Ruth recognized the woman's perfume.

Buy something pretty for your girlfriend.
Olivia.

Ruth dropped the money and the card in a drawer. She needed a hot bath. She felt dirty.

The days turned into weeks and the weeks into months.

Things settled into a reassuring routine. Work at the office, sometimes lunch with Charlie. Maybe a movie on a weekday night. Clara Bow. Ramon Navarro. And then, on the weekend, Ruth would shed her everyday skin and don her jacket and tie. Charlie had given her a fine trench coat as a gift, and she had bought more shirts, and another hat, using the money from Olivia. She also bought Charlie perfume and a pair of pearl earrings.

And sometimes a dead body would land on the slab, some sad forgotten man or woman. Ruth would pick up the phone and slip a new form into the typewriter. She had her own stamp now. She had asked one of the guys in the Southside, and he'd suggested an old Polish man, who made her a copy of the records stamp. She carried it in her bag. No more sneaking into other people's offices at lunchtime.

Everything was fine.

Ruth was maybe drinking a little more than before,

smoking more cigarettes. When she was out with Charlie, dressed like a man and with her lover on her arm, she was aggressively cheerful. She danced and made a racket and ordered more "tea". But it was alright. They'd sometimes stumble to Charlie's place, a little smashed, and fall in bed, giggling.

Later, Charlie snoring gently at her side, Ruth would stare at the ceiling, questions running through her now sober mind.

What were they doing with the bodies?

Olivia and Collins did not look like Arkham's own Burke and Hare. But one heard things, about fraudsters and criminals. Ruth believed they were involved in some form of insurance scam, the ramifications unseen to her and impossible to fathom.

"Leaving so early?"

Olivia was standing in the doorway, her hand on the knob. She was wearing a deep maroon coat with a soft fox collar and a matching cloche hat.

Surprised, Ruth put her bag down. "What do you want?" she hissed.

Olivia pouted. "Let's call this a social visit."

Ruth glanced at her wristwatch.

"Yes, I know, it's late," Olivia said. She unbuttoned her coat, revealing a black dress, a long string of pearls. Like she was coming from a gala night. "They will be here soon."

"Who?"

"Our... associates. I guess it's high time you met them. Get acquainted. Learn more about our circle."

"I am not interested."

"Liar." Olivia came closer. "You are too intelligent not to be curious. And tonight–"

There was a sound from the service corridor. The metal door at its end opened, hinges creaking.

"Ah, here they come."

Fear like a spike of ice pierced Ruth's chest, cutting her breath short. Sharp, unexplained, a feeling of helplessness, an urge to flee. Run away. Hide. Irrational. Paces clicked in the corridor. Feeling the other woman's eyes on her, Ruth stepped back from her desk, and Olivia moved to her side and, unexpectedly, took her by the hand.

The corridor door creaked, and the handle moved.

"Do not be afraid," Olivia ordered, a quavering note in her cultured voice.

Ruth wished she could turn and look at the woman's face, but her eyes were glued to the door as it slowly opened.

And then in they came. A slow procession of hunchbacked shapes, walking on hoofed feet, ember-like eyes burning in dog-snouted faces. Black fur, flashing teeth. They moved like apes, their paws' knuckles sometimes touching the floor. Sometimes their talons clicking on the marble tiles. There were six of them, two undoubtedly male.

Ruth wobbled, and Olivia's hand squeezed her own. "They mean us no harm. Look at them."

Ruth's voice was broken. "I–"

"Look! Don't you dare turn your eyes away... Look at them if you want to live!"

The creatures crossed the room in single file. One of

them, Ruth noticed, wore wire-framed glasses. Another sported a wristwatch. Ruth choked on a laugh at the incongruity.

"Good," Olivia whispered. "Keep looking."

The creatures opened the two icebox drawers where the recent unclaimed bodies had been waiting. A man and a woman, drifters by their clothes. Found by the railroad after a chilly night. The black creatures pulled away the sheets and remained for a moment in contemplation of the remains. One of them stretched out a hand and caressed the face of the dead woman, almost affectionate. They stood like that for a minute, as though in prayer. Then, effortlessly carrying the bodies, the things walked back to the corridor.

Thank you, they said. Or so Ruth believed. By now, her mind had completely dissolved.

"See?" Olivia whispered in her ear. "There is nothing to fear."

Ruth missed five days of work, claiming a bad cold. In fact she spent the time curled up in her bed, her arms wrapped around her folded legs. Laying perfectly still, breathing slowly, and moaning rhythmically. When fatigue overwhelmed her and sleep came, she was shaken awake by the dreams screaming in her mind.

Charlie found her like that, when she came to visit after work on the evening of the fourth day. Ruth was still wearing her office clothes and her shoes, and was soaked in sweat, and trembling. Her moans were like a frightened animal's.

"I'm calling Doctor Howard," Charlie said. There was a telephone at the bottom of the stairs. But Ruth caught her by the wrist. "No," she croaked. "Just stay with me."

Charlie frowned, worried. Then she slipped out of her shoes and lay down with Ruth in the bed, holding her tight. They spent the night like that, both awake. One of them worried sick, the other slowly going crazy.

After that night, and the fever days, Ruth did not care anymore. She went through her days like they were somebody else's.

She called the number and handled the paperwork and collected the money from her mailbox. She no longer had any qualms spending it. She stalled Charlie's questions at her gifts, and all the rest. She danced and drank and smoked and partied harder than ever. She became notorious at the Southside Speakeasy.

She started wearing slacks at work, and ignored the raised eyebrows. She started smoking in her office. "It covers the smell of the disinfectant," she explained when a surprised Lumley caught her lighting up. He could not deny that it did.

She carried a hip flask in her handbag. Sometimes she came to work dead hungover. Sometimes she was tipsy by lunchtime. But nobody noticed, nobody cared. She least of all.

She tried not to think of the nightmares. The dark shapes dancing in the dusk, the strange chanting. And on the nights when the bodies were taken, she no longer vacated the offices. She would just sit at her desk and watch as the creatures came. It was better than be at home alone, and dream.

It was on the third night they came that she started talking to them, and they answered back.

The Devourer Below needs feeding, the dog-faced creature explained, during one of their conversations. He moved his lips, but his voice sounded in Ruth's mind like her own thoughts. *And we are Those That Feed the Devourer.*

There was pride there, and duty. A sense of belonging. And Ruth knew she was one of those "we", just like Olivia or Collins or the others. Because there were others.

Surface Dwellers, the creatures called them.

But that did not matter to her. Only Charlie mattered now.

The creature she called Bob caressed Ruth's face, and she did not shrink or start. His touch was delicate, like a friend's. *Protecting your mate,* Bob said. *Feeding the Devourer. This is good.*

She offered him a cigarette, but he declined.

After they left with the body, she locked up the office and staggered back home.

She hoped she would get at least two hours of dreamless sleep.

Their first row was terrible, and started from nothing. They had come home from the Southside, where they had danced until they were dizzy, and everybody clapped and sang along. They sat together on the bed, and Charlie slowly undid Ruth's clothes. Took off her jacket, loosened up her tie. Helped her out of her shirt.

"I think the landlady is getting suspicious," Charlie whispered, and kissed Ruth's shoulder.

Ruth shrugged her off, instinctively.

"Hey! What's wrong with you these days?"

Ruth turned to her, her eyes two steel spikes. "What do you mean?"

Charlie shrugged and huddled closer. "You are strange," she said softly. "It's like there's always something going on, in here."

She caressed Ruth's temple, her fingers light and cool. Ruth pushed her back.

"Hey!" Charlie screeched. She chuckled, but Ruth's expression smothered her mirth.

"If you weren't this insistent," Ruth said, "people wouldn't be suspicious."

"You got it bad tonight, huh?" Charlie snorted. "Well, sorry for loving you."

"This is it, right? You're sorry about this."

Charlie's eyes widened. "Are you insane?"

And Ruth started screaming at her, words that cut like blades, until Charlie broke down crying, and Ruth finally realized where she was, and what she was doing. She stopped mid-phrase, her mouth suddenly dry. "I am sorry," she said next. "I'm sorry, my love, I am so sorry–"

She sought Charlie's hand, and the redhead pulled back, her face streaked with black eyeliner, her eyes reddened and puffy. They looked at each other, both of them more sober than they had been for weeks. More sober than they wished to be.

"I am sorry," Ruth said again, and finally they held on to each other.

•••

There was a fire in the Rookeries on French Hill one night, the flames painting the clouds red. The fire truck tore through the streets screaming and later, as the greasy black smoke rose from the wreckage, the bodies were brought to the morgue.

"You want to stay where you are, miss," the fireman said. Fatigue colored his voice. Ruth was standing behind her desk, her hands on the desktop, her face pale. "It's not a pretty sight."

Men with soot-smeared faces brought in the stretchers. Three bodies, under dirty sheets. The smell was awful.

The creature under the desk moved and brushed Ruth's leg.

There had been four of them in the morgue, when the firemen had come. Now two were hiding in the supply closet, and one had made a dash for the staircase. Bob was huddling under the desk.

The firemen put down their stretchers, opened the ice drawers.

"We will get you the reports and paperwork tomorrow." The chief walked closer, and Ruth retreated. She could smell the musky tang of the creature under the desk. Felt his breath, hot against her leg. But the fireman just looked her in the eye and frowned. "For the moment, put down in your registers we've got three of them, male, in their thirties by the look of them."

"Shouldn't there be an autopsy?" Ruth asked, her voice shaking.

The fireman shrugged. "It's pretty clear what killed them," he said. "I doubt the city will waste too much time or money on them."

"Poor bastards," another man said, pushing the drawer closed.

They were folding up the stretchers. They nodded to her as they filed out, and in a moment she heard the trucks starting. She sat down with a sigh.

Three more, the thing under the desk said.

The closet door opened, and the other two peered out.

"You can't take these," she replied. "Not yet."

They are cooked, Bob conceded. *The Devourer would reject them. But we can consume them anyway. Honor them. Share them.*

Ruth's heart skipped a beat. She had always known, of course. The knowledge had been festering at the back of her conscious mind for weeks, months now. But now she could no longer hide from it.

They ate them.

The Devourer Below was a greedy master, but he did share his food with his servants.

Ruth pushed back a bout of nausea. "Does Olivia… and Collins…?"

Sometimes, her confidant said.

She closed her eyes. "And am I expected to?"

Where had that thought come from?

When the time comes. Soon. In the woods.

"I don't think I could."

The creature gave a brief shrug. *Your time will come. You are a lot like us. You hide away. Secretive. You are not used to being seen. You would feel at home with us, down below. You could share the food with us.*

Ruth laughed. "Are you flirting with me?"

Bob's eyes were like dying embers in the dark. *You have a mate already.*

Ruth shuddered. "What do you know of her?"

She has a nice smell. We feel it on you. His gaze lingered on her face. *She would be welcome too. In the woods. And Below, too, where the Devourer awaits.*

That was when Ruth decided she needed a way out of all this. She wished she still believed in God, in any god that need not be fed dead bodies. Then she could pray for some form of deliverance. For herself, and for Charlie.

"Some guys were here looking for you."

Ruth stared at Chuck Lumley, the feeling of déjà vu washing over her. "What people?"

He shrugged and picked up his hat and his bag. "Two guys, one Black, the other looking like a cop, and a woman. They were here this morning. Asked a lot of questions."

Ruth felt a pressure in her chest. "What sort of questions?"

He shrugged and glanced at the door. His shift was over, and he wanted to go home. "Questions. About how we run things hereabouts. You know, the paperwork, the routines. They might be back. I told them you're the one to see about the unclaimed bodies and the rest."

Then he wished her a good evening, and left her alone with her fear.

The three strangers called about one hour later.

"Miss Turner?"

She looked up. A man in a trench coat, a young woman in a cheap coat and comfortable shoes, and a tall Black man in suspenders stood at the door of the office.

"Yes, I am Ruth Turner."

The two men looked at each other. "Can we have a bit of your time?" Trench Coat asked. "Your colleague said you are the one we should talk to."

"Mister Lumley," Comfy Shoes added. She had short red hair, and large brown eyes.

"I think he mentioned you," Ruth said. "I don't know–"

"It won't take long," Suspenders said, with an affable smile. "You can call me Calvin, and my friends here are Roland and Lita."

Ruth gave them a wary nod.

"So this is where the bodies are kept, huh?" the man named Roland asked. He gave her a look. "Before they get buried, I mean."

Ruth arched her eyebrows. "This is the morgue," she said.

"She's not wrong, you know," Calvin chuckled.

"Do you get many unclaimed bodies?" the other man asked. The same question Olivia had asked, a lifetime before.

Ruth crossed her arms. "You should define 'many'," she said, keeping her tone professional and detached. "I am not aware of the average figures across the country. We do get an unidentified body once in a while, but it is not a common occurrence. I am sure the police have better figures than I do right now."

Calvin frowned. "And what about the bodies that are identified, but not claimed by any family member?"

"The lonely and the forgotten," the woman, Lita, said. It sounded like a quote from somewhere.

"Once again, we can have one of those, once in a while. I do not have any figures at hand. If you could call again–"

"What happens to them?" Roland asked. He was slowly walking around the room, and asked his questions without watching her.

"The Town Council arranges for their burial. On the Hill, or in Christchurch."

"What's the difference? Why choose one or the other?"

Ruth shrugged. "A matter of convenience, I presume. We have no say in these arrangements."

The man in the trench coat was standing by the filing cabinets. "And I guess this is where all the records are kept, right?"

Ruth stood. "Why are you asking me these questions? Who are you?"

He looked at her from underneath the rim of his fedora. "Just… you know, concerned citizens."

"Concerned about what?"

Roland put his hand on a filing drawer handle. "I guess we couldn't take a look at the records, right?"

"Your guess is correct, mister–?"

The Black man placed his hand on his friend's shoulder. "I think we have inconvenienced Miss Turner enough," he said. "Let's go."

They wished her a good night, and before she could ask her own questions of them, they were gone. Ruth sat down heavily, her heart racing.

"And what have you told them?"

Ruth took a drag from her cigarette. She was leaning

on the wall by the telephone. Her landlady gave her a hard look, and she answered with what she hoped was a reassuring smile. "What should I tell them?" she hissed into the receiver. "They wanted to know about the unclaimed bodies. And how they are assigned to the different graveyards."

Olivia was silent for a long moment.

"You have done right," she said finally. "Just keep acting normal. Everything's fine."

Ruth doubted it. The strangers were certainly not done with her.

"We must be careful," Charlie said in a low voice when they met for lunch the following day.

Her luminous smile was gone, and she kept looking around.

"What happened?"

"A guy came to the shop," she said. "Asking questions."

"A guy? Questions about us?"

Charlie nodded. "Tall, wearing a trench coat and a slouch hat. He did not look like vice squad, but he certainly had a cop feel to him."

Two nights before there had been another raid at the Southside. Another hectic scramble, another wild run through a maze of darkened alleys, police whistles and frantic footsteps. Another sharp stab of panic that had dissolved in a burst of frenzied release.

But in the cold daylight, this was different.

They walked towards the campus grounds, neither of them feeling like lunch.

"What did he want with you?" Ruth asked.

Charlie looked at her and frowned. "What do you think?"

"Maybe he's not vice," she said.

"Maybe we should stop going out for a while."

Ruth stopped, like she was rooted to the ground. A young man carrying a stack of books dodged her and kept running past. "Watch out!" he shouted, and was gone.

Ruth listened to her own voice, dead and toneless. "You want to call it quits?"

Charlie's cheeks were aflame. "Don't be stupid," she hissed, and squeezed Ruth's hand.

She sat down on a bench, and Ruth sat by her side. "I just say, we should start being more careful. More private about… about everything. About us."

Ruth stared at the tip of her shoes. "I don't want to hide anymore."

She was feeling again at the brink of a precipice. The endless fall was calling to her.

Charlie placed her hand on Ruth's forearm. "I know, love. But we must be careful." Her usual mischievous spark lit her blue eyes. "We can be together at my place. Dance to the radio."

She was suddenly serious. "But we must be careful."

"Yes," Ruth agreed. "Very careful."

According to the police, whoever broke into her office was scared away by the night watchman. Ruth wondered if any of her friends from Below were also involved. A chair had been smashed, and the place was in a mess. Lumley was standing in a corner, holding his black bag like a shield over his chest.

"They cracked the locks," the uniform cop said. He walked to the filing cabinets, trampling the spilled sheets on the floor. "And then they had a go with a crowbar on these here drawers."

The files from the community burials.

Ruth interlaced her fingers, hoping the policeman would not notice her trembling hands. He did not.

"Not much to steal here anyway, what?" he said, genially. "Young punks, probably. Or some student prank."

"Do we need to come down to the station?" Lumley asked. He glanced at Ruth.

The officer shook his head. "We might need a statement. You check out if anything's missing. But as I said, this is not the crime of the century, what?"

"At least nobody got hurt," Ruth said, trying to sound calmer than she felt.

The cop scoffed. "Kids. It's those pulp magazines they read, if you ask me. And movies too. All those gangster stories."

The knock on the door cut short Bob Haring's crooning about Tahitian skies, and put a stop to their dance. "Don't–" Ruth whispered.

The knocking came again. Charlie hugged Ruth harder for a moment, then they let go of each other, and the redhead went to answer the door.

The man in the trench coat pushed her back and walked in, ignoring her protests, the Black man in suspenders and the young woman in the sensible shoes right behind him.

"Sorry to interrupt," Roland said. He gave a long look

at Ruth, taking in her neatly pressed trousers, her jacket, her tie. "Well, well," he said, and pushed his hat back on his forehead.

Charlie stepped in front of him, her hands closed into fists. "What does this mean?"

"We need to put a few questions to your girlfriend," he said.

"You can't come into my house like this!"

"Really? And what are you going to do? Call the police?"

He flashed a badge at her, and put it back in his pocket. She barely got a glimpse.

Calvin grimaced. "Awkward."

Ruth stood by Charlie's side. "What do you want?"

Roland snorted. "Like you don't know."

"She's not one of them," the woman said. She had a steady, authoritative voice. Lita, Ruth remembered.

"Yeah, sure," Calvin smirked.

"She's not. I can feel that. You know I can. She's tainted, but not yet–" she waved her hands, "corrupted."

"Tainted?" Charlie turned to Ruth, sharply. "What does this mean? You know these people?"

"It's OK," Ruth said in a low voice, her eyes on Roland's. She squeezed Charlie's hand. "This has nothing to do with you."

He grinned. "Yeah, sure."

"She's right," Lita said. "The girl is clean."

Charlie was no longer listening to them. "What is happening?"

Calvin sighed. "Your friend here, miss. She got involved with some bad people. Bad people indeed."

Charlie turned to stare at her. Ruth felt a tightness in her chest, but it slowly dissolved in a cold spike of resolve. She leaned closer, and gently kissed her on the lips.

"Well, I'll be damned!" Roland blurted.

"I need to talk to these gentlemen," Ruth said, like she was talking to a child. "It will be alright." She looked at the Black man. "Not here. Let's go out."

Roland was about to say something, but the other man stopped him. "We'll go for a walk," he agreed.

"I will stay here with her," Lita said. She was staring Ruth in the eye. "I'll make sure she's safe."

Ruth whispered a thank you, and followed the two men outside.

They walked slowly along the street. With Ruth in her coat and her fedora, they were just three men taking a stroll after dinner, having a smoke.

"How long have you been with the cult?" Calvin asked.

Ruth was feeling strangely lightheaded. This was not the way she had imagined it would be. "I don't know what you are talking about."

"We've seen the registers," he said. "You're good, but we knew what to look for."

"Why use a crowbar?" Ruth asked. "Why not get a warrant?" She looked closely at Roland. "This is not official, is it? Who are you? What do you want?"

They were silent for a moment. "We want to do the right thing," the grizzled man said. "Cut the snake's head."

"We want the top people," Roland said. "Madame Dyer, Collins. All the others. Professor Warren too. Put a stop to the madness. For good."

"We need to know where they meet, when," the other explained. "Sweep the whole thing clean."

"I know nothing of this," she said. She felt like she was slowly sinking in deep, cold water. Her breath came out in ragged bursts. "I met Collins and, I think, Madame Dyer. Olivia. But apart from that– They only use me to get the bodies."

"This is really a pity," Roland said.

He stopped, his hands in his pockets. "She looks like a nice girl, your girlfriend. You think you'll be able to keep her out of all this? You think they will let you go? Her too?"

"They threatened my family," Ruth whispered.

Calvin placed a hand on her shoulder. "We want to help you."

Ruth straightened her back. This was what she had been praying for. She took a bold step over the brink. "There is going to be… something. In the woods," she said. "I do not know the details. Some kind of celebration."

She had gone with the flow for too long. Not anymore.

"When?"

"I don't know. Soon. I can learn more. I have been invited. So to speak."

The two men traded a glance. Then the man in the trench coat handed her a calling card. Special Agent Roland Banks. And a phone number. "OK, Miss Cinderella," he said. "You're gonna give us a call as soon as you get your invitation to the ball."

They talked long into the night, holding on to each other, after the three strangers had gone.

Ruth told Charlie of Collins, and Olivia, and their racket. An insurance fraud, she explained. They bought insurance for people that did not exist, and then provided a body, and burial details, and collected the money.

"It's horrible," Charlie breathed.

Yes, horrible. But not as much as the truth.

"And now the feds…"

"Yes, they have been on the case for a while."

"What will happen to us?"

Ruth smiled, and kissed her on the top of her head. "Nothing. I will help them. I am just an accessory. I will testify. They will let me off the hook."

Charlie was slowly rocking back and forth.

"Why didn't you tell me?"

Ruth took a deep breath. "Because I love you."

Ruth lit a cigarette, filling her lungs with warm courage.

"Is your invitation still on?" she asked. Bob's burning eyes drilled into her. She hid behind a cloud of smoke. "To the feast."

Yes.

"Good!" she smiled. "I'm curious. When will this be? Where?"

When the stars are right. Where the shadows are deeper. In the woods.

"It's a bit vague."

You will be told. The woman that smells of dead flowers will tell you.

"Olivia? Is she going to be fine with me coming?"

The lips of the creature curled up to reveal a thick, sharp, eye-tooth. *You will come. We will welcome you. She won't question this.*

Bob lifted his hand, and his sharp talons ran along the curve of Ruth's jaw.

You could be one of us. Your mate too.

"She won't come," she said, a little too sharply.

Why?

"She's not ready yet."

The creature nodded. *But you are.*

The others had carried an old woman's body out already. Her friend was getting ready to go.

It will be glorious, he said.

Olivia's expected visit was three days later. "Have they found out who broke in here, then?"

"Students from one of the Miskatonic Greek societies," Ruth replied. The lie came naturally, her tone light, her voice steady. "Some kind of dare or initiation. You know how students are."

Olivia arched an eyebrow. "No, not really. But talking about initiations... In five days, on the next new moon. Your presence has been requested. It seems our friends down below have taken a shine to you." Olivia Dyer sounded peeved. She touched a strand of hair that escaped her powder-blue cloche, and gave Ruth a poisonous smile. "They want you along for the next ceremony. Remember, in five days."

Ruth crossed her arms, expectant. "Where?"

A smirk. "Out in the sticks. We will send a car for you. It will be an informal thing. No black tie or anything – come as you are. But come on an empty stomach." She licked her lips, a quick flick of her tongue. "There will be a buffet."

Collins drove a wobbly old Model T with one headlight on the blink. Ruth climbed aboard and he gave her one of his yellow-toothed grins. The engine coughed and belched black smoke.

"No tie?" he asked. "Someone might mistake you for a woman."

His laugh turned into a cough, and he spat out of the side window.

Ruth did not deign to reply. She had opted for slacks and sensible shoes. She adjusted her hat, and glanced in the rear-view mirror, trying to spot in the dirty, cracked glass a hint of Banks and the others following them. She had found an excuse with Charlie. A providential headache. No movie tonight. She repeated to herself that all would be well.

Collins drove the car out of town, along the road to Dunwich. The trees closed around them, and the road wound through the hills, all twists and turns.

"Is it far?" she asked.

"Nervous?" He looked at her, and she wished he'd keep his eyes on the road.

"Curious, actually."

"We'll be there in a quarter of an hour. Then there's a short walk up the hill."

The rearview mirror reflected only darkness. Collins started humming a repetitive, dirge-like song. Ruth lit a cigarette and ignored his coughing.

They drove in silence, the road trying to surprise them

with humps and tight bends, and finally they passed a standing stone, placed in the ditch like a sentinel. Collins gave a satisfied sigh and turned right, into the woods, past a narrow wooden bridge. He parked in a small clearing, next to three other cars.

"Come," he said. He took a lantern from the back, and she offered him a light. Then they started through the trees. "Mind your step," he said, holding the light high.

They followed a dirt path uphill through the undergrowth, and passed two more standing stones. Ruth tarried for a few breaths, leaning on the rough surface of one of these. She strained to catch a sound of someone following them, but all she heard was a faint breeze through the bushes, and an owl hooting in the distance.

"Are you coming?" Collins snapped.

Up ahead, she caught the faint glow of more lanterns.

"Here we are!" the man announced, waving his light and coughing again.

A broken chorus of greetings welcomed them.

Olivia was standing in front of a grassy knoll, a perfect inverted bowl, crowned with stones like fingers pointing at the sky. There was a passage, like a corridor leading down into the earth. A distant sound, coming through the ground, like a rhythmic humming.

"Oh, here comes the special guest of the soiree," Olivia said, when Ruth entered the circle of lights. She turned to the side and gave a sign. With a faint cry, Charlie was pushed forward, and staggered on the uneven ground, trying to keep her balance. Ruth was fast to catch her in her arms.

"What does this mean?" she blurted. Her heart raced and her mind reeled. This was not supposed to happen. She felt momentarily lost.

"You make such a great couple," Olivia leered. "Our hosts insisted you share tonight's feast. They seem to have a strange romantic streak."

"The more the merrier," Collins chuckled.

A balding man in a tweed jacket harrumphed at their mirth, and scoffed. There were others waiting around, black shadows among the black trees.

"Are you alright?" Ruth asked, in a whisper.

Charlie nodded. She was pale, and her heart beat like a mad drum against her ribs. Like that first time, the night everything began, Ruth thought. "Hush," she breathed, like she had done back then. She ran her fingers through Charlie's disheveled hair.

"Here they come," she said. The man's laugh died.

Hunched shapes were emerging from the earth. Ape-like and silent, they fanned out in front of them, standing just outside the glow of the lanterns. They smelled of earth and musk and something sweet and sickening.

"All is ready," the man in the tweed jacket intoned.

One of the black shapes detached itself from the shadows and came close to Ruth. Charlie went rigid, her eyes wide, as the thing stretched out a clawed hand and caressed Ruth's face.

You have brought your mate. This is good.

"Oh, God–" Charlie moaned, "It's in my head!"

Suddenly she was pushing against Ruth, trying to disentangle from her embrace. The black dog-faced ghoul took a step back, looking at her with his burning red eyes. He tilted his head to the side, frowning.

There was a bang, loud, like a thunderclap. A bullet caught the ghoul in the shoulder, and it spun around and crashed into a bush.

Ruth tackled Charlie, and together they rolled on the ground as bullets started flying, the rattle of the automatic weapons tearing through the night. The cultists and the ghouls scattered screaming as a flame arced through the air and smashed into the entrance to the barrow, erupting into a ball of fire. Pressing Charlie down, Ruth caught a glimpse of Collins staggering back, the front of his shirt soaked in darkness.

"Let's get away from here," she hissed, and she ran in a squat, dragging Charlie along. Hunched over, using her free hand and feet, she scampered through the undergrowth. She slipped and fell, and Charlie helped her up. They ducked behind a tall tree as the tight beam of a reflector swept the vegetation. Fear and anger were a taut ball of cold in her belly.

They stood motionless, holding on to each other, pressing against the bark. Charlie was crying. Ruth tasted her tears with a kiss, and hushed her.

Then the guns were silent. Light beams cut through the dusk. Voices were calling. The fire was roaring, eating at the trees. The whole top of the barrow was aflame, the stones standing out black against the liquid brightness of the fire. Men were coming in from their hideouts. Ruth thought she caught a glimpse of Special Agent Banks, holding a Tommy gun, and the woman, Lita.

"Let's go," she hissed.

They ran through the ferns, not caring about the noise, the low branches slapping at their faces. Charlie squealed as she stumbled and fell, her hand slipping from Ruth's.

"Come!" Ruth gasped. She tried to pull Charlie back to her feet, but the redhead pushed her away with both hands. A question lingered on Ruth's lips as a line of fire seared through her side. She cried out in pain, and turned.

"I guess we owe all this to you."

The dancing light of the hilltop flames turned Olivia Dyer's face into a grotesque mask, her eyes wide and crazed, her makeup smeared in dark streaks, her lips a ragged gash. She had lost her hat, and her hair was a wilderness of dirt and twigs. She had lost her shoes, and her dress was torn. She held a large knife in her hand, the ornate triangular blade glinting, red with Ruth's blood.

Ruth pressed a hand to her side, wet, her heart pounding in her fingers.

"Two more bodies," Olivia leered.

She lunged, pushing the blade forward. Ruth dodged, her side burning, and slammed into a tree. The blade swished close to her face, and she kicked out at Olivia. The other woman backed away and moved in a circle. With a snakelike twist, she grabbed Charlie by the hair, pulled her head up.

"The girlfriend first, then," she hissed. She poised her blade to cut through Charlie's throat. "I want you to see this."

Charlie's eyes were liquid pools of fear. "Run!" she cried. Instead, Ruth jumped at Olivia, crashing into her.

Charlie cried again as the two women rolled through the undergrowth, grappling with each other. They stopped against a tree stump, Olivia sitting astride Ruth. "I always knew it would end like this..." Olivia chuckled and lifted her knife. Charlie rushed her, screaming, grabbing her arm and wrenching the knife free. Olivia hit her in the face with her other elbow. Charlie fell back to the ground.

Olivia took a deep breath and looked around for her knife. From beneath her, Ruth grabbed her by the wrists. Olivia cursed and tried to wrestle free.

Then two large furry hands cradled Olivia's face and twisted her head around. Her neck broke with a sound like a dry branch. Her face frozen in a surprised expression, Olivia fell to the side and was still.

Charlie scrambled to Ruth's side, and the two women crouched in the bushes, holding each other. A familiar ghoulish face looked at them. There was dark blood pouring from a wound in his shoulder, and his eyes burned brighter than ever.

There was the noise of people moving in the underbrush. *They are coming*, he said. *Come with me. Below. We will be safe. Your mate too.*

Charlie was shaking as though in a fever. Ruth held Bob's gaze and shook her head.

"I can't," she said.

Bob was still for a moment. The hunters were coming closer.

One day, maybe.

Ruth's breath was ragged. "Maybe."

And why not? she thought. The dog-faced creatures

were honest, clean. Pure, in their strange way. They saw the world for what it was, and did not try to change it. They did not blackmail or betray each other. They had no guns, no knives. Maybe they'd let her make amends for what she'd done to them. It would be good, to finally live without hypocrisy. Free.

Ruth squeezed Charlie's hand. "We're safe now," she said, slowly. Just like that night, a million years before. But different.

Ruth cast a glance at the dead, pathetic remains of Olivia. She was already free, she realized. She cleared her voice. "I will not hide anymore," she said.

It would be good, she thought, when the moment came. Good for the both of them.

Her heart was slowing down. "One day," she nodded to the ghoul.

The creature held her gaze for a long moment. Then he walked away into the dark, dragging Olivia's body with him.

THE DARKLING WOODS
Cath Lauria

There was something decidedly *strange* about this place.

Wendy thought it might be the effect of the woods. She'd never been this close to the woods beyond Arkham before. The docks were where she made her home these days, she and James. Not that the docks didn't have their fair share of strangeness, with odd patches of lurking darkness that smelled like anything but the sea, and strangers striding off boats with eyes too deep and far too bright, with dull, gray-skinned fingers that swayed like seaweed on the ends of their arms.

There was *plenty* of creep on the docks, people and things to look out for. It was different when you were used to it, though. Riverside was made of a strange that Wendy recognized, and did her best to avoid. There were lots of ways to keep out of the path of the ones that seemed wrong, lots of other people to make a living from.

Back in Riverside, people called kids like Wendy and James "urchins" if they were feeling charitable or "little thieves" if they were being, well, rather more honest. Wendy had learned early, after her mother was taken away, how to lighten her fingers so a mark never felt her lift a watch or a wallet. When her usual feathery touch turned unfortunately hammer-handed, she learned how to dodge a grasping arm or duck a blow from a cane and run to a safe place – leastways, as safe as anywhere was in Arkham.

It was a risky life, but it was all danger she knew and understood. Wendy hadn't been living on the docks by herself as long as lots of the other kids, but she was a fast learner. When she felt that warning tingle, when a situation was going bad, she knew to hotfoot it.

But she couldn't count on that tingle working the same in all places. What was odd in one part of Arkham might be normal in another, the same way all the kids along the docks knew not to steal from the laborers there, just the travelers. Maybe strangers got treated the other way around here in Uptown. There was no other explanation Wendy could think of for why, in this run-down hostel, which was just a few short steps away from Arkham Woods, she and James were being treated like actual *guests*.

It was very unsettling.

"Oh, you poor things, get in out of that rain," the woman serving a drink to a glowering man at the back of the room had exclaimed as soon as Wendy and James stepped through the door of the hostel. She'd smiled brightly at them, the friendly look marred a bit by the numerous gaps where she was missing teeth. Being out a few teeth was nothing new, but most people, full set or not, didn't go around beaming like that at strangers.

"What's a pair of sweet children like you doing out by themselves on an evening such as this?" the matron went on, leaving her sole other patron behind and coming over to shut the heavy wooden door behind them. It closed with a bang that startled James so badly he jumped, and cut them off from the fading light of the sun. Without it, even though there was a fire lit and candles here and there on the tables, the inside seemed terribly dark. No fancy electric lights for a place like this.

"I know everyone who lives in Uptown," she continued, wiping her hands off on the dark fabric of her skirt. "But I've never seen the pair of you before. Are you... vagrants, perhaps? Orphans?"

Well, they sort of *were* vagrants, but Wendy had never heard anyone sound so excited before about wandering children. It made the hair at the back of her neck prickle. And as for the other...

"We're not orphans," she said firmly, although James actually was. The younger boy looked enough like her that they could fool people into thinking they were siblings, and right now Wendy wasn't too keen to let this woman think they were all alone. "Our mother sent us ahead to get a room," she lied blithely, and James squeezed her hand so hard her knuckles cracked. "We can pay," she added. It was true for a single night, at least, although one night away from Riverside wouldn't be long enough to cool Marvin's wrath. Wendy would think more about placating the leader of the Water Street Runners later, though.

"Hmm." The woman's expression went from overly warm to cool, the light of interest in her eyes waning into something distant. "I suppose I can put you up for the night, although your mother had better hurry. Doors around here tend to close as soon as the sun goes down, and this place is no different."

"I'm sure she'll be here," Wendy said. When their "mother" inevitably failed to show up, she would bank on the woman not kicking out a paying customer until morning.

"Right." The woman's eyes narrowed a little as she looked them over more carefully. "No bags?"

Wendy shook her head, soggy red curls falling across her forehead. "They're with her."

"Show me your coin."

Wendy pulled a few silver coins out of the little coin purse she kept in the biggest, most obvious pocket in the front of her gingham skirt, careful not to let anything in her hidden pockets jingle. One of a pickpocket's cardinal rules: always separate your stash.

"Good enough." The woman snatched the money from her hand so fast Wendy flinched. "I'm Mrs Duncan," she said, more genial once again – probably because there was money to be made. "Dinner's not quite ready yet, but if you sit over there I'll have it out to you fast enough, then take you upstairs to your room once you've eaten."

"Thank you, ma'am." Wendy led James over to the rough-hewn oak bench Mrs Duncan had pointed them toward and sat down, gripping the edge of it hard enough to threaten her palm with splinters. The room was warm, almost cloyingly so after a day spent cadging lifts on the backs of passing Model T's and darting down alleys on their way from Riverside to Uptown.

"Wen, what are you doing?" James whispered, as Mrs Duncan disappeared into what smelled like the kitchen. "We don't have a mother coming! I don't have a mother at all! I thought we were going to play the 'poor alone children, let 'em work off their room and board' roles with her."

"I know, but..." Wendy bit her lower lip. "I don't think that was the right way to go for this one. Didn't you notice how happy she seemed when she thought we were alone?"

"Maybe she just likes children?" James suggested, a pitiable note of hope in his voice. "Stranger things've happened."

That was certainly true, and Wendy had seen more of them than she cared to think about. "It's done," she said at last, and James sighed. "And we're getting a meal and a room out of it, at least. It's better than sleeping out there."

James shrugged, wiping his running nose on his sleeve. He'd been fighting a cold for what seemed like ages now. "We've slept outside plenty of times. There's always someplace that keeps the rain off ya."

"It's not the rain that worries me," Wendy said, more to herself than to her companion. James was a carefree child despite living on the streets, not tough and rough like so many of the others. He didn't see the badness in things unless they were right in front of him, and even then he didn't hold onto them long, always content to flit on and on. Wendy... she had learned caution, after what happened to her parents. To her mother Penelope, who wasn't crazy no matter what people said about "that Adams woman."

Wendy pulled at the neck of her dress to get a bit of extra air. The only other person in the hostel's dining area was the man across the room, who was scowling down at the table as he nursed his drink, yet it was warm enough in here to make her sweat. Was she running a fever, or just still hot from their mad dash across town earlier today?

Arkham was a big place, and getting from one side of it to the other took a lot of effort, especially when you were trying not to be seen. She and James had a real need not to be seen right now, particularly by the Water Street Runners, the gang of kids who ran the streets down by the docks. Marvin, their leader, had mouthed off to one of the burly, bad-tempered stevedores last week and been hit so hard for his daring that his face had puffed up like bread dough.

He'd been holed up for days, his crew shadowing him anxiously, and it had been almost like a holiday for Wendy and James. No one stealing their scores, no one threatening them, no one talking bad about them and their family – or lack thereof. It was downright pleasant to work the streets for a few days there.

Once Marvin could get around again, though, he was meaner than ever, lashing out at everyone smaller than him and demanding more and more tribute from people like Wendy and James, who were just barely able to get by. The night he caught sight of her amulet was the last straw – he'd instantly demanded it, even though it didn't look like anything special. If he could take it, he would… but Wendy couldn't let him. The amulet was more than just a memento from her mother – it helped her feel safe when the bad things got too close. She and James had run for it, Marvin's curses following them the whole way down the street.

They *would* go back to Riverside again, of course. This wasn't permanent, this little detour of theirs. Wendy couldn't leave the docks for good, not when she was still waiting for her father to come back. He had left her a message not long ago, entreated her to stay safe. He was coming back, and she would be waiting for him. Then they would get her mother out of the sanitarium and be a family again, fighting off the darkness together.

Wendy let go of her collar, letting her hand rest briefly on the amulet hidden beneath the thin cloth of her blouse. Compared to the surroundings, the necklace felt surprisingly cool to the touch. It got that way sometimes when she passed by one of those dank, dark patches set back in the fog of the docks, and Wendy wasn't at all surprised that it was reacting the same way here in Uptown. There was something *off* about this entire place.

"She's coming back," James hissed, and Wendy dropped her hand immediately. It was second nature to hide the amulet's existence at this point.

Wendy had no reason to suspect Mrs Duncan of anything like that, but then...

"Here." The woman carried a tray in one hand, and as she got close she set down two bowls of stew on the table in front of Wendy and James, each accompanied by a slightly dented pewter spoon, and two pewter mugs of water. "Eat up," she advised, a strange smile crossing her face. "Your mother wouldn't want you to go hungry, I'm sure."

"Thank you, ma'am." Whether the woman was odd or not, her food smelled good. Wendy and James tucked in, and she sighed heavily as the first bite of stew graced her tongue. It was thick and meaty, with chunks of potato and carrot and a hint of garlic, and so salty it might preserve her tongue, but it would be worth it for food so rare and rich.

They ate and drank up the water, which tasted only a little bit musty, and Wendy tried not to think about how the sun was surely gone now, and how dark it was in here, and how the longer they sat alone, the sharper the look in Mrs Duncan's eyes as she watched them from her place near the door.

Wendy was finished, but James was still scraping the bottom of his bowl when Mrs Duncan came back over, lighting a fresh, fat candle and setting it on their table to provide a bit more light. "You must be getting worried about your mother," she said with an exaggerated frown. "Perhaps we should go out and look for her."

"No," Wendy said firmly, pressing her leg against James' to remind him to keep quiet and let her do the talking. "She must have gotten held up, but she said if she didn't arrive today, she'd meet us here tomorrow morning."

Mrs Duncan's eyes glittered like black beetle wings in the candlelight. "Is that right."

"Yes." Wendy held the woman's gaze, and after another moment Mrs Duncan stood up.

"You two still look hungry. Water isn't enough for growing children like you." She whisked the mugs away into the kitchen.

James looked a little excited. "D'you think she's going

to bring us *beer*?" he asked, then turned his head to cough against his shoulder. "I hear there are bootleggers who have secret hideaways in Arkham Woods and make all kinds of booze!"

"Ha!" The man at the far table scoffed and pointed a finger at them. Wendy's eyes widened – she hadn't even realized he was paying attention to them. "Bootleggers, yeah, there's bootleggers in them woods… fewer now, though. Ever since that damn *thing* got wise to us… shoulda run early on, not hung back like a pillock." He tipped his mug back and swallowed its contents down, like he was trying to drown whatever memory had captured him. Wendy felt a reluctant pang of sympathy – she'd seen folks like this before, who'd witnessed more than they could handle.

Most of them ended up dead.

"There's things in that wood," he went on, staring toward Wendy and James but somehow seeming to look right through them. His eyes were glassy, and his hands were clenched tight around his mug. "Things that defy nature itself. Things that can fight off a hungry flame… things that…"

"Oh, quiet down, you old fool," Mrs Duncan said as she returned from the kitchen, frowning ferociously in his direction. "There's no call to go scaring the children with your wild, drunken tales." She came over to their table, shaking her head. "Men like Mr Edwards over there are exactly the reason that we're all better off without alcohol," she said firmly, setting two small mugs down in front of them. "It's milk for the pair of you, fresh and warm." James sighed and slumped a bit, but reached for the milk anyway.

"There you are." Mrs Duncan stood back and folded her hands across her middle. "Go on. A little treat on a cold night."

James was already downing his milk in great gulps, his reticence vanished in the face of an extravagance they rarely tasted. Wendy had a few sips as well, but she'd never cared for warm milk, and pushed her mug over to James after a moment. He needed it more anyway, being smaller and sick.

"What, is milk not to your liking?" Mrs Duncan asked with a haughty sniff. "I should know better than to – wait." She leaned in closer. "What's that around your neck, girl?"

"It's…" Wendy glanced down at her amulet, almost completely covered by the neckline of her dress. Just the chain was showing… why would that be enough to interest Mrs Duncan? "It's nothing."

"It doesn't look like nothing to me," Mrs Duncan said, a strange gleam in her eyes. She reached a knobby hand out for Wendy's neck, and the amulet shivered a warning against her chest. Wendy abruptly stood up, putting more distance between her and Mrs Duncan.

"It's just a trinket from my mother," she said stiffly. "I'd rather you not touch it."

"A *trinket*, you say? Is that right?" Mrs Duncan's eyes narrowed, but she didn't make another grab for the amulet, even though her eyes lingered there for an uncomfortable amount of time. As soon as James finished off the second mug of milk, Mrs Duncan grabbed both of them up and stalked back into the kitchen without another word.

The man at the table in the back – Mr Edwards – raised

his mug toward them in solidarity. "'Ware harridans bearin' gifts," he said with a snicker.

"What's a harridan?" James asked – slurred, more like. Wendy looked at him and was alarmed to see he was listing on the bench, swaying back and forth like he could hardly hold himself upright.

"James?" She reached out and grabbed his shoulder, steadying him. "What's wrong?"

"Nothing's wrong," he said irritably, batting at her hand. "I'm just ... sleepy, s'all."

"Sleepy?" He'd become sleepy fast. All of the running on top of being sick, and now a full meal and two mugs of milk had knocked him off his feet.

"Poor little thing, he looks exhausted."

Wendy whirled around to face Mrs Duncan again, who was once more wearing her kind and genteel expression. "Why don't I show you to your room?" she continued, pointing at the stairs. "It's right up here."

Wendy really didn't want to do anything that Mrs Duncan recommended. This woman had been strange from the very moment they stepped through the door, and Wendy didn't like the way she'd honed in on the amulet, as if she could sense its powers somehow. She wanted to grab her friend and run, to take their chances in the night rather than stay in a place that made her skin crawl with a sense of ever-increasing danger.

But James – he was practically asleep right now, and Wendy wasn't strong enough to carry him very far. There was no way she'd leave him here alone, either. "All ... alright."

"Good, good." Mrs Duncan reached for him, but Wendy put herself between James and that woman's grasping hands and wrapped one of his arms over her shoulders.

"Stay upright," she said in an undertone. "Stay awake just a little longer."

Mrs Duncan grabbed the candle from their table and led the way up the stairs, which squeaked so much with every step it was as if a whole colony of mice were being tortured beneath them. There were six doors in the hallway they entered, and Mrs Duncan brought them to the one at the very back right of the row. She pulled a broad ring of skeleton keys out from beneath her apron and stuck one in the keyhole, twisting sharply. The door opened with a creaking sigh, and, reluctantly, Wendy brought the staggering James inside.

There was a single high window in the wooden wall, and two beds on either side of the room with a small table between them. The table had a mirror on it, and a basin and jug. "Chamberpots are under the beds," Mrs Duncan informed Wendy, as she laid James down on the nearest bed. He immediately went limp, totally asleep before Wendy could even get his shoes off. "But there's an extra fee for cleaning if you use them. The outhouse is just behind the hostel."

Wendy said nothing, just pulled the thin, grayish wool blanket over James' body. In the dim candlelight, with him gone so still so fast, the material reminded her of a shroud. She shivered at the thought of James lying on a slab in the coroner's, just another body set aside to be identified or slid into an unmarked grave. She'd known other children on the streets who'd ended up like that, killed by pneumonia or an infected bite.

Wendy knew she wouldn't get any sleep tonight.

"As long as you're up," Mrs Duncan went on, resting one hand casually against the doorframe, "I wonder if you might be willing to assist me with something. It's been quite a while since I restocked my store of firewood, and I could use a helping hand in getting it all back here to the hostel. I would return half the price of your night's stay as compensation," she added.

It was a generous offer… or it would have been, if Wendy wasn't positive that this woman was as dangerous as a viper. "I'd rather stay with James, thank you," she said stiffly.

Mrs Duncan smiled thinly. "I think he'll sleep far more soundly with you gone, my dear. You wouldn't want to wake him with your thrashing around, after all. Come and help me."

Wendy didn't want to go. She didn't want to leave James by himself, and she *really* didn't want to go anywhere at all with Mrs Duncan, but if she refused her hostess, Wendy wouldn't put it past the woman to simply grab her and pull her out of the room. What did she want? What was her plan? For there had to be some sort of plan, or why else would the woman be so terribly *interested* in her?

Wendy was trapped. The man downstairs – Edward, or whatever his name had been – didn't seem like he'd be much of a help if things went bad. She couldn't run once she got outside, because that would mean leaving James. She couldn't stay in the room either, because there was no way to keep Mrs Duncan out of it.

She would have to play along, for now at least. Until James had slept off his post-meal malaise and she could get him to run. Perhaps she could lose Mrs Duncan in the woods…

"Well, girl?" Mrs Duncan snapped.

"Yes, I'll help you, ma'am," Wendy said slowly. "Of course." Her amulet suddenly quivered against her breastbone, and it took every bit of self-control she had not to clutch at it.

"Good, good!" The bright, pleased expression was back on Mrs Duncan's face, as out of place there as pearls on a pig. "Come downstairs and I'll get what we need."

Wendy took one last longing look at James, hoping to see him coming out of it, stirring and ready to run… but he was so deeply asleep now that he was snoring, drool starting to pool in the corner of his mouth and run out onto the bedclothes.

"Coming, girl?"

Wendy nodded and straightened her shoulders, then turned and walked out of the room. Mrs Duncan stayed behind long enough to lock the door again – lock James *in* – before they both headed down the stairs. "It's for his own protection," Mrs Duncan said blithely as she caught Wendy's worried look back. "I've had issues with sleepwalkers before. Wouldn't want him to tumble down these stairs and crack his little head open, would we?"

Once they were onto the main level again, Mrs Duncan opened the door of the closet built under the stairs and reached inside. Her hand emerged wrapped around the haft of a wood axe, probably three feet long, with a thick handle and a crusty blade that seemed to have… *bits* sticking to it.

Bits of wood? Bits of… something else? Wendy couldn't tell.

The man at the table watched the two of them with bleary, unconcerned eyes. It would do no good to appeal to him. If he wasn't drunk, then he was so lost in his own head he probably couldn't see what was happening anyway.

Mrs Duncan took out a strange reddish cloak and threw it over her shoulders, fastening the clasp in the corner to hold it in place, then shouldered the axe and smiled again at Wendy. "Let's be off, then. The sooner we get the firewood, the sooner you'll be back safe with your little brother."

"Woods ain't no good place t' go at night," the man at the table suddenly opined. "The things there… the ungodly things, the men with the… with the…"

"Shut up, you fool," Mrs Duncan hissed at him as she grabbed Wendy by the shoulder and propelled her toward the front door. "Don't scare the girl. There's nothing in that wood to be afraid of, nothing at all."

"Not if you're on *its* side, I reckon," the man mumbled, just as Mrs Duncan slammed the door shut behind them.

She took a deep breath, then looked at Wendy and said, "I should know better than to take in people like that. People who've been stricken by delirium," she added. "He's been out of his cups for too long, I daresay. Probably get quivers and shivers and who knows what next?" She smiled again. "Aren't you glad your little brother is locked up safe and sound, just in case?"

"I… Yes," Wendy choked out. She was starting to tremble herself. *All we wanted was a safe place to rest for one night, just one.* Now it seemed like she'd fallen into Hell instead.

She looked anxiously up and down the street, checking to see if someone, if *anyone*, could be called out to, could be appealed to for help.

There was no one out at all, no one other than a dog gnawing on something long and thick near the alley. Mrs Duncan shouted at it and the dog shied away, whimpering, then ran as they walked past where it had been chewing at a bone of some kind. It was a surprisingly big bone, long enough to belong in a human arm or a leg. Wendy shivered, unable to hold back from grabbing her amulet now. It was dark enough out that Mrs Duncan probably wouldn't notice.

"Come along, then." Mrs Duncan tightened her grip on Wendy's shoulder and propelled her toward the edge of Arkham Woods. Despite how close the forest was to the main street of Uptown, there didn't seem to be any visible paths leading into it, nothing to show where people had gone before.

The moment they stepped under the canopy of trees, all the moonlight filtering through the patchwork clouds above seemed to vanish completely. It was as dark as a sewer or the bilge of a ship, dark as a *tomb* in here. Wendy tripped over a root, then another. "Please, I can't... I can't see where we're going," she pleaded, shying away from Mrs Duncan's heavy hand. The woman's fingers only dug in more firmly, pressing bruises into Wendy's clammy skin.

"Just stay close to me," Mrs Duncan instructed her in a brisk voice. "I know the way. I've traveled this route plenty of times, and no one's broken anything on the way there yet."

Her phrasing wasn't at all comforting. Wendy knew she had to escape… but she needed to get Mrs Duncan deeper into the woods before she made her play, or her chances of beating her back to the hostel became even fainter.

Courage, my darling girl. Courage!

The memory of her mother's last words as she was pulled away from Wendy stuck with her, and the amulet was a source of warmth and comfort in the startling chill of the eerily silent forest. Wendy firmed her aching shoulders and did her best to steady her steps, looking around to search for landmarks among the trees. The darkness made her efforts next to useless, but having something to do helped her control her fear.

They walked for another few minutes without speaking before Wendy finally gathered the breath to ask, "Haven't we gone far enough?"

Mrs Duncan chuckled, her voice deep and strangely resonant against the trees, as though it were being amplified by something. Or wait… was that just *her* voice that Wendy was hearing now, or was someone else out there? Multiple someones, singing… or no, wait. Chanting.

"I think you know by now that we aren't here for firewood, child," Mrs Duncan said, her smug satisfaction plain to hear. "Your little 'trinket' made that clear, didn't it? You're going to play a much more important role than acting as my mule."

There it was. Confirmation of Wendy's fears, straight from the mouth of the loathsome woman herself. If she had been James, she would have been surprised and dismayed to experience such a betrayal. As it was, Wendy felt oddly vindicated. *My amulet was right. It's always right about danger.*

Mrs Duncan went on, "And if you don't want your little brother to be next, you won't–" Whatever threat she'd been about to level was cut off as she herself suddenly slipped on the mossy ground, cursing as she fell forward. Wendy's already racing heart leapt against her chest, and she seized the moment to wrench her shoulder out of Mrs Duncan's grasp.

As soon as the woman wasn't holding onto her, it was somehow a little easier to see. She noticed a fallen branch just a few feet away and bent down to grasp it, but before she could wrap her hand around it, Mrs Duncan grabbed her by the hair and wrenched her upright.

"You're trying to run the wrong way," she hissed in Wendy's ear, brandishing the axe menacingly. "You're needed in the clearing, child. Now come along nicely and don't try to escape again, or… *Argh!*"

Wendy raked the heel of her boot along Mrs Duncan's shin, stomping down hard enough to stagger the woman as she jerked away. Mrs Duncan tried to swipe at her with the axe, but she was bent forward over her injured leg and didn't have the reach. Wendy grabbed the branch, hefted it once, then walloped Mrs Duncan across the middle with it as hard as she could, breaking the makeshift weapon over her back and knocking her down. The woman screamed with pain and rage as she fell, her free hand clawing in Wendy's direction.

"You horrible child! I'll make you pay for this! I was going to make your death gentle, but now I'll let the ghouls gnaw you down to the bone before I take your head with my axe! *Get back here!*"

Never.

Wendy turned and ran.

She didn't know where she was going. The woods were as unfamiliar now as they had been when she was first drawn into them, and although it was marginally easier to see, that didn't seem to make much of a difference to her feet. She tripped over what felt like every second root and fallen branch, and everything she touched was covered in a slimy moss that clung to her skin even when she scraped at it with her fingernails. Twigs caught in her hair and pulled at her face and shoulders, like they were trying to hold onto her. It made her fight harder to get away, her heart pounding so hard that she could feel the thud of it in the tips of her fingers and the end of her nose. By the time she emerged from the thickness of the forest onto the bank of a completely unfamiliar creek, Wendy was exhausted and utterly out of breath.

A *creek*... She certainly hadn't come anywhere near this on the way in. Where had she gone wrong? Where did this creek emerge from the woods? Wendy considered trying to cross it – it couldn't be more than six or seven feet wide, and the current didn't look terribly fast. She took a step closer to it and gazed into the water, hoping to get a feel for its depth.

The water was black, even in the wavering light of the moon. Not green touched with silver like the waves out in the bay, or even the oily brown of the murky water around the docks. This water was simply black, swallowing all hints of light. Even her reflection barely had a chance to appear on the surface of the slow, sludgy water before it vanished.

Right. That's settled. Wading across it was not an option, and there was no way Wendy was touching that water if she could help it. She was too short to have any hope of jumping it. Perhaps if she followed it downstream she would get back to the edge of Uptown.

Wendy turned around and promptly screamed, so startled that she nearly did *herself* in by falling into the water. Coming forward at a shamble as she exited the line of trees was Mrs Duncan, her teeth bared in a grim rictus, one hand gripping the top of the axe like the head of a cane.

"You," she snarled, pointing a knobby finger at Wendy. Any hints of satisfaction in her face were completely gone, evaporated in the wake of their earlier, violent encounter. "Do you have any idea what this pathetic show of force of yours could cost me? They're *waiting* for us, waiting for *you*, and the longer they wait the greater their hunger. I won't be responsible for leaving Umôrdhoth in need, do you hear me?"

Wendy's amulet was practically vibrating against her chest. She gripped it with one hand, holding the other out for balance as she backed away from Mrs Duncan. "I won't go with you!" she shouted, finding strength in her own defiance.

Mrs Duncan straightened and lifted the axe over her head. "Then I will carry your corpse there across my own back!" she shrieked, and threw the axe end over end straight toward Wendy.

Wendy wasn't sure how she saved herself – whether her sudden fall was from her old worn boot slipping on the slick surface of the mossy forest floor, or whether her amulet had really become as heavy as it suddenly seemed to be, dragging her down to the ground just in time for the axe to sail over her head and into the water behind her. There was a splash, and a few droplets of water hit the back of her neck. They were so cold on her skin that they seemed to burn.

"My axe!" Mrs Duncan sounded stricken, her cruel expression melting away into fear as she stared at the dark water. "No, my axe!" She started forward, as though she might somehow retrieve it from the terrible waters, when a dark, sibilant laugh seeped out of the woods.

Wendy stared in astonishment as two pairs of darkly shining eyes blazed into existence behind Mrs Duncan, who spun awkwardly to face the sounds coming from a yet-hidden mouth. "I was bringing her," she said quickly. "I promise, I was bringing her for the master, like you asked me to."

"You speak the same words so often, they cease to have any meaning," the beast on the left said as it stepped into the moonlight, hard to understand through its mouthful of jagged teeth. Wendy stared, unmoving, caught somewhere between horror and a terrible sense of satisfaction by her worst fears being realized. Her mother had warned her about creatures like these.

"*I will bring, I will bring, I will, I will…* but you have brought us nothing but a chase," the beast went on accusingly.

"I swear, I was leading her straight to you!" the woman pleaded. "I am one of the truly faithful, I would never try to cheat you or the Devourer Below! Please, you must believe me."

"Umôrdhoth hungers," said the creature on the right, its shining eyes rolling like marbles within their sockets as it looked back and forth between the two of them. "And *we* hunger."

"The girl shall go to him," the first one said decidedly, a twisted smile stretching its lips. "While *you* shall be for us."

"No!" shrieked Mrs Duncan, rearing away from the monsters in a last-moment effort to escape their hungry maws. "I am faithful, I am a good servant of Umôrdhoth, you *cannot do this to me!*"

Wendy almost reached out to grab Mrs Duncan by the hand, to pull her away from the beasts in a hopeless attempt at evading death even though the woman had admitted to leading her into the woods to be killed, but it was too late. The monsters fell on her, their ravenous mouths poised to rend, and a second later the screams started.

Wendy fell back against a nearby tree and shut her eyes, gripping her amulet so tightly she had to be nearly crushing it. No amount of wishing could block out the noise of Mrs Duncan's grisly end, the way her screams became bubbling gasps and finally one last moan before dying off altogether. Wendy's own breath stopped for a moment and she just stood, shuddering, for a long second, before she finally opened her eyes and peeked out at the grisly scene.

The feasting hadn't stopped. The beasts were gorging themselves. Wendy should try to run while they were distracted, and hope that they didn't care to hunt her down. Or...

It had been a long time since she'd used Mama's amulet like this. She hoped she remembered the right words... She hoped her efforts were enough to save herself.

Wendy opened her eyes, opened her mouth, and began to speak the secret words passed on to her by her mother. The amulet's shivering slowed, taking on a more familiar cadence, a secret heartbeat that Wendy somehow recognized and that knew her in return. She stared at the beasts, who were slowly pulling away from Mrs Duncan's mangled corpse, casting their eyes around the edge of the creek as though...

As though they couldn't quite tell where she was, even though she was chanting not five feet in front of them.

Wendy never quite knew what the effect of using the amulet would be; it seemed to give her different results every time. Distraction was good, but could she do more? She increased the force of the words, putting more power into her voice, more determination into her own will.

She was not going to die in Arkham Woods. Not at the hands of Mrs Duncan, not sacrificed to some ancient god, and not eaten by monsters. She was going to survive and save James, they were going to make it back to Riverside, and soon she would get her family back. She just had to keep her faith, and, most of all, she had to keep her nerve.

The beasts stopped twisting their heads and sniffing. They stopped moving altogether a moment after that, falling as still and silent as statues. Even their glittering eyes looked as dull and cloudy as shards of sea glass. *Perfect.* Now all she had to do was quietly pick her way between them, find her way out of these hellish trees without alerting any other monsters or their followers to her existence, and break James out of his locked room.

Right. Simple.

Wendy straightened her back and inhaled deeply, ignoring the scent of decaying wood and coppery blood that invaded her nose as she did so. She took one firm step forward, then another, then–

Crack! Crack! The heads of the two quiescent beasts burst apart like rotten melons, spraying foul effluvia all over the nearest trees, the ground, and Wendy herself.

What in the–!

Wendy spun wildly, looking for the source of the shots. Was she next? Should she run? Surely she wasn't next, otherwise she'd be dead... But who could have done it? Who out here could possibly be interested in helping instead of harming her?

There was a noise of crackling twigs in the shrubs just to the left, and Wendy stared at them, still holding her amulet and wishing to the heavens that Mrs Duncan's axe hadn't gone into the creek. "Who's there?" she called out, hating the tremors in her voice but unable to still them completely.

A tall, indistinct silhouette appeared, a creature with horns protruding from the top of its head and a hand filled with fire, and for a moment Wendy's heart froze with fear. Then the man stepped out of the tangle of branches, and the horns were only two twisted limbs behind him, and his fiery hand was the torch that he held.

Just a man… a man that Wendy recognized. He was staring fiercely at the carcasses of the two ghouls, like he was searching them for something.

"Ah… Mr Edwards?" she said after a moment. As he looked over at her, with the grim lines on his face deepened by the flickering torchlight, for a moment Wendy was convinced she was done for anyway.

Then his eyes widened and he holstered his gun then held the torch farther out in front of him, lighting a clear path for her. "Wendy, ain't it? Ha! I was hoping I'd find you 'fore that old devil-worshipper sank her claws in too deep. Took me a bit o' time to work up the nerve, if I'm honest," he added, scratching the back of his neck with his free hand.

Oh, heavens. What had a man like Mr Edwards seen that made *him* scared to be out here? Not that it mattered right now – all that mattered was the fact that he *was* here. He'd come to help her, which was far more than anyone other than James had bothered to do in what felt like forever.

He was a hero.

Right now, her hero was walking over to the corpses and taking a long, hard look at what was left of their hideous faces. "Damn," he muttered. "Ghouls. Not the creatures I was hopin' for after the time I 'ad out here, but still, better 'em gone than you or me." He looked at the leftovers of Mrs Duncan lying between them and grimaced. "Reckon we'll leave 'em and the lady here for the night, eh? Although she didn't turn out to be much of a lady, in the end. We can tell the undertaker about 'em tomorrow, if you even wanna bother."

He straightened up and nodded his head back the way he'd come. "There's a trail runs right next to Hangman's Creek through here," he said, then set off back into the trees. After a final look at the murderous creatures – all three of them – who had nearly killed her tonight, Wendy hurried after him.

It felt *less* terrifying with Mr Edwards as her companion instead of the terse Mrs Duncan, but lighting a single torch didn't turn the darkness into day. She heard scritches and snuffles in the distance, and for a moment she thought she detected the sound of chanting again. Oh lord, was he going to lead her to the cultists? Was he one of them too? But… no, he didn't seem the type. A bit of a scoundrel for sure, like a ship's captain who always saved a little space in their hold for something of dubious legality, but not an actual murderer. Except of monsters, apparently.

"Who were you looking for?" Wendy asked as they headed back toward what she hoped was the hostel, where, with luck, James still slept. It wasn't her business, but the way he'd stared at those ghouls had made her curious.

Mr Edwards turned his head and grinned at her, a little manic to be sure, but also with an edge of anticipation in it. There was violence in that grin, but Wendy was quite sure it wasn't violence that would be directed toward her. Her amulet was completely still against her chest. "When we get back to the hostel, I'll tell you all 'bout the goat man," he promised.

Goat man? What in heaven's name was a *goat man*? Some special kind of ghoul? Wendy had a sneaking suspicion that whether she stuck with Mr Edwards or ran back to

Riverside at first light, she was going to learn a lot more about the underbelly of Arkham over the coming days.

She reached up and grabbed her amulet.

I'm going to need an axe of my own.

PROFESSOR WARREN'S INVESTITURE
David Annandale

The anthropology department's council meeting was over, and there were going to be drinks in the faculty lounge. "Some conviviality will do us good," said Reginald Pyx, the department chair, as he ended the meeting. "A chance for us to toast the end of another term, and the start of the holidays."

A chance for you to grandstand some more, Peter Warren thought. Stretch the day out a little bit longer for us. Go on. Why not?

"What odds the wine is going to be more of his personal production?" Vera Flemyng said quietly to Peter as they made their way down the hall, hanging at the end of the line of professors. Their footsteps echoed on the polished wood floors. Electric chandeliers hung from the vaulted ceiling, bathing the hall in a warm glow, though the far ends of the hall seemed to tremble slightly in deeper shadow. The classrooms were empty, but the smell of chalk dust hung in the air, making Peter's throat dry and scratchy.

"I'm not taking that bet," he said to Vera. "We already know that's what it's going to be." If Prohibition were ever repealed, Reginald would surely weep. For years now, he had used the absence of wine in stores and the legality of brewing it at home to foist his creations on the other members of the department at every opportunity.

"It's going to be mulled wine again, isn't it?" said Vera.

"In keeping with the season." Peter sighed. "Did you try it last year?"

"I was away sick, lucky me. I heard about it, though."

"It tastes like sweet tar."

Vera made a face. "Stop it. You're going to put me off tar."

The faculty lounge was on the top floor of the humanities building. It had a good view of Miskatonic University. The December afternoon was dark, and a few snowflakes drifted down over the quadrangle. Peter took up a position near the window, a cup of the mulled wine in hand, determined to hold off drinking it as long as possible. In the center of the lounge, surrounded by a circle of dark-brown leather armchairs, Reginald held court, his voice loud and expansive, smothering all other efforts at conversation in the room.

The chair of anthropology was five years younger than Peter, though he wore the gravitas of his position as if it granted him twenty years' experience over everyone else. His hair had turned silver early, and was luxuriant, perfectly coiffed and swept back over his ears. Peter's hair was gray, not silver. Gray. And it refused his efforts to comb it, sitting on his forehead in an unruly tangle. Reginald had no beard, his pencil mustache a statement of assumed glamour. Peter's beard came to an aggressive point. He knew it made him look older. He knew it made him look angry even when he wasn't. Only that happened less and less often these days.

He also knew he should not be comparing himself to the chair. Or, if he did, it should be from a position of superiority. Reginald was an unworthy chair. He wasn't a scholar. He was the performance of a scholar, an empty suit cavorting for an ignorant audience. He had published widely, oh yes. He was good at that. He had had articles in journals, but most of all, he wrote for general interest magazines and newspapers. His work had even been featured in the *Saturday Evening Post*. He brought anthropology to the masses. He made it exciting.

He made it puerile.

There was no originality in his scholarship. It was a regurgitation of all the standard orthodoxies, dressed up in a style that readers found *inviting*. The word made Peter's gorge rise. Those readers didn't know any better, and they never would, if this was all they had to read.

"You should tell us a ghost story," said Reginald, grinning at Peter. "What better time of year?"

Peter blinked, caught off guard. "What?"

"A ghost story. Tell us one." That grin. Infuriating. Insulting. "You must have plenty to draw upon. I won't believe that you don't."

"He's baiting you," Vera warned under her breath.

I know. He took the bait anyway, as he always did. He couldn't help himself. "I am not a collector of ghost stories," he said.

"Come, Peter," said Reginald. "Don't be disingenuous. You aren't going to pretend *again* that you believe in all the occult nonsense you've been so assiduously gathering."

Peter drew himself straight. He raised his head, his beard jutting accusingly at Reginald. "I believe that we close our minds to secret knowledge at our peril," Peter said, his voice louder than he intended. He believed what he said, and the words had seemed good and strong in the instant before he spoke them.

Then Reginald chuckled, and his cronies joined in, and the words sounded defensive and trite.

"I'm sure you're right," Reginald said, making a show of trying to keep a straight face. "I'm sure you're right."

Condescending pig.

"But tell me," Reginald went on. "Where stands the work on your mighty tome? I mean, if we are to benefit from your wisdom on secret knowledge, then we need to be able to read the fruits of your labor, don't we? Don't we?"

"Don't say it," Vera whispered.

"The work is going well," Peter said through clenched teeth.

Laughter. Applause. Reginald bowed, accepting the praise of his sycophants. He held a hand out to Barry Fitzroy, who theatrically pulled out his wallet and handed a dollar to Reginald.

"What did I tell you?" Reginald crowed. "Every year! Word for word! I told you I could get him to say it."

Peter stormed out of the lounge, leaving behind the shredded mass of his dignity. His head throbbed with anger. His face burned. And the worst of it was that it was true. He had said the same thing last year, and the year before that, and the year before that, going back and back. He had been working on the book for more than twenty years, and it was still not even close to being done.

It wasn't his fault. The work was too important to be done badly. The stakes were too high. No one in the department, not even Vera, could understand that.

But the fact remained that it was unfinished. It was dozens of notebooks filled with his jottings, and a score of attempted pages of the first chapter. That was all he had to show.

That, and the mockery of his colleagues.

Goaded and frustrated with himself, Peter was in the university's Orne Library the next day. He was going to make headway today. He was going to end the year in a way that would give him hope for the new one. He looked up at the gargoyles poised over the entrance of the library, and promised them that things would be different now.

He had made them that same promise many times before.

An hour later, seated at a table in the restricted area, leafing through the books the librarian's aide had brought to him, the energy of the morning had passed, and the morass of inertia had returned. He stared at the pages, but the words that he had once read with the thrill of forbidden discovery were stale. They inspired nothing. All they did was remind him of the monumental scale of the task, of the uncountable tributaries of knowledge and rites that resisted all of his attempts to arrange them into a meaningful system. But he had to find the system, the order that would tame the chaos, and become the bulwark of reason against the threat of the occult.

He slumped back in his chair with a groan and tossed his pen onto the table.

"There is the look of a man who thinks he has read it all."

Peter looked up. He did not recognize the woman who had stopped beside him. She eyed his books with a look of knowing amusement. "Do I know you?" he said.

"Theodora Marlowe," she said cheerfully, not put off at all by his brusque tone. "Department of English. You would be Peter Warren."

The name didn't ring a bell. Perhaps she was a recent hire. Then again, there were many faculty in the other departments that he didn't know. Theodora was in her early thirties. Her black hair was in a bob, her nose was sharp, and she wore a black skirt and blouse, giving him the impression of being observed by a raven.

"What do you want?" Peter asked.

"I saw what you were reading. You seemed like someone I should speak with. I thought maybe I could help."

"Help me with what? Our fields are not the same."

"No, but there are avenues of research that will draw the disparate together. I should think you would know that by now."

He gave her a curt nod. He sat forward and took up his pen again, as if he were going back to work.

Theodora didn't take the hint. "This is a good library," she said. "A very good one. But there are other books than the ones you can find on its shelves. Even in this area. Books this library should not have."

Peter put his pen back down. She had his attention. "Why shouldn't it?" he asked.

"Because knowledge can be dangerous."

With those words, she struck at the heart of what he was trying to achieve, and why his work mattered more than anyone understood. "No," he said. "That's wrong. No knowledge is dangerous in and of itself. It's how it is used that matters. A hammer is a tool for construction, and it can also be a murder weapon. That is determined by the wielder."

Theodora pulled out the chair on the opposite side of the table and sat down. "How do you plan to use it?" she asked quietly.

She really wanted to know. She was interested in a way no one else had ever been. For the first time in years, he felt truly respected. Here, finally, was someone who understood the task he had set for himself. She might also understand why it was so important that *someone* do this. It was the most important thing in the world.

"I have made a study of the occult since my student days," Peter said. "When I first began the work that has been the object of my professional life, I thought my goal was to dispel the superstition I studied."

"Then you discovered your mistake," said Theodora.

"I did. There is real knowledge held by the secret cults that have nestled in the cracks of our societies for all of human history. It has been misused, to our cost. I fear for our continued existence, if that misuse is not combatted. We have already come close to the end."

"You think the Great War was caused by occult forces?"

"Caused, exacerbated…" He shook his head. "I'm not sure. But can anyone deny that our world trembled during those years? Can anyone deny that so much ended forever?" He shuddered. He had not seen combat, but even from the safety of Arkham, he had felt everything burn. He thought of all the certainties of order and faith that had died in those four years. "If there is even a chance that such forces were involved, then they must be combatted. And I have come to believe that they can only be properly fought with the same powers that they wield."

"Fire with fire."

"Yes. If you do not understand how you are being attacked, how can you defend yourself? And a sword will not help you if you are being shot from across a field. You must shoot back. Malefic cults must be combatted by the enlightened use of this knowledge. There is no other way."

"I agree," said Theodora.

"You do?"

"What you have just said is nothing less than what I have believed for years. I have something you must read."

"What is it?" He spoke quickly, already excited, a dog responding to the promise of a walk. He couldn't help himself.

Theodora stood up. "Give me your address," she said, speaking even more softly than before. They were co-conspirators now. "I will have it sent to you tonight."

The knock on his door came after ten that night, when Peter had almost given up expecting anything to come.

He had spent the evening trying to focus on other work as a distraction, and trying to choke down a meal, but he was too excited, even though he didn't want to be. Every enthusiasm for the last decade and more had ended in disappointment, frustration, and the guilt over more failure to move the work forward. He should know by now not to get his hopes up.

They were up all the same.

He ran to answer the knock. There was no one there when he opened the door. His house was on a street that ran along the west side of Miskatonic University. It was a road of old, comfortable homes, favored by the more long-tenured faculty. The yards were small, hidden behind high stone walls that made each house an enclave of shadowed privacy. Peter looked up and down the street. No one in sight. Not even the sound of retreating footsteps. Falling snow shrouded and blurred the streetlights, and the pools of darkness between them were thick with imagined watchers.

Peter grabbed the brown-wrapped parcel that sat on his porch step and went back inside, slamming the door's deadbolt home so he heard the loud *chunk* of the night being locked out.

He took the parcel back to his study, cleared a space on his desk, and, in the glow of his banker's lamp, unwrapped the book.

It was thick, heavy, and old. It smelled faintly of something more unpleasant than mustiness. Peter couldn't place it, but it made his throat tight. The book was bound in leather that was soft to the touch in a manner he found disgustingly familiar. It felt *intimate*. He dropped the book on the desk, unwilling to hold it a moment longer. As it slipped from his fingers, he had the sensation of brushing against raised veins.

Swallowing back his revulsion, he opened the cover and began to read. The book was called *Devoratio*. It was written in a patchwork of Latin, Greek and Middle English. He thought it might be a translation, worked on by many hands, of something older. There were turns of phrase that were odd for any of the languages in which it was written, as if they were being twisted by the force of the tongue that lurked behind them.

Or if some part of the translators was still capable of being horrified by the words they were committing to paper.

Peter was horrified. And he was mesmerized. The *Devoratio* put to the test the principles he had propounded to Theodora. The knowledge in here was powerful. It was also hideous. There were revelations here that he regretted learning as soon as he read them. Could he really turn what he learned to the necessary ends?

"Knowledge is neutral," he croaked. "Power is neutral. The ends and the wielder are what matter." He kept telling himself this as he read. At first, the words seemed like the weakest of rationalizations, a broken shield that would not protect him from the taint of the *Devoratio*. But the further he read, the stronger the credo became, and the more excited he grew.

Theodora had been right. This was a book he *had* to read. It was the most important book he had ever encountered.

The power here was real. The implications were enormous.

He finished with the coming of dawn. The light through his study window was sickly, gray as bad flesh, as if he had harmed the day in his reading.

Perhaps he had. He had never pretended to himself that the acquiring the knowledge he sought would not have a price. There would be sacrifices. There always were in war.

He was exhausted. He was revolted. He was exhilarated.

He had to know more.

Tucked inside the back of the *Devoratio* was a card with Theodora's address. Her street was not far away, though it was one that Peter found, to his surprise, that he did not remember ever having visited before. The houses here were more tightly crowded, their walls more smoke-stained, their walls higher and thicker. Theodora's home was where the street dead-ended. The building was a deep frown of gray stone.

Though it was barely day, the door opened before Peter could knock. "I thought you would come by," Theodora said.

She led him to a dark lounge. The air smelled of candle smoke. The windows were dirty with soot, and barely let in enough light for Peter to make his way to the armchair Theodora pointed at. She sat in its twin opposite him, a cold hearth between them. Behind Theodora, a dark, heavy curtain covered the entrance to another room. Peter felt no draft, but the curtain shifted slightly, and he wondered if there were someone else about to join them. The movement of the curtain stopped, and Peter thought he heard the scrape of something heavy against stone. But the sound was faint and brief, and perhaps he had imagined it. He hadn't slept for almost twenty-four hours. His eyes burned with fatigue, and his mind burned with horror and excitement.

"You read it, then," said Theodora.

"It's horrible."

"Yes," she said. "Yes, it is. I'm glad to hear you say that. That tells me you meant what you said yesterday, when you said there are powers abroad that must be fought."

"I never imagined…" Peter stopped, his stomach churning at the thought of what he had learned. "Can these things truly be?"

Theodora nodded. "They can be, and they are. The *Devoratio* is a dream, too. The dream of what some would wish the world to become."

Peter shuddered. "They must be stopped."

"Yes." Theodora said simply, and waited.

"They must be fought."

"And there is only one way to do that. Only one way to be sure."

"Yes."

"This is what you said to me in the library. Do you still believe it?"

"More than ever," said Peter. "There is power in that book, and it must be claimed."

"By you?"

"If need be." *Yes.*

Theodora was silent for a moment. "You do understand what you read."

"I believe so."

"And that there is a price to pay to claim that power."

He had been thinking of nothing else. "There will be a worse price, paid by many more, if someone does not do what is necessary."

"Then we are agreed."

Peter hardly slept for the next week. He spent his nights reading and re-reading the *Devoratio*, and then tossing and turning for a few, fitful, nightmare-plagued hours. The days he spent with Theodora, discussing individual passages, teasing out their implications, and bracing himself for what had to be done. She gave him more to read, too, old exegetical texts written by devotees of the *Devoratio*. They were almost as horrifying as the primary source, but they were necessary too. He was learning, and what he was learning was powerful.

The following Friday, it was time to act.

"Are you ready?" Theodora asked.

"I have to be," he answered.

It was snowing heavily in the late afternoon as he trudged up the street from his house to the home of Reginald Pyx. He paused about a block away. Doubts racked him. Guilt twisted a vise in his gut, and for a few moments he couldn't breathe. He dragged air into his lungs, forced it out slowly, and fought back his rising gorge.

I can't do this.

I have to. This is the worst of it. This is the price.

He rocked back and forth, grateful the street was empty of other pedestrians, caught between fear and duty. Finally, he leaned forward until he almost lost his balance, and made himself walk on.

I have to. I have to.

Harriet Pyx answered his knock. "Hello, Peter," she said. "This *is* a surprise."

His smile felt sickly. "I'm just as surprised to find myself here. Is Reginald in?"

In the hall behind Harriet, two children, a girl in her teens and a boy a few years younger, chased each other up the stairs to the second floor. From somewhere else in the house, Reginald bellowed cheerfully at them to keep it down.

"Certainly," Harriet said. She let him in, and Peter waited in the entrance hall while she went to find her husband. He wasn't long, and arrived with a grin that was equal parts incredulous and curious.

"Well, well," said Reginald. "This isn't a visit I would have predicted."

"I imagine not."

"Or maybe I should have. Are you here to berate me for having some fun with you after the department council?"

"No," said Peter. "I need your help."

Reginald blinked. After a few moments, his smile grew even broader. "You're not joking," he said.

"I wish I were."

"Now what, in the name of all that is wonderful, could you possibly want my help with?"

Peter took a breath, then plunged ahead. *This must be done.* "I've run into something. I think it's important."

"Then, and let's be honest here, I'm hardly likely to agree that it is."

"I know. That's exactly why I want your opinion about it. Because if you *do* agree…"

"Then it really is important."

"Quite."

Reginald shrugged and reached for his coat where it hung on a hook near the door. "You intrigue me. Let's go see this discovery of yours."

"It's not quite ready to show you yet," said Peter. "I wanted to be sure first that you would come."

"And I am."

"Can you give me an hour?"

"Sure."

Peter hesitated. "There's one other thing."

"And that is?" Reginald sounded really eager now. He was a man looking forward to great personal pleasure in the very near future.

You think you're going to humiliate me again. You think you're going to make me a laughing stock. Is that really the reach of your ambition now? It must be, to judge from the drivel you put out as scholarly work.

The thought of Reginald's anticipation made him angry, and the anger gave him strength. "If this really is something… If this really is important…" He grimaced helplessly, exactly as he had practiced in front of a mirror before heading out.

"You want it to be a secret," Reginald said, with all the force of his condescension. "You don't want the unwashed rushing in on it." He chuckled.

"That's right," said Peter. "Secret knowledge has always had to be protected. There are good reasons for this…"

Reginald held up a hand, forestalling explanations and boredom. "Say no more, Peter. Please. Say no more." He struggled to keep a straight face. "Your secret is safe with me. I'll find an excuse to pop out, make sure my hat shadows my face, and sneak over to your house in an hour."

"Thank you," Peter said curtly. He let his irritation show. It would add to the lure he had dangled in front of Reginald. "I'll see you then."

He walked home with a lighter step. His chest still felt tight, but he was committed now. There would be no going back. And Reginald had made his decision easier just by being Reginald.

I can pay this price. I can and I will.

He didn't take his coat off when he returned home. He didn't turn any of the lights on. He stood just inside the door for the entire hour, watching through the diamond-shaped window for the department chair. The moment he saw Reginald appear, he went out.

Now comes the moment of truth.

"Here I am," said Reginald. He stamped his feet, shaking off wet snow. "You certainly picked a night for it."

"Thank you for coming," Peter said. His heart was beating so hard, he half-expected Reginald to hear it, and it was a miracle his voice didn't shake. He strode off. "This way," he said.

Reginald followed, and in a few minutes they were outside Theodora's. Reginald looked around. "Funny thing," he said. "I'd swear I've never been here before. Only a few blocks from my house, but I don't recognize the area at all." He turned to the dark windows. "Whose place is this? I don't think they're home."

"She's home."

Peter let himself into the house. A few candles created a path of faint illumination from the hall to the sitting room, where the drapes were drawn to keep the light from leaking into the street.

"Why are we here?" Reginald asked. "Are you *collaborating*?"

"Yes," said Peter. He walked slowly toward the entrance to the next room, and the heavy curtain he would finally put aside for the first time. That was the Rubicon he had to cross.

"With whom?"

Reginald's insistent questions made him pause, his hand on the curtains, and he did not know if he had the strength to move them. "With Theodora Marlowe," he said. "From English."

"Don't know her. Did you convince her of your nonsense, or was she already a believer?"

"She knows how serious the work is."

"Wonderful. More crackpots in the humanities. That's all we need." Reginald sighed. "Alright, then. Go on. Don't keep me in suspense. Let's see your discovery."

Reginald's mockery and his command gave Peter the impulse he needed. He drew the curtain. There was a short hall beyond and, on the immediate right, an open door to the basement stairs. Peter took them, and Reginald followed.

There was even less light here. They had to take the steps

carefully, hands firmly holding the bannister. The descent into the darkness was Peter's descent into the unknown. The *Devoratio* had told him something of what to expect, but to read it and to live it were states of knowledge and experience a universe apart. The steps under his feet were stone, not wood, and he thought again of the scraping sounds he had heard on his first visit to Theodora's. The house felt wrong, as if it were a thing in imperfect disguise, the details of an Arkham home just a little bit off. Mystery enveloped Peter. There was power at its heart, and it was at its heart that he was about to arrive.

The staircase went down too far.

"This is ridiculous," said Reginald, sounding irritated, not afraid. "How deep is Marlowe's cellar?"

Deep enough, and dark enough.

Were those Peter's thoughts? Or did he hear them whispered?

He was hearing things now. There were stirrings down below.

"Is this a gathering of the cracked?" Reginald asked.

Up above, the door slammed shut.

"Uhm…" said Reginald, finally sounding uncertain.

They reached the bottom of the stairs. Lanterns flared suddenly as their covers were removed. Peter stopped breathing when he saw the words of the *Devoratio* become flesh.

"What…" Reginald whispered. Now he was afraid.

The basement was prepared for a ritual. It was almost completely bare, but there was an altar at one end. It was a roughly hewn block of marble, polished smooth by centuries or more of use, and stained dark with blood. Standing around the basement were figures in dark, at least a dozen of them. They had hoods pulled forward, casting their faces in shadow. Peter was just able to recognize Theodora to the right of the altar. The others, he didn't know.

Some of them were hunched forward unnaturally. Their limbs were too long, and their mottled-gray fingers ended in dirty claws. They breathed in snorting, gurgling pants, like pigs at the trough.

Behind the altar, stacked chunks of stone formed a crude throne. A figure in red robes crouched on it. Even on its haunches, it was taller than a man. Its robes were crimson, and it wore a mask fashioned from the skull of a deer. One pallid hand held a staff of gnarled wood, surmounted by a crescent-shaped carving that made Peter think, at once, of runes, of the moon, and of a sickle.

This was the reality of the words Peter had read in the *Devoratio*. His head swam, and his pulse beat a deafening rhythm in his ears.

"What is this?" Reginald demanded, loudly, as if indignation would shield him. He was also shrill with fear.

"This is where knowledge becomes power," said Peter. "I'm sorry."

The red-robed priest cocked its head, the dark sockets of the skull fixed on Reginald. The priest pointed with its staff. It gibbered with a voice harsh as a dog's, and thick with phlegm.

"I'm truly sorry," Peter said. And he was. *It must be done.*

Four of the human cultists stepped forward and grabbed

Reginald. They dragged him to the altar and forced him down. They held his arms and legs against the stone. He struggled in their grip. "Peter!" he yelled. "Stop this! Get them to stop!"

Theodora produced an athame of mirrored obsidian. She cut Reginald's coat and shirt open and tore the cloth away, exposing his torso.

The cultists began to chant. Voices human and inhuman formed a hymn that twisted around Peter's mind like a net of worms. The air began to thrum, as if it might tear, and with it the veil of reality. The verses of the hymn were rot and torn flesh, and its chorus was the coming of a devourer.

The priest leaned over Reginald. It sniffed and then cackled wetly.

Peter turned away and covered his ears. He did not want to witness what came next.

Theodora pulled his arms down gently and handed him the athame. The hilt felt warm and slick. Its carving squirmed in his grip.

"No," said Peter.

"You must," Theodora whispered. "You see what surrounds us. If we do not seize the power, it will flow through them. We can't allow that."

Peter took a shuddering breath. "No, we can't."

He steeled himself. *It must be done.*

Peter walked to the altar and stood over Reginald. The other man was still screaming, but his cries were muffled beneath the force of the chanting.

The priest hissed and pointed at Peter, and then at Reginald.

"Peter," Reginald pleaded. "Why are you doing this?"

"To save us all from the Devourer. I have to fight fire with fire. And you cannot reform a church from without."

The chants rose to a shriek, and Peter brought the point of the athame down hard, silencing Reginald with a single blow. It was easier to follow the priest's commands than he had expected. He shouted the words of the hymn, the words that the *Devoratio* could not translate into any human tongue, words he could suddenly pronounce, and know them to be true and strong.

Peter completed the act of sacrifice, doing what must be done, joining in the ritual with all his heart. He was committed now, and he was glad, and he felt his spirit burn with knowledge. Power surrounded him. It was the foreshadowing of something greater and more terrible to come, and it was power that he had joined now.

I will control this power one day. I will use it for the good of all.

The inner voice was faint. It could have been someone else's echo.

When the feast began, he did not hesitate. He took and he ate of the body that was given to him.

SINS IN THE BLOOD
Thomas Parrott

It was night by the time that Joe Diamond left the Orne Library. All the other readers had gone. The welcoming lamp above the door turned off as he walked away. There were no stars overhead; a ceiling of clouds had swept the sky. A cold gust of wind tugged at his trench coat. Thunder rumbled, and a first drop of chill rain spattered him.

"Figures," Joe sighed.

He pulled his coat tighter around himself and turned the collar up against the wind. His thoughts turned back to the case. Nadia Leandros, an exchange student at Miskatonic University, was plagued by dark visions and spectral harassment. Dismissed by the police as a crank, a mystery person had brought her troubles to his attention. Joe had seen too much to dismiss the horrors of Arkham out of hand. He had decided to dig deeper.

Nadia shared a birthmark with a recent murder victim here in town. Researching that had brought him to Orne

Library, and the librarian Daisy Walker had been able to guide him onward from there. The tale she unveiled was a wild one. The mark had quite a history, dating all the way back to Ancient Greece and a time of myth. Nadia, it seemed, might be a descendant of Princess Ariadne of Crete, and inheritor of a dangerous pact made with a real nightmare.

Umôrdhoth, the Devourer Below.

It was not Joe's first encounter with this eldritch monstrosity. A cult that served it had been tied to a recent spate of violence, and led to a night of terrors he'd just as soon forget. If he had been fortunate, that would have been the last they'd see of the ancient menace. Luck had never been his strong suit.

A sound pulled Joe from his thoughts. The rain had picked up to a steady, unpleasant drizzle. It draped the world in a muffling, gray veil. There had been something else, though. Footsteps? He paused with a frown and glanced over his shoulder. Had something moved back there? It was hard to be certain in the dark.

He hurried onward, picking up the pace. He would stop into his room at Ma's boarding house. A change of clothes might be in order by that point, and even if not, an umbrella would be welcome. There was a shared telephone he could use there, too. He needed to contact Nadia and convince her to meet him at ...

There it was again. He was sure of it this time: the clack of a heavy tread against the cobblestones. Someone wearing hobnailed boots, perhaps. Or, his mind put forward in an unwelcome interjection, something with iron-shod hooves. Something like the monstrous cult priest from the tale Miss Walker had found.

Joe's thoughts raced. It might be nothing. He did not own the streets of Arkham, after all. Something twisting in his gut demanded a more paranoid interpretation, however. If the Devourer Below wanted Nadia, it would not appreciate an incorrigible meddler like him getting involved. Might it have dispatched someone – or something – to take him off the board as a precaution?

He took a sharp turn down the first side street that came up on his right. A few steps into the alley and he turned to face the entrance with his left side. Joe pulled one of his Colt 1911s from the shoulder holster under his coat. He kept the weapon concealed by his body for the moment. If it was an innocent bystander he'd only make a headache for himself drawing down on them. If it wasn't…

Joe could hear them clearly. Tackety footsteps following in his wake. The gait seemed wrong for a human being. Would a person take such long steps? He knew all too well that such things weren't impossible. They were close now. He focused on keeping his breath steady.

Silence.

Joe frowned. Unless his ears betrayed him, his pursuer had stopped mere feet short of the alley. Did they suspect an ambush? Had he played his hand too obviously? He flexed his fingers around the grip of his pistol. He could feel sweat on the back of his neck despite the chill in the air.

He struggled to remain patient, but there was only the sound of the rain pattering all around and the pounding of his own heart. That twist in his gut curdled into a cauldron of nausea. He couldn't take it anymore. Joe swept out of the alley, weapon raised, to confront his follower.

There was nothing. The street and sidewalk were both empty.

"You're going crazy, Diamond," he whispered to himself.

A sound overhead snatched his eyes upward. A gust of wind or the beat of wings. Something even darker than the overcast sky swept in a circle far above, before turning to the west. Joe blinked, and it was gone.

Could have been a bat, he told himself. Just a massive bat. Sometimes perspective made size hard to gauge, right? He huffed out a sigh and holstered his pistol again. Ma's wasn't far now. It would be good to get out of the rain.

It was coming down in a full pour by the time he reached the boarding house. A few lights shone in the upstairs rooms, other lodgers going about their lives. Joe stepped under the overhang at the front door with heartfelt relief. He took his fedora off and shook rain off it to the side, before knocking the mud from his boots. Only then did he proceed inside.

The warmth of the common room enveloped Joe like a hug. The house was old and thoroughly lived in. It escaped being run down only via the constant efforts of Ma and any boarders who made the mistake of looking bored. Footsteps were audible overhead, and low chatter came from all directions. There was a comfortable humanity to the hubbub. He took a deep breath.

"Got yourself caught in a downpour, Mr Diamond?"

Joe turned to face Ma. She was sitting over by the radiator with some knitting in her lap. Her wrinkled hands kept the needles busy as she looked him over with a measuring eye. A faint furrow of her brow conveyed a dollop of disapproval.

"Afraid I did, ma'am." Joe bowed his head in quick apology. "Hate to track some wet into your home here. Gonna head right upstairs and get myself cleaned up."

Ma sniffed. "See that you do." She gestured with a needle towards the kitchen. "Afraid you missed dinner. You know the rule: if you're not at the table, you don't get fed."

Joe clicked his tongue regretfully. "Hate to hear that. Work kept me real late today."

"Something to be said for hard work," she allowed. "Also something to be said for being punctual."

"Very true." A thought occurred to Joe. He phrased it carefully. "Wonder if I could ask your help, since I missed dinner and all? Nothing troublesome, I'd just like to borrow the car so that I could stop by Velma's. I'd walk, but the rain…"

The needles stopped as Ma considered. "Suppose I could see my way to letting you do that. Keys are–"

"On the peg in the kitchen," Joe finished. He grinned. "Thanks, Ma. You're an angel."

She sniffed again. "Don't let it become a habit, Mr Diamond."

He held up a three-finger salute. "It won't. Scout's honor."

Ma turned her attention back to her knitting. "Have a good evening."

"You too, ma'am."

Joe hurried up the stairs towards his room. A plan was already forming in his mind. He'd call Velma's first and talk to Agnes, to make sure she was willing to help. From there he'd try to get in touch with Nadia and ask her to meet with them. Given that she didn't know him from Adam, that might be a tough sell. Hopefully, the public location would make her feel more comfortable.

He pushed the door to his room open. It was dark inside. A misty gust caught him in the face. The window was open, letting the rain-damp wind in. Joe frowned. He hadn't–

Something barreled into him at full speed. The attack caught him low and lifted him up off his feet. He smashed into the wall, driving the air from his lungs in a painful gasp. Stars exploded in front of his eyes. The boarder on the other side of the wall pounded back angrily.

Joe caught hold of his attacker in a desperate grip around the neck. Both of them toppled to the ground. He could catch only blurry glimpses of his foe in the dark. They were robed and masked. Something glinted in their right hand – a knife. It swept towards his face and he caught that arm by the wrist to hold it off.

Joe swung with his right hand balled up into a fist. He dealt a series of fierce blows around his attacker's head and shoulders. The shadowy figure grunted and some of the strength went out of their knife hand. Joe seized the chance to smash it against the bottom board of the bed. One, two, three times, and on the third the knife came loose and dropped to the floor.

His opponent recovered with a snarl. They dealt him a series of painful body blows. The layers of his coat and clothes muffled the impacts a little. Something gave in his chest with a crisp snap and pain pulsed through him. Joe elbowed his attacker in the neck to push them back, and went for one of the guns under his jacket.

His efforts earned him a headbutt to the face. It snapped his skull back into the floor with a dull thud. His world went white for a moment. When his vision cleared, his foe was winding back for a punch down towards his nose. Joe jerked his head out of the way at the last second, and knuckles met hardwood with a crunch. The masked figure let out a low groan of pain and reeled back, clutching at their hand.

A shine caught Joe's eye: the knife. He lunged and grabbed the blade. When he came back around, the figure was charging him again. Joe rolled out of the way and lashed out. The dagger sank home into his foe's right thigh until metal crunched into bone. His assailant gave a muffled screech of agony. His neighbor pounded the wall again angrily. If this went on much longer, he was going to draw attention from others. That would bring suspicion he didn't need.

The attacker staggered away, ripping the knife from the wound. The two of them glared at each other across the space of the room.

"Devourer take you," rasped the masked person. "You're already dead, detective. You just don't know it yet."

They hurled themselves at the window. Joe lunged to try and catch hold of them, keep them from escaping. He came up just short, and the shadowy figure plunged out of the opening. Joe leaned out the window and watched them pick themselves up painfully. They limped away into the night, soon lost in the darkness.

Joe shut the window firmly. The lock on it was broken

along rough lines, as though it had been frozen and hit with a hammer. He sat down on the foot of the bed and let loose a deep sigh. He regretted it instantly, the breath making his chest ache. His head was already beginning to beat a painful tattoo from the hits he'd taken.

"You know you're on the right track when someone's trying to kill you," he told himself. It was an encouraging sign, if not exactly a comforting one.

There was no time to rest. Joe dragged himself to his feet and made his way to the small, shared bathroom. The mirror showed an unwelcome but familiar sight. His lip was split and there was a cut above his eyebrow. Half his face would be purple by morning, and he'd broken a rib if he was any judge.

"Gotta find a new line of work one of these years, Diamond," he muttered.

There was a first aid kit among his things. He washed his face and applied Mercurochrome, wincing as the stinging liquid touched the broken skin. The kit had some of those clever little adhesive bandages that they'd come out with after the war. He applied one of those above his eyebrow. He put some gauze over the rib for padding and taped it off carefully.

Joe took a moment to assess. None of it was pretty or perfect, but it would hold for now. He'd just have to try not to breathe too deep. The thought brought a grin to his reflection. Add in a few aspirins and a swig of water, and it would have to see him through the night. There was no other choice. Something stronger would have been nice, but he needed a clear head for what was coming.

He grabbed a bag of supplies from his room and headed back down the stairs. The phone was near the bottom.

Joe picked up the phone and dialed the operator. "Can you put me through to the women's dormitory at Miskatonic? Thank you." It was getting on in the evening. He had to hope he was in before phone curfew.

A young woman answered. "Hello?"

"Hi. This is Joe Diamond, private investigator. Could I speak to Nadia Leandros, please?"

There was a pause. Distant from the receiver he heard: "Nadia, someone on the phone wants you. Some private eye?"

Another woman came on the line. "Hello? This is Nadia." Her voice still carried a heavy Greek accent. She sounded nervous. He couldn't blame her.

"Thank you for speaking to me, Nadia. My name is Joe Diamond, and I heard about your... troubles."

She hesitated. "The police told me it was nothing. That it was all in my head."

"I don't believe that. What's more, I'm hoping I can help you."

"How do I know this isn't a trick?"

Joe smiled. Smart kid. "You don't. That's why I'm hoping you'll agree to meet me at Velma's and hear me out. The diner over on the East side. You know it?"

"Yes, I know it," she said. She didn't even hesitate. Joe figured she didn't feel like she had a lot to lose at this point. "I'll be there in a half hour."

"Sounds like a plan."

Joe hung up and headed out through the kitchen. He

snagged the keys off the peg and made his way out of the back of the boarding house. Better to avoid any awkward questions from Ma about the condition of his face for as long as he could.

Nadia sat back in the booth opposite him and blinked. She was a young woman, dark haired and olive skinned. She had full lips and aquiline features. There was a piece of Velma's cherry pie in front of her, only half-eaten. She'd stopped picking at it about halfway through Joe's story. She scrubbed her hands over her face.

"All of that sounds…"

"Crazy," Joe finished for her. He took a sip from his cup of black coffee gone cold. "I know. I wouldn't blame you if you walked away from me. I hope you don't, though."

Nadia took a deep breath. "Because if you're right, this ends with me dead."

"Seems to," he said regretfully.

"The things I've seen, that I've heard… I haven't had a good night's sleep in weeks. And it does seem to be getting worse." Her eyes were ringed with dark circles, heavy with the truth of her words.

"Well, this curse seems to be carried in the bloodline," Joe said. "What about your folks?"

Nadia looked down. She picked at the pie with her fork. "My mother vanished when I was a kid. She… was just gone. We never saw her again. So…"

Joe nodded. It hurt to walk her through all of this, the grim possibilities. For a moment, he desperately wished for a return to blissful ignorance. It faded. That wasn't his lot.

She pinched the bridge of her nose. "OK. Let's say I believe you. Am I supposed to die? Because Ariadne let it kill her."

"No," he said gently. "It didn't work then, and it definitely wouldn't work now. The bloodline has spread who knows how far at this point."

"So, what?" Her voice was tight. A brittle control over desperation. "What do I do?"

Joe took a deep breath. "Well, that's where things get interesting, isn't it? I'm not much one for spells and sorcery. I'd sooner trust in steel and gunpowder."

Nadia gave him a flat look. "You brought me here to tell me you can't help me?"

Joe held up a hand. "Easy. I wouldn't waste your time that way. You're not the first person to encounter nightmares in this town, and I'm not the first person to try to do something about it. There's a few of us who know each other, and we all have our own areas of strength. For instance–"

The waitress stopped by their table. "Warm up your coffee?"

"I'd be obliged." Joe waited until his coffee was topped up to the brim, steaming once more. "For instance, Agnes is a bit of a specialist in these areas."

Nadia looked around with a frown. "Agnes?"

"Pleased to make your acquaintance." The waitress' eyes sparkled with amusement. She had sharp features and pale skin amidst a tumble of dark curls. They didn't quite reach the shoulders of the green shirt she wore under her apron. There was a silver chain around her neck, but whatever was on it was tucked into her collar. "Agnes Baker, that's me."

Nadia's eyes focused on the woman, and she blinked. "Oh." She glanced at Joe, then back. "I'm sorry."

Agnes smiled wryly. "Don't sweat it. I wouldn't expect me either."

Nadia smiled back uncertainly. "So you're a–"

Agnes clicked her tongue, cutting her off. "Easy does it." She glanced around. No one was sitting nearby. "No need to rush to put a label on things, especially when they're hard to pin down."

Nadia swallowed and nodded. "Right."

Agnes motioned for Joe to scoot over on the bench. He obliged, and she sat down with a sigh. "Feet are killing me. Long night. Guess it's not getting any shorter, huh?"

"Afraid not," Joe said.

Agnes nodded and studied Nadia closely. "Joe told me about your problem. Heck of a thing. I can almost see it hanging over you like a dark cloud. I've been mulling it over, and I think I have an idea."

"So you can help me?" Nadia leaned forward.

Agnes frowned. "I don't want to give you false hope. These things I deal with, the unseen world, it's dangerous and unpredictable at best. There's a lot that could go wrong."

"I have to try, right? What other choice do I have? Wait to die, if I don't go insane first?" Her voice shook on the last words.

Agnes nodded. "I understand. We'll do what we can."

Joe took another sip of his coffee. "So what's the plan?"

"Agnes!" It was Velma over behind the cashier, wearing a frown. "I'm not paying you to flap your gums!"

The waitress sighed and got back to her feet. "The plan

is, first I finish my shift. You two just hang out for an hour, and we'll go."

"Go where?" Joe asked.

"Well, the first stop is going to be City Hall. After that?" Agnes smirked. "The cemetery."

The rain had stopped by the time they were ready to go. It had left the night chilly in its wake. Agnes had swapped the apron for a worn coat. She had a book under one arm as she came over to meet them by the car. It was a ponderous tome bound in black leather. The sight of it brought a frown to Joe's face.

"You're bringing that?" he asked.

"This isn't the kind of ritual you wing," she said.

"Fair enough. Do you just keep it in your locker at work?"

Agnes snorted. "Well, I don't keep at home by my bed, I can tell you that much."

Joe started to reply but paused, thinking it over. He shrugged. "Yeah. Makes sense."

The waitress eyed the vehicle. "Isn't this Ma's car?"

It was a beat-up Tin Lizzie with a faded paint job. It had the same air around it as the boarding house: kept going more by Ma's force of will than anything else. Even inanimate objects did their best to not get on her bad side.

"Could be," Joe allowed.

"No wheels of your own, detective?" There was a gleam of mischief in Agnes' eyes.

"Most months I'm happy to keep the lights on at the office," Joe noted dryly.

"Gotta quit taking these pro bono jobs," she offered.

"Maybe tomorrow." Joe gave an amiable shrug. "We can walk if you'd prefer."

"Or we could not," Nadia interjected. The jacket she'd brought was a thin thing, unsuited to the cold. Joe wasn't surprised. Students never had much money, and she'd come from a warmer clime.

"Come on, let's go," Joe said. He went around to the driver's side to climb in.

"Sure thing," said Agnes. "But if anything happens to it, keep my name out of your mouth when you're explaining to Ma."

The waitress climbed into the passenger side while Nadia got into the back. Joe got the engine started after only a couple of tries, and they were off. The clatter and roar of the running vehicle made for a noisy ride. It put a damper on conversation while they rode to City Hall.

The building was located downtown, just off Independence Square. It was nondescript and rundown, marked out only by a clock tower that rose from the top. The timepiece was so poorly maintained that it was barely legible. It was also tightly closed up for the night, all lights off. Joe surveyed it all with a frown.

"So what do we need here?"

"I need to get into the records," Agnes said.

That wasn't much of an answer. Joe pushed down a surge of irritation. He had to remind himself that while he might not trust Agnes' methods, he did trust the woman herself. He stepped up to the door and tried the knob. It rattled but didn't turn. Locked.

"Got an idea on how we'll get in?"

The waitress grinned insouciantly. "Gonna let something like a locked door stop you, Joe?"

Joe glowered at her briefly before turning back to the door. Now, he probably could just kick it off the hinges, but that'd be quite a racket. The trick was to figure out how to break it without making too much noise. He might be able to just break the inset window and reach through to–

"Excuse me," Nadia said.

The detective stepped out of the way, blinking. The young woman moved forward and took a hairpin out of one of her pockets. She fiddled with the lock for a few seconds, her eyes closed. Her tongue was stuck at the corner of her mouth in concentration. The door clicked, and she turned the knob. It creaked open, revealing darkness beyond.

"That's a handy talent," Joe said. "Where did you …"

"Life hasn't always been easy. Sometimes you do things you aren't proud of to make sure there's food on the table." Nadia shrugged self-consciously. "You pick up things living like that."

Agnes patted Joe on the shoulder. "Don't worry. There'll be a need for manual labor before the night's over."

She swept past him into the building, and the other two followed in her wake. Joe shut the door behind them. No reason to make it obvious to anyone passing by that someone had gone inside.

"Dark as pitch in here," Nadia commented.

"My moment of triumph has come sooner than expected," Joe remarked dryly.

He pulled a flashlight out of his coat. The beam was

briefly dazzling as he turned it on. It caught dust motes drifting in the air. He swept it back and forth across the room. City Hall was no more impressive on the inside. It was a confined area, cluttered with worn desks and too many filing cabinets.

"Perfect!" Agnes said brightly. She plucked the flashlight from his hand and began walking from cabinet to cabinet. She stopped to inspect each one in the light.

"You know, we could help more if we knew what you were looking for," Joe said with some exasperation.

"All will be clear in time," the waitress singsonged. "Patience is a virtue."

"So is clear communication," he replied.

Nadia had fallen quiet. Joe glanced back to check on her. She was hard to make out in the dark, but it looked like she was rubbing the part of her neck where the birthmark was. A surge of sympathy rose in Joe. She hadn't asked for any of this. He knew what it was like to be young and in over your head.

"You alright?" he asked.

The young woman startled before smiling, her teeth flashing in the dark. "Just thinking about all of it. Doesn't seem real."

"That's good," Joe said.

Nadia tilted her head. "Good?"

"Yeah," Joe said. "As long as you feel that way, maybe you return to a normal life after this. Like waking up from a bad dream. Just leave it behind you. Because once you accept that it's real, that the monsters are out there…"

"Then there's no going back," she said softly.

Joe nodded. There was a sadness in her eyes as she looked at him. Someone past that point of no return. He turned away from it. He couldn't afford self-pity. The nightmares were bad enough as it was.

"Aha!" Agnes said from across the room. She'd settled on a particular filing cabinet and was in the process of pulling drawers open.

"Found it–" Joe started to ask.

A creak cut him off from overhead. All three of them froze, looking upwards.

"Could just be the building settling," Agnes said quietly.

"Yeah, or it could be Santa Claus," Joe said. "We're not that lucky."

"What do you think it is?" Nadia's voice was barely above a whisper.

"I don't know. I'm going to take a look." Joe tossed the keys to Agnes. "Find what you're looking for. If I don't come back, get the kid out of here and see this done."

The mischief was gone from the waitress's face. She handed him the flashlight and got a lighter out of her own pocket to replace it. "Be careful, Joe."

He nodded. "I will." He pulled one of his guns.

Joe set off up the stairs. They creaked under his feet as he went up. He fought the urge to curse. If there was something up there, it was going to know he was coming. He stepped through the doorway to the second floor. This level was broken down into distinct offices. He crept past their doors, trying each one as he went. They were all locked.

There was the clatter of tackety feet up ahead in a sudden

rush. It took him back to the alleyway earlier that evening. The hair on his neck stood on end. The unmistakable sound of a door followed. Joe turned the corner in a rush to find another hallway. A door at the end was open, revealing another staircase up. It must go into the bell tower.

He ran forward, darting to the base of the stairs. He looked up just in time to see a shadow vanish into the maintenance chamber for the clock mechanism itself. It was a brief glimpse, but it was enough to see the shape of it. It was wrong. Inhuman. He got the impression of wings. His heart pounded in his ears.

The urge to turn back was strong. It seemed like the smart play. Joe pressed onward instead. He couldn't stand mysteries. It was what made him so good at what he did. Besides, he had never been one for making good calls. Be a shame to break with tradition tonight.

The sound of the clock tower's mechanism was loud in the staircase up. It was as poorly maintained as it looked to judge by the sound of grinding gears. He went up step by step, flashlight and gun held at right angles in front of him. There was a final doorway to the room at the top. Joe took a deep breath.

He kicked the door. It slammed open with a thud. The sound echoed loudly, and Joe cursed his own nerves. Someone could have heard that. The chamber beyond was empty. There was a ladder leading up a hatch to the roof. It was open, letting in cold air and rain. Joe stared at it for several seconds. There was nowhere to go from up there.

Nowhere for a human being to go, anyway.

The bell tolled. The sound was sudden in the darkness

and Joe jerked backwards, swerving to face the mechanism. He sighed as it rang again, deafening in the confined space. With a glower he shut the hatch to the roof and latched it. He turned and headed back down the stairs.

Agnes and Nadia waited at the bottom with wide eyes.

"Anything?" Agnes asked.

"I don't know," Joe admitted wearily. "Any luck on your end?"

She held up a manila folder. "I have what we need. Let's get out of here."

Once they were back on the road, Joe fixed Agnes with a firm look. "Going to let us in on this plan of yours?"

"And lose my air of alluring mystery?" Agnes gave a crooked smile. "Fine. You're not gonna like it, though."

"If it saves my life, I like it," Nadia called from the back.

"Might want to hear it before you say that," Agnes said.

"Spill it," Joe said.

"We need to perform an exhumation. We have to dig up the other victim you told me about," Agnes said.

For a few minutes the only sound was the clatter of wheels against stone. Joe cleared his throat. He shuffled through a number of possible responses in his mind, ranging from "no" to "hell no". He even made a brief stop on "do you understand how illegal that is?"

Instead, he settled on something more diplomatic. "OK," Joe said. "I'll bite. Why?"

"The mark on Nadia's skin is only a symptom, not the source. Her essence – her soul, for lack of a better word – is stained with the pact her ancestors made. We have to excise that taint, but, once we do, it isn't going to just vanish."

"It needs somewhere to go," Nadia said.

"Bingo," the waitress said. "The curse is defined by bloodline, so we need a vessel that suits it."

"It's a dead body," said Joe. He felt like it was a reasonable point to make. The idea of digging up some poor sap was already a less than pleasant one. He wanted to be damn sure it would actually work before they went through with it.

Agnes cleared her throat. "Yeah. That's the tricky part. The transfer has to be from like to like. Living essence can't go into a dead body. So we're gonna have to finesse it up a little if we want the Devourer to take the bait."

"Dress it up how?" Joe asked.

Agnes mumbled a response, lost in the clamor.

"What was that?" he asked.

The waitress scrunched up her face. "We have to breathe a little life back into it too."

Joe's head snapped to face her fully. "What?"

"I told you you weren't going to like it!"

"We had that covered with the digging it up part! I was already there!" Joe snapped.

"Watch the road!" Agnes said. She sighed. "Look, the piece of essence we have to take from Nadia is going to carry some energy with it anyway. All I have to do is breathe on those sparks a bit! The Devourer Below will sense that something is tampering with the curse, it will come to claim its due and snatch the body. The body seems alive, so the essence transfers. Then the Old One devours it, and she's safe."

"Something's wrong," Nadia said. There was a lot of tension in her voice, verging on fear.

"You got that right, kid," Joe said. He shook his head vigorously. "There has to be a better way, Agnes."

"We're meddling with dangerous stuff here, Joe! It's not gonna be safe, clean, or pretty, no matter how you slice it."

Nadia pushed up between them from the back. "Something is wrong!"

"Yeah, we–"

"No!" the student snapped. "Look around!"

Joe had become so focused on arguing with Agnes that the drive had faded into the background. He glanced around hastily. Something was indeed wrong. The surrounding town had vanished.

An all-encompassing darkness pressed in on all sides of the car. The headlights flickered pitifully in the face of it, unable to even illuminate the road ahead. Unreasoning terror welled up in him, yammered in his ears. Joe did his best to shove it aside and slammed on the brakes. They squealed, but the sound faded to a whisper and was gone. The darkness brought with it a terrible cold like an arctic wind. Frost was already forming on the outer parts of the car. His heart pounded as he stared at the spreading crystalline patches.

"This isn't natural," Agnes warned.

"Yeah, I got that part," Joe snapped.

Something struck the vehicle with terrific force. It rocked, and glass splintered. Someone screamed. Joe was slung forward against the wheel. His already-wounded chest exploded with pain. The world narrowed to soundless starbursts. All he could do was wheeze.

Joe!

He breathed in, breathed out. The world spun dizzily. It was as if that shattered glass had settled below his throat and filled up his torso. He cradled an arm across his chest, gasping.

"Joe!"

The scream punched through the daze he was in. It was Agnes. She was half out of her seat, draped into the back of the vehicle. He turned around to see for himself. The waitress had a desperate hold on Nadia's legs. The student was being dragged out of the vehicle, inhuman hands snagging her around the canopy and yanking on her.

Joe's chest was still afire with agony. He ignored it. He clambered up onto his own seat and leaned around the canopy. A horror waited there to meet him. In shape, it wasn't altogether inhuman. Its skin shone with an oily black sheen. Great wings spread from its back, buffeting the night air soundlessly.

The face was what struck Joe the most, though. There wasn't one. There was only a terrible blankness instead. It was as if whatever misbegotten deity had made this thing had gotten that far before giving up. The emptiness did not stop it from sensing them. Its head turned towards Joe, and a barbed tail lashed at him.

He threw his left arm up just in time. The stinger slashed against his coat and carved straight through it to the flesh underneath. Joe nearly fell back but kept his wits about him. He wanted to scream. Instead, he went into his pocket with his other hand and came up with a 1911. He brought it to bear and squeezed the trigger.

The weapon spoke, flash and thunder somehow muffled

by the enshrouding darkness. At this range he couldn't miss. The .45 ACP round tore through the thing's chest in a gout of glistening black blood. It fell away, shriveling in on itself like a dying spider. Revulsion and horror warred in him as he kicked it off.

Nadia's terrified face stared up at him from under the canopy.

"Agnes, can we–" Joe started.

Prehensile paws seized him under the arms and snatched him skyward. The ground lurched away from him in a terrifying surge. It tore a choked-off yelp of terror from him. Great dark wings beat around him: another of the creatures. It had him. He kicked his legs wildly, and one foot caught under the side mirror. It was all that stopped him from being hauled bodily into the dark. Metal creaked and bent, an insufficient anchor against an uncertain fate.

There were screams from below. Joe had his hands too full to worry about that. Terror made for quite a distraction. He flailed wildly, desperately managed to hook a foot into the car's canopy. It stabilized him just a little, but there was no countering the thing's inexorable pull. He aimed his 1911 over his shoulder and fired blind. All it got him was dazzled eyes and a deafened ear. A barbed tail struck and smacked the gun from his grasp. It fell away into the shadows.

Fear ignited into anger, the desperate urge to fight back. Joe struck backwards with his elbows. He connected with something, but the substance of the thing seemed all wrong. It was like trying to fistfight with a curtain, too gauzy and insubstantial to find purchase. Another beat of powerful wings, and the mirror broke away under his left foot.

His other slid inch by inch towards coming loose. Joe grasped desperately for his other gun. His hand hit something metal, and he pulled it out. It wasn't the second 1911, but instead the knife he'd gotten from the cultist earlier. There was no time to be picky. There was a sick certainty in his stomach that if the monster dragged him into the sky that would be the end of him. He cut at one of the arms holding him, and oily liquid sprayed. That hand fell away, but the other still had him. He hung painfully, caught between one foot and his shoulder, between the ground and the sky.

Agnes had climbed onto the top of the car. Joe grabbed at her frantically. She ignored him. Instead, she stood her full height, one hand held over her head. Something glinted silver in her grasp.

She spoke a single Word.

Light flared. It had a physical presence, hitting like a wave on the ocean. It tore the surrounding shadows asunder and bleached the world bone white for a single eternal moment. Heat came in its wake, a wash of hot wind that flung Joe's trench coat up and outward.

Somehow, without a mouth, the thing holding him screamed.

It was gone.

Joe fell. His heart lurched into his mouth. He barely managed to get his hands under him before he struck the cobblestones. The impact was still enough to leave him dazed. He laid there on the ground for a few seconds, coughing. His one leg was still caught behind him, sticking into the car. He yanked it loose and staggered to his feet, as unsteady as a drunkard.

They were in the middle of an Arkham street. The car was parked in the middle of the road at an angle, black marks behind it showing the sudden braking. Lights were coming on in the buildings all around them. Joe could hear raised voices in some. Their assailants had left no trace, not even a few spatters of dark blood to show they had ever existed. All he could do was laugh in disbelief. The sound had an unhinged edge to it that made him choke it off hastily.

Agnes was crouched on top of the car. Her face was drawn with effort, head down and eyes closed. Nadia was sprawled on the back seat, shaking uncontrollably. Her arms were crossed over her face.

"Arghu." His voice came out strangled. Joe coughed and tried again. "Are you alright?"

The student slowly lowered her arms and stared at him with wide, white eyes.

"Right," he said. It had been a stupid question. He raised his eyes to the top of the car. "Agnes?"

The waitress blinked her eyes open. "Yeah," she rasped.

There were sirens in the distance. There was no way to explain any of this, no evidence that would begin to suffice. Stories like this one were how people ended up in sanitariums behind locked doors.

"We gotta go."

"Right."

Agnes nodded once, then again more firmly. She clambered back down off the top of the car and climbed into the passenger side. Joe saw his pistol lying nearby and stooped to pick it up. He returned it to the holster, then tucked the knife back into a pocket too. He climbed back into the driver seat.

He tried to start the car. The engine sputtered. It wasn't until the third try that it caught, and they could set off again. They raced down the road towards the cemetery.

Joe's face felt raw. He touched it and winced. It was like he'd been sunburned.

"That was a hell of a thing," he said.

"Yeah," Agnes said.

Nadia nodded wordlessly.

"How did you–"

"Joe," Agnes cut him off. "Shut up and drive."

"Right," he said. "You got it."

They arrived in French Hill, one of the richest neighbor hoods in Arkham. The elevated terrain was covered by decaying mansions and old money estates. Joe had to hope that would throw the cops off their trail; not many people ran for the upscale part of town. The graveyard was located near the foot of the eponymous landmark. It was a site rich in history; they said some tombstones dated all the way back to the original colonists of the seventeenth century.

Joe didn't know if that was true. All he knew was that it wasn't the kind of place he'd hoped to spend a night. He climbed out of the Model T and winced as his chest throbbed.

"Ma's going to murder you," Agnes noted.

Joe glanced at the vehicle. The canopy was bent inwards.

The back windows had been shattered. The side mirror, of course, was gone completely. He pursed his lips a moment. It was hard to argue with the assessment.

"If we actually make it to daybreak, I'll be delighted to let her have her chance."

Nadia got out of the car on shaky legs. "I have a question."

Joe went around to the rear of the vehicle. He dragged the bag of supplies out and opened it to take stock. He'd started putting the kit together after that one insane night. Enough people around town owed him favors that not much was really beyond his grasp. He hauled a shotgun from within and loaded it with practiced movements. Then he snagged a few sticks of dynamite for good measure.

"What's on your mind?" Agnes asked.

"Is this normal for you people?" Nadia demanded.

"This isn't normal for anybody," Joe said wearily. He didn't know what else to say. She must feel like her world had gone insane, and she was right to.

He stepped up to the fence that surrounded the graveyard. The place was shrouded in mist. Tombstones and mausoleums stood out in silhouette. Great trees grew among them, branches stretching forth like bony fingers against the night sky. The wrought iron gates were locked.

Joe turned back to the two. "Anyone want a hand up over the fence?" He offered laced hands as a step.

"Such a gentleman," Agnes said.

She stepped into his grip and climbed up and over. Nadia followed suit. Joe handed them his stuff through the bars, and then with some huffing and puffing managed to haul himself over as well.

"So how do we find the grave we need?" he asked.

"That is why we stopped in at City Hall," Agnes said cheerfully. She held the manila folder up triumphantly.

Joe gave her a flat look.

She ignored it, busily examining the documents. She pointed off ahead to the right. "That way. It's the same shadow that clings to Nadia, faded but lingering. Must be where the body is."

"Are we sure I'm not just going crazy?" Nadia asked. "That seems more and more preferable as we go."

"We are not the best judges of that," Joe replied.

The mist swirled around them as they headed inwards towards the grave they needed. The whole place had a deep stillness about it. Joe couldn't place if it was the sanctity of sacred ground, or just the calm before the storm. Either way it made him feel uneasy, like an intruder.

They passed a grave only half dug. Shovels had been left to finish the work later. Joe snagged three of them and handed them out. Faces were grim all around. No one wanted to think about what they were shortly going to be using the tools for.

"So, this thing, this… Devourer." Nadia's voice seemed loud against the quiet of the grove. She must have felt it too because she spoke quieter as she continued. "It takes people, right?"

"Sort of. Last group of cultists we ran into were feeding it bodies. Things got ugly when they decided to supplement with the freshly murdered." Joe shrugged. "This group seems to try for food that's a bit more fresh."

"Food. Right," the student muttered. "Anyway, so why

didn't it take my... you know. My relative's body."

"I've been wondering that myself," Agnes said. "I do have a theory."

"A delightful one, I'm sure," Joe remarked. "Feel free to share with the class."

Agnes hesitated. "You've been tormented by visions and such, right, Nadia?"

The student nodded. "Awful ones. Dark presences. Voices in the night. They would say things..." She trailed off, shook her head.

"Well, I'd guess he got desperate. Didn't see a way out." The waitress left the rest of the thought unsaid. "They'll still come for the body eventually, I'd imagine. Just less urgently."

"I remember some notes on the file," Joe said softly. "He was an indigent. A drifter. Who knows how long this madness had been chasing him from place to place, never finding rest."

They continued in silence for a way.

"My mother..." Nadia said.

Joe looked over at her. "You said she vanished."

"She did. 'Ran off.' You can imagine all the things people said." She shook her head. "Greece has not been a peaceful place. It is easy for people to become lost."

Joe nodded. What could he say to that? To the weight of sorrow it represented?

"I've been thinking about it, though. She was tormented too, I believe. I remember arguments. Sleepless nights. I wonder now if she ran to try to protect us. To protect me." The young woman hugged her arms around herself. "No one would have understood."

"This isn't going to go like that," Joe said firmly. She had every right to be shaken, but he couldn't let her follow that dark line of thought here and now.

Nadia managed a smile. "Thank you. Even just not having to face this alone is… I'm grateful to both of you. No matter how this turns out."

Agnes rested a comforting hand on Nadia's shoulder. She motioned with the other hand towards a grave up ahead. It still looked fairly fresh; new grass had yet to grow on the churned soil.

"That's it."

The three of them gathered around it and looked down. They had moved beyond the cemetery proper into Arkham's potter's field, where the unclaimed dead were buried. There was no tombstone, only a simple wooden cross staked into the dirt. A pauper's grave. Joe shook his head with weary sadness.

"There's no fairness to any of this. I hope you know that, Nadia. You don't deserve what's happening, and neither did this fellow." Joe crouched and rested the shotgun against his shoulder. This freed a hand to pat the soil. "Wish I'd known. I'd have done what I could for him, too."

"You can only do what you can do," Agnes said somberly. "He's beyond our help now. And we have someone here tonight that we can still change things for."

Joe nodded. He pulled off his trench coat and set it aside, propping the shotgun against a nearby grave marker. Then he rolled up his sleeves and picked up one of the shovels.

"Let's get to work."

The shovel bit deep into the dirt. The other two joined

in, and they worked without talking. The only sound was the labor itself. It was hard work; all of them were soon sweating and panting. The mound of dirt next to the grave grew steadily and the pit grew deeper and deeper.

The work set all of Joe's injuries to aching anew. His chest was a sharp suffering that wouldn't go away anymore. His eyebrow and lip stung where sweat ran into the cuts. He paused once to wipe his face on his sleeves and left a streak of red in his wake; the scab had broken, and the cut was bleeding fresh.

"The university… has not… prepared me… for this," Nadia wheezed.

Agnes gave an exhausted laugh. "Maybe graverobbing is in a later class."

"If we could not call this graverobbing, that would help my peace of mind a lot," Joe said.

His shovel clunked against something hard. The trio's eyes met. Joe pushed the earth aside to reveal the top of a coffin. It wasn't terribly deep. The poor rarely got a proper six feet. It was cheap pine too, the better to save the city money. He could see where it had been nailed shut around the edges.

"You both might want to climb out. Body's been in here for several days. It's not going to be pretty."

"As opposed to everything else we deal with, which is such a sensory delight," muttered Agnes.

Nevertheless, she scrambled out of the grave and offered Nadia a hand up as well. Both looked on with drawn faces. Joe wedged the tip of the shovel into the edge of the coffin lid and began to lever with all his strength. On the third heave it tore away with a crunch and a creak, wood splintering around the nails.

The stench hit Joe before he ever saw the body. He stumbled back against the edge of the grave with a hand clamped over his mouth. It was not his first time dealing with the dead, but most of them hadn't had as much time to ripen. This one was green and bloated, lying in a pool of its own leaked fluids.

Agnes flinched and muttered something in a language he didn't recognize. Nadia was not so restrained; she whirled and staggered a few steps away to vomit noisily. Joe looked up to the dark sky, struggling not to join her. He swallowed hard a few times, trying to clear his mouth of nauseous saliva.

"Are you sure this is going to work?" he asked Agnes once he thought he had his stomach under control.

"Joe, I haven't been sure of anything since I learned monsters were real," she replied.

"Yeah, that's fair," he said. There were still mornings where he woke up and told himself that all these things were just nightmares. It was a nice illusion while it lasted.

Joe went to climb out. For a moment loose earth slid under his hands at the edge. All he could picture was toppling backwards into the sloppy mess in the coffin. The idea gave him a desperate strength that let him cling on and heave himself up and out. Agnes helped pull him the last bit.

"Hey!" Nadia called and pointed off into the distance, back towards the entrance to the graveyard.

Joe looked in that direction. Lights were approaching

through the mist, the sweeping beams of flashlights. His shoulders tensed immediately. They'd hardly begun and already drawn attention. No matter who it was, that was bad news. They'd made too much noise along the way through Arkham. It would have been easy for someone to have followed them here. The question was who.

"Damn." Agnes had obviously reached the same conclusion. "Do you think you can distract them?"

"Depends on who it is," Joe said. He scrubbed a dirty hand over his face. "I'll do my best. You and Nadia stay back. Try not to start chanting in the background, if you would."

Agnes gave him a wry look. "I'll do my best."

She went to collect Nadia. Joe walked on ahead, stopping only to collect the shotgun. He kept the weapon low. Whoever it was could well be an innocent bystander, and he had no urge to frighten them.

He passed out of the edge of the potter's field and back into the stone markers of the cemetery proper. The approaching figures resolved into the shape of people through the mist. A beam swept onto Joe, dazzling him momentarily. He raised a hand to shield his eyes.

"Hold up there," one of them called.

Joe did as he was asked, stopping. He tried to adopt a relaxed posture. It was easier said than done. He knew he looked a frightful mess. He was battered, bruised, and covered in dirt. Not exactly a soothing portrait at the best of times, much less in the dark of a graveyard at night.

"Well, well. If it isn't Joe Diamond."

Joe recognized the voice now. Officer McClury, one

of the policemen who patrolled the beats in Arkham. The light shifted down out of his eyes and he saw the man, confirming his guess. Middle-aged and redheaded, McClury was a bluff fellow with a remarkable mustache. His left hand held the flashlight, while his right was hooked into his belt. Not close enough to his gun to be a threat, but not too far away either. Another policeman stood a bit further back, though Joe didn't recognize that one.

"Officers," Joe said steadily. "Good evening to you. Can I help you somehow?"

"Funny thing, that," McClury said. "I was about to ask you the same thing. Look like you've had a rough night, Joe."

Joe mustered a smile. "Well, I am working a bit later than I'd like, I'll be honest."

"Working a bit late, he says!" McClury chuckled with what seemed like genuine good humor. He glanced back at the other officer. "Did you hear that?"

"I heard," the other cop said flatly. No amusement there.

Something about that one's voice was familiar, but Joe couldn't place it. His skin crawled. He frowned.

McClury continued, "Been a busy night for us too, Joe. Would you believe someone was screeching around town in some jalopy, scaring all kinds of folk? A few people even thought they heard gunfire."

"Is that so?" Joe asked.

He glanced off towards the gate. They had come from that direction and must have seen Ma's car. McClury might be toying with him, or just trying to avoid a confrontational approach. Joe got along with most of the police in Arkham well enough, but some resented "freelancers" like him. McClury seemed relaxed enough, but his pal fidgeted with ill-concealed impatience.

"Sure is," McClury replied. "Don't suppose you've seen anything strange yourself?"

"Strange? In Arkham? Perish the thought," Joe said.

"Righto, righto. Perhaps, just to set my mind at ease, you could explain what you're doing in a graveyard late at night?"

Joe gave a humorless smile. "I already told you. Working."

McClury gave him a wounded look. "Oh, come now, Joe. Don't make this hard on me. I'm just doing my job."

He might well be, Joe mused. McClury didn't seem to be lying. Joe wasn't sure he had it in him to draw down on a cop just doing his job. He resisted the urge to glance over his shoulder to where the two women and the exhumed body were. The most important thing was to keep Agnes' work from being disturbed. If he could pull these policemen away somehow...

"It's a gloomy place to have a conversation. If you're concerned about my activities, I'd be happy to come down to the station and make a statement," Joe offered.

McClury's eyebrows went up. "Would you now?" He scratched at his jaw. "That's kind of you to be so accommodat–"

"Where's the girl?" growled his compatriot.

Joe tensed. It didn't take a detective's insight to see something off about that question. "What girl?"

McClury seemed almost as surprised as him. He frowned

at the other cop. "There were reports of women involved in that car incident I spoke of–"

The other cop limped forward. Favoring his right leg, Joe noticed. The skin between his shoulder blades crawled.

"You know he's involved, McClury. Probably kidnapped a woman. We have to find her."

The familiar voice. It clicked into place, the last piece of the puzzle. He'd heard it before, alright. Tonight, in fact. There was a dark stain on the man's uniform pants over the thigh. Blood, soaked through a bandage and clothing alike.

"Hurt your leg there, officer?" Joe asked.

The man's face was still in shadow, but Joe could see his expression tighten. The realization that the cultist had said too much and given himself away. The false cop's hand dropped to the butt of his service pistol.

"Easy does it there," McClury said. "There's no call–"

The second cop drew his pistol in the blink of an eye. Joe dove for a nearby tombstone as the gunfire rang out. Bullets impacted on the granite surface, chipping away at the stone. Joe hunched up and brought the shotgun around for a blind shot, forcing the two policemen to scatter into cover as well.

"What in the devil do you think you're doing, Cooper?" roared McClury at the other cop. "Stand down!"

Cooper replied by shooting him. Joe blanched as McClury's body sprawled out across the moist soil, dead before he hit the ground.

"You son of a bitch! You didn't have to do that!"

"You're all grist for the mill," snarled the revealed cultist.

There was chanting in the distance now. Agnes was

smart enough to have kicked off the ritual the moment she heard gunfire, Joe reasoned. No point in wasting time when things had obviously gone south.

Cooper clearly heard it too. "Give me the girl and I might let you walk away."

Joe glowered and leaned out to take another potshot by way of answer. The cop responded with a series of blasts that forced Joe to duck his head down.

"Besides, who's to say I did it?" the cultist laughed coldly. "Who do you think they'll blame? The decorated officer, horrified to see a fellow policeman gunned down? Or the shady detective always sticking his nose where he shouldn't? I'll be a hero for bringing you down."

"You actually have to bring me down first," Joe snapped. He was caught between anger and fear, and fell back on bravado to cover it.

He glanced down at his shotgun. There were three more rounds in the Winchester Model 12's magazine. The cultist's gun had looked like a Colt .38 Special. Six rounds to the cylinder, but Cooper had been more liberal with his shooting. He must be almost out.

Something shrieked in the distance, intruding on Joe's thoughts. The inhuman sound chilled him to the core, an instinctive fear of a predator's cry. More of the screeches responded from all directions. A whole pack of somethings were headed in this direction, and they didn't sound friendly. His heart sank. Whatever edge he'd had evaporated in an instant.

"Doesn't sound like I'll have to worry about you at all, detective," Cooper laughed.

"Hell's bells," swore Joe.

Agnes had warned him, he recalled. Umôrdhoth would feel the ritual once it began and dispatch its minions to collect what it considered its due. He desperately wished she'd been wrong for once. He sighed. He couldn't stay pinned down here. The priority now had to be getting back there and protecting the waitress until the ritual was finished.

The time for subtlety was past. He reached for a dynamite stick and froze. They were in his trench coat, back at the grave. His options narrowed rapidly.

"Hell of a thing," he muttered.

Joe took a deep breath and bolted from cover. Cooper rose and took his shot. Joe heard the hiss of the bullet and staggered. A bleeding line had been drawn on the outside of his thigh. He stumbled into a gravestone and nearly fell.

He came around to see the service revolver pointed dead center at him. Cooper had a murderer's grin on his face. He pulled the trigger. It clicked down on a spent cylinder. Caught up in celebration of his victory, it took a second for the cultist to realize nothing had happened. His eyebrows went up.

That moment was everything. Joe brought the shotgun to his shoulder, aimed, and squeezed the trigger. It was a series of smooth, practiced movements. The blast caught Cooper in the chest. He pitched backwards in a spray of blood.

Joe wavered. He didn't feel much triumph, only a weariness. This hadn't been a slavering monster, just a human. It wasn't the first life Joe had been forced to take.

It probably wouldn't be the last either. More of those wavering howls sounded, closer now. He set off again, limping, towards the grave-turned-ritual-site.

An auroral glow was building there. It wasn't bright, but it hurt Joe's eyes if he looked directly at it. That wasn't the only sign that strange energies were afoot. There was a vibration to it. He couldn't hear it, but he could feel it in his bones, like the deep tolling of an unseen bell. As if in response, the ground rumbled beneath his feet.

A mausoleum door burst open to his left. A snarling figure loped out of it, at once human and animalistic. Its limbs were elongated and ended in broad claws, suitable for digging and tearing. Red eyes gleamed in a canine face. Joe didn't hesitate. He shot the thing before it could close with him. It fell away with a shriek, and he caught a glimpse of the open crypt behind it. There was a mouth of a tunnel within.

Either they were digging their way out, or they had such passages prearranged. There was no telling. For a dizzying moment he imagined Arkham as nothing but a thin rind on a termite's mound of tunnels, all of it crawling with monsters. All Joe could do was wonder how many of them would be coming, and how long it would take him and his friends to be overrun. He shoved the thoughts aside. None of that changed what he had to do.

He was within sight of the grave. He carefully avoided looking at the growing maelstrom of aetheric energies and instead focused on a blur of activity nearby. Nadia was fighting fiercely with one of the monsters, bludgeoning it with her shovel. Each blow drove it back only briefly. For a heartbeat he cursed his own lack of foresight. He should have left her with a gun.

Another was coming up behind her. Joe blew it away with the last of his shotgun shells. Then he lunged for the one that the student was battling, bringing the butt of the shotgun around to strike it between its twisted shoulders. The blow knocked it to its knees. It came around towards him, snarling. Hot breath blew in his face, stinking of carrion.

Nadia seized the opportunity to smash it directly in the back of the skull with the shovel. It slumped to the ground with a squelch.

"You're alive!" she said.

"Let's not get ahead of ourselves," Joe said. "Know how to use a gun?"

"I'm Greek," she said simply.

Joe considered that for a heartbeat. "Fair." He pulled one of his 1911s from a holster and tossed it to her, then drew the other for his own use.

The ground was shaking constantly now. Both staggered against the force of the earthquake. Cracks erupted in the dirt, and pure darkness vented from them like steam. To Joe's dizzied gaze, the shadows seemed to form great tendrils. They reached for the boiling light in the grave with a mindless hunger, primordial and terrible.

A ring of the beasts was closing in all around them. They approached at a lupine lope, calling back and forth to each other with their uncanny cries. Their eyes glowed crimson in the mist. The shimmering energies of Agnes' ritual illuminated them all too well, every gaunt rib and slavering fang. The two humans pressed back-to-back against this tide. Joe shot the closest one and it spun away. There were two more to take its place.

He fired again and again. The bullets were well placed, but all they could do was buy seconds. He could hear the thunder of the other gun behind him as Nadia fought too, but he couldn't spare her more than a thought. A red-eyed horror climbed over a tombstone, and he shot it in the face. The gun clicked empty, and he ejected the magazine to replace it with his last reload.

As suddenly as it had begun, the chanting stopped. The light in the grave died. Without it the graveyard plunged into preternatural darkness. Blind, Joe could only listen. What he heard burned into his brain with a hateful indelibility.

Down there in the grave, something that shouldn't be alive took a deep, shuddering breath. It was a noisome sound, thick with mucus. It coughed, trying to clear lungs that scarcely existed anymore. Then, impossibly, it screamed. A wail caught between a newborn's innocence and the howl of the damned. He clapped his hands over his ears to try to shut it out. It wasn't enough.

A great wind blew, and the earth roared. They fell to their knees. There was a moist slurping. In Joe's fevered imagination he saw those tentacles of darkness grasping into the grave, seeking the morsel laid out for them. Nadia was screaming, he realized, and clutching at him. He screamed too, and they huddled together in that tenebrous hell, human contact the only comfort available to them.

The world blurred. It took Joe several seconds to realize the sounds had stopped. The darkness was gone. He was shaking uncontrollably, laid out on the ground. Nadia was curled against his side, trembling. He looked around. A few red-eyed shadows were fleeing back to the deep places. Whatever drove them on in their attack had withdrawn.

"Agnes," he rasped.

Joe staggered to his feet and limped to the grave. The waitress-turned-sorceress was slumped against the side of the hole. At her feet was a pit. It opened down into unfathomable darkness. A glimpse into impossible depths. She slid towards it, inch by inch, as the earth crumbled. Joe tore his eyes from it and grabbed the other investigator by the shoulders. He pulled her from the grave with a last surge of strength.

When he looked back, the grave was just a grave. The terrible pit was gone, and only splinters remained of the coffin and its occupant. He looked down at the waitress. She was terribly pale, as though the efforts of the ritual had drained something vital from her.

"Agnes," he whispered, and patted her cheek.

Her eyes blinked open. For a moment they were lost, staring into nothingness. Then she focused on him and took a deep breath.

"Joe."

Nadia had found her feet. She looked around, clearly dazed. "Did we make it?"

Joe coughed. "Seems that way."

"Hell of a thing," the student said.

They dropped her off at the university in the mangled Model T. Agnes and Joe watched as she limped off towards her dorm. She painted a rather horrifying picture of grime and misery. He supposed that all of them did.

"Will you be able to get in?" Agnes called. "You're past curfew."

Nadia glanced back with a lopsided smile. "I'll manage." She held up the hairpin she had used at City Hall.

The waitress laughed quietly and sat back.

"Did it work?" Joe asked as she continued on.

Agnes nodded slowly. "Yeah. I'm pretty sure it did."

Joe managed a tired laugh at that. "'Pretty sure.' Well, I'll take what I can get."

The waitress turned to look at him. "This is twice now, you know. That night with the zealot, and now this. These terrible things, they're going to keep happening. This isn't the end, and we aren't always going to get lucky like this."

Joe thought that over. *Lucky*. Worst part was he knew she was right in that description. Nadia was safe, and both of them were still alive. It could have been a lot worse. For a moment he imagined these events continuing on, time after time. Always desperate, always scared. He sighed deeply.

"You're right," he said. "But all you can do is what you can do. And this time, we saved somebody.

"For now, for tonight, that's enough."

A CHILLING EXCERPT FROM

LITANY
of DREAMS

BY ARI MARMELL

The aromas of life, rich and cloying and congealing in the back of his throat, danced arm in arm with the stink of putrefaction and death.

Wilmott Polaski, a pale and scrawny figure whose element included musty books and dusty shelves, jabbering students and bickering academics – and most assuredly did *not* include copses of thick boughs, glittering eyes peering from the shadows, swarms of insects and waterlogged socks – found himself uncertain as to which collection of scents was worse.

The boots he had hurriedly purchased for this sojourn fit poorly, and his coat was woefully inadequate. Mosquitoes, for which he would have thought the lingering winter chill would be too cold, hovered in thick clouds over the languid waters. Strange birds, or what he assumed to be birds, called in the distance. Ragged moss sagged from tired branches that always seemed to be reaching his way, perhaps attracted to his warmth in lieu of a spring thaw that refused to come.

Did Hockomock have alligators? He didn't think so, couldn't recall ever hearing of such creatures here. With every glance toward the dark and rippling surface, always lapping uncomfortably close to the roadway, however, he grew less and less confident.

In short, the good professor deeply did not wish to be here. With any luck, he wouldn't have to be for long.

Another twenty minutes' walk produced nothing akin to an alligator, nor anything more hostile than those mosquitoes, but it did – finally! – bring into view the community he'd caught the train down from Arkham to find.

If, he observed with some disdain, one could even dignify it with the term.

It had no name, so far as he knew. No fixed borders, no shops, no municipal center or identity. Just a collection of scattered homes and tiny farms huddled on the edge of the Hockomock Swamp, a "community" only in the sense that the several dozen families who lived in these ramshackle domiciles interacted with one another on a somewhat regular basis, and seldomly with anyone else.

The houses were old, rickety, shingles and walls beginning to rot, the supports that held them above the muddy flats and potential floods bowing like the legs of a tired grandfather. While Wilmott heard sporadic sounds of labor in the distance, the striking of tools on wood or wet soil, he saw no one.

Nervously, he dug into his coat pocket, once more checking a bundle of handwritten notes and a hastily sketched diagram. He'd anticipated an unfriendly reception – from Henry Armitage and other fellow academics, he'd heard many a report of just how mistrustful some of these insular Massachusetts communities could be – but somehow the total absence of reception was more disturbing still.

According to his haphazard little map, however, he was still on course. With a sigh he returned the papers to his pocket and continued.

The water of the swamp puddled before him, occupying a shallow dip in the roadway. Mud squelched under his steps, threatening to yank the ill-fitting boots from his blistering feet. Wilmott swallowed a stream of profanity. Damn the useless Arkham police, damn Chester and damn himself for getting caught up in the young fool's endeavors!

He glanced skyward, hoping to estimate the time of day, how long he had to accomplish his self-assigned mission before he had to turn back if he wanted to beat the sunset. The sun, however, skulking behind layers of white cedar branches and fat, ponderous clouds, told him nothing. With more silent cursing, he turned his gaze once again to the path ahead...

Was that it? That house there, hunkered at the very edges of the deeper waters? Its wood sagging, windows sloping like sleep-heavy eyelids?

It could be. To judge by his last look at the map, it should be. Defying the nervous agitation in his gut and drawing himself up to his full, impressive – if woefully spindly – height, Wilmott marched forward and pounded his knuckles on the door.

It shuddered. Paint flecks snowed down to his feet. Nothing more.

Wilmott waited what he judged a polite interval, then knocked again, harder still.

And again.

What to do if nobody was home? Somehow, in all his deliberations about whether to even come, all the time it took him to pinpoint and then reach his destination, he'd failed to consider so basic a hurdle. Perhaps this sort of thing was more complicated than he'd given–

The door finally swung open, with less a creaking than an angry and fiercely startling *crack*, as he raised his fist to try once more. Wilmott found himself staring at a yellowed shirt under frayed denim overalls.

He craned his head upward. An angry, reddened face, covered in the thick stubble of untended weeks, glared down at him.

"What?" The man's voice was as coarse as his chin and cheeks.

Wilmott removed his hat – as much to give himself a second to recover as out of courtesy. "Afternoon. Are you Woodrow Hennessy?"

"Who's askin'?" He spoke with a near-impenetrable drawl; Wilmott, for all his efforts to be kind, couldn't come up with a better term than *backwoods*.

"My name is Professor Wilmott Polaski, from Miskatonic University. I–"

"Got no use for university folk. If you're lookin' for a guide, go back'n ask over in Taunton." The door began to shut.

"No, you don't understand. I'm searching for a missing student. Chester Hennessy."

The door halted.

Taking that as an invitation to continue, Wilmott bulled on. "Chester's been gone for several weeks now, and I'm afraid the authorities have been stymied. I recalled that he'd mentioned you on occasion, and I thought perhaps–"

"Ain't talked to Chester in years. He an' his don't have truck with our side of the family."

Well, *that* wasn't right, not based on what Chester had said. "Mr Hennessy, perhaps if I might come in, we could discuss–"

"I said I don't know. Leave."

And now Wilmott was growing irate, not merely at the constant interruptions but the man's entire attitude. Did he not recognize the seriousness of the circumstances? Was he not concerned for his kin?

Perhaps the man somehow failed to understand. He was, after all, but an uneducated yokel.

"Mr Hennessy, I think perhaps I've failed to make myself clear. Chester is–"

The door opened all the way once more, and while Wilmott might not have been clear, the message conveyed by the pair of steel barrels that now hovered mere inches from his suddenly pallid face was unmistakable.

"Leave!"

Hands rising in sudden terror, one of them still clutching his hat, Wilmott backed away from the shotgun. Sheer luck prevented him from tripping over his own heels, or the rickety steps, as he retreated from the porch. He'd barely reached the roadway when the door slammed, hiding Hennessy – and his weapon – from view. The professor barely even heard it over his pounding heart.

He released a long, shaking breath.

"Well," he muttered. "That could certainly have gone better."

Instinct and rationality both urged him to turn around and leave, to head back to Taunton, check into a hotel for the night and hop aboard the first train back to Arkham in the morning. He'd already gone above and beyond the call of any duty owed a student by his professor.

But the project...

Nor was it merely his own ambitions that made Wilmott hesitate. He knew, absolutely knew as surely as if he'd read it in one of his own textbooks, that Woodrow Hennessy was lying to him.

It wasn't merely the man's behavior, though that, even for so isolated and unfriendly a community as this one, was certainly suspicious enough. It was Chester himself. On one of the rare occasions his relations had come up in conversation at all, Chester had specifically told him that he got on much better with the low side of the family than his parents did.

While "better" didn't necessarily mean "close," it certainly implied a stronger relationship than Woodrow claimed.

Although he turned and walked away from the Hennessy house, although it ran counter to his better judgment, Wilmott Polaski had already made a decision.

He didn't go far. Perhaps a mile at most, distant enough that Hennessy should think him gone, that no random member of the community – not that he'd seen any – would connect the stranger with that particular house.

And there, sitting upon a log at least marginally free of mildews or fungi or other swamp substances, he waited.

He knew the delay would mean stumbling his way back to civilization in the dark of night, at best; and at worst, genuine bodily harm. He deliberately shunted those thoughts aside. He felt himself on the verge of answers, possibly of saving not only his prize student but the project that would cement his own name in the textbooks he so valued.

Night fell, the avian and insectile songs of the Hockomock changed from one chorus to another and Wilmott Polaski shuffled his way back toward the crooked house.

He approached at an angle, wincing as he deliberately set his path through the cold waters, soaked almost to his knees. Should Hennessy open the front door and gaze out through the curtained, drooping windows, he ought to notice nothing amiss. And thankfully the sodden earth rose again around the house proper, if only just, so Wilmott shouldn't have to remain long within the muck.

The back of the place was, if anything, even more dilapidated than the front, whole sections softened with moisture and inner rot. The good professor had to remind himself more than once that such disrepair didn't necessarily reflect a slovenly nature on the part of the inhabitants, that the environment might well seep into the wood, strip the paint, bestow a patina of filth, regardless of all efforts to hold it at bay.

Not that he was *too* terribly inclined to give Hennessy the benefit of any doubt.

Lamplight leaking out from the ill-fitting shutters, and a bright moon glowing through the clouds that had grown thinner as dusk fell, provided just enough illumination for him to get by. Enough to note details of the house that he'd failed to observe earlier, when his focus has been entirely on the front door and the man within.

The most salient of those details was the lower level, beneath the house proper.

It had, perhaps, been constructed at a time when the surrounding waters were a bit lower than today. Standing mostly above ground, it couldn't rightly be called a basement, yet it was too large and structurally sound to be simply an under-floor hollow someone had bricked up. Whether it had existed since the structure was built, or whether someone had added it later, Wilmott wasn't architect enough to say.

Neither could he say with certainty why that lowest level didn't fully match the width of the rest of the house, creating a peculiar combination of partial cellar, partial crawlspace. It wasn't unique to the Hennessy place, either, as he'd seen similar construction on some other homes he'd passed. Perhaps it was to do with the inconsistent earth here at the swamp's edges, with portions solid enough to support construction standing adjacent to others that were far too soft? He didn't know.

He knew only that, beneath the sagging floor and between the wooden supports, stood walls of uneven stones and thick mortar.

A half-sunken cellar certainly felt like a good place for Hennessy to hide his secrets, and, if nothing else, one of its own narrow windows might provide ingress. Crouching low, shuddering at the slick mud beneath his fingers as he scrabbled for balance, Wilmott slid beneath the house's outer edges.

Picking his way between puddles and discarded, rusted tools, biting his lip to keep from exclaiming his revulsion at the cobwebs and skittering bugs, he neared the first of those windows...

"*Isslaach thkulkris, isslaach cheoshash... Vnoktu vshuru shelosht escruatha...*"

It might have been five voices or fifty; he knew only it was more than one. Resonating off one another, echoing in brick-walled rooms, filtered through cracked wood and the natural songs of the swamp, it seemed somehow more than the foreign tongue – or perhaps simple gibberish – that reached his ears.

"*Svist ch'shultva ulveshtha ikravis... Isslaach ikravis vuloshku dlachvuul loshaa... Ulveshtha schlachtli vrulosht chevkuthaansa...*"

On it went, intertwining until he couldn't tell one phrase from the next, and then repeating once more from the beginning.

Over and over as he sat and listened, trying and failing to make the slightest sense of it, growing somehow *heavier* with each repetition even though it never varied in volume. Something about the litany was... off. Unclean. He felt violated, as though something slick had wiggled on the back of his tongue as he swallowed a bite of what should have been a mundane meal. He found himself lightheaded and nauseated, staggering back a few steps from the window as he struggled to restrain his rising gorge.

The handle of the old shovel on which he stepped was rotten most of the way through, but with enough of a solid center to resound like a gunshot when it snapped beneath his foot. Disoriented and now terrified of being discovered, the professor turned and fled, splashing through the swampy waters and into the night, leaving the Hennessy house behind.

The house, but not the ghastly phrases, which now seemed determined to dog his every step.

"*Isslaach thkulkris, isslaach cheoshash... Vnoktu vshuru shelosht escruatha...*"

Two nights later, he returned yet again.

As before, he'd initially intended to flee, and found himself unable. Thoughts of Chester Hennessy and their shared endeavors occupied his waking hours, most of which he spent staring at the walls of his rented room or aimlessly wandering about town. When sleep had finally claimed him, he'd tossed in the grip of horrific nightmares, shivering so violently he'd bolted awake from vistas of frigid ice... howling winds... endless shadow... *something* reaching out for him, stretching, grasping…

And always, asleep or awake, nesting at the back of his mind, winding and twisting and coiling around itself over and over, that abhorrent, damnable verse. Had he been honest with himself, Wilmott would have admitted there was something to the mantra itself, far more than his concern for his missing student or even their endeavors, that kept him here.

Even when preparing his return to the house, however, he never allowed himself to consider it.

This time, thanks to a quick trip to Taunton's shops, he came prepared. A set of screwdrivers and miniature blades sat tucked in a bag at his belt, and he clutched a small lantern in one fist, an iron prybar in the other. Flimsy as the wood was, the last was almost overkill. The window frame scooped away like oatmeal; he could practically have made entry with his bare hands.

Wiggling, grunting, he wormed his way through the window and flopped to the mildewed stone floor, flinching from both the impact and the choking scent.

Only as he picked himself up did he realize that the odd recitation continued, that the people down here, whoever they were, were still repeating their mindless refrain. Up to that point he'd thought the words were merely in his head, as they had been for the past days.

That realization brought with it another wave of disorientation, as if the thought itself made him more susceptible. The hallway tilted around him, splintered in a kaleidoscope of fragments, before pulling itself back together and leaving only dizziness in its wake.

Wilmott staggered forward, one hand on the wall while the other clutched the lantern that now seemed a woefully insufficient source of light. The uneven floor made the vertigo harder to deal with, as broken stones reached up to trip him or sudden dips threatened to topple him. More than once the swamp crept in between the stones at the lowest points, resulting in puddles to splash or, on one or two occasions, even wade through.

Surely the passageway couldn't be this long? It must be his own confusion that had him nigh convinced he'd taken scores of steps already, rather than a mere handful.

When he stumbled yet again, glancing down angrily at his traitorous feet, he discovered it hadn't been the floor that tripped him this time.

The blue-gray of a Postal Service uniform, now tattered, hid most, but unfortunately not all, of the half-stripped skeleton beneath. Nor had it been time, the waters, nor even vermin that had torn away the flesh and tissue. Even through his disorientation, his horror, Wilmott clearly saw the jagged indentations on the bone that could only have been left by human jaws.

He found himself continuing, with only the faintest memory of clambering back to his feet. He couldn't remember at precisely what point he'd collapsed, nor did he recall vomiting, though the acrid taste on his tongue suggested he had.

He thought, too, that he might have seen the remains of other savaged corpses beyond that of the unfortunate postman, had flashing, sporadic images of additional limbs, additional skulls, but once more his memory refused to cling to them well enough to be sure it was anything more than overwrought imagination.

His head ached, the skin uncomfortably tight around his skull. By the time the obvious notion of "Turn back! Get out!" penetrated his feverish mind, he'd already reached the end of the hall.

A cage of some sort, or a makeshift cell. He couldn't seem to focus on it clearly, or at least only bits and pieces stuck in his memory. He recalled stone walls and haphazard iron bars.

He recalled the stench of old sweat, of human filth.

Recalled not the one young man he sought but a small collection of faces, caked in mud and spit and blood and worse, some merely soiled but others subtly misshapen. If Chester had been among them, Wilmott never saw him.

It was from them, from chapped lips and ragged throats, that the alien chorus emerged. Over and over, almost but not entirely in unison so that the words seemed to vibrate in the ear.

"*Svist ch'shultva ulveshtha ikravis…*"

And Wilmott stepped toward them, his empty hand outstretched to tug at the chain and padlock that sealed them in, his own mouth beginning to move, no thought or instinct in his head save to *join them.*

The vicious report of a shotgun, and the patter of stone fragments falling from the buckshot-marred ceiling, shook him from his trance.

In the entryway to a perpendicular hallway Wilmott had previously overlooked in his distraction, stood Woodrow Hennessy. He gripped his weapon in corpse-knuckled fists, and twisted fabric of makeshift plugs protruded from his ears.

"I told you to leave, God damn you!"

Had Wilmott been more together, more himself, he might have heard not only the fury but the horror and grief burdening the man's outburst.

But he was not, and did not. Howling in confusion and in fear, the professor spun and raced back the way he'd come.

He sloshed through pools, stumbled over corpses, scraped his hands as he scrabbled back through the open window. Even in the pitch dark, he only barely remembered to keep hold of his lantern. His thoughts – all those not wrapped up in the litany, endless, pounding – were of escape only. In his panic, then, it seemed to make sense that the monstrous rustic with madmen locked in his cellar would be far less keen to pursue him into the wild than back along the road.

By the time his pounding heart had slowed and his head ceased spinning long enough for him to recognize the downsides of such a plan, he was already hopelessly lost.

Hours passed. Wilmott shivered violently, soaked to the waist. Beneath the dark waters, the mud had finally sucked the oversized boot from his left foot, forcing him to limp with fear that he would step on something piercing, slicing... or biting.

Unnamed creatures shrieked in the distant dark. The swamp rippled in the wake of swimming things.

From the muck below and the cedars all around, limbs snagged at his clothes, at his skin, making him start with frightened cries no matter how tightly he tried to keep his lips shut. Surely they were only branches, roots, vines. Yet in the flickering light of his lantern and in his thoughts – which felt ever warped, ever more sluggish, compressed in some mental vise – he could have sworn he saw them moving, flexing as they reached for him.

And that light itself had begun to fade, its dancing growing ever more frantic, as the flame licked thirstily at the last few traces of oil.

They both flared, then, the firelight and the panic together, in a final burst.

Before him, half-sunk in the swamp, vine-wrapped and coated in slime, was a black stone. He peered at writings carved in an alphabet unlike any he had ever seen before and could not possibly read – and yet which seemed, at some level below the conscious, perhaps even beyond the sapient, familiar. It tugged at him, a sensation that felt as physical as it did emotional. A shiver began at the back of his neck but died before it traveled far, as though his body no longer remembered how to move.

His lantern died, to reveal another source of illumination, coming up through the swamp behind him.

"Professor!" Woodrow Hennessy's voice was hoarse. He must have been calling out for some time. "Professor, can you hear me?"

He stepped into view, water sloshing around his calves. Wilmott Polaski tore his gaze from the stone, advanced toward the newcomer, and responded in the only way he could, with the only words he knew.

"*Isslaach thkulkris, isslaach cheoshash…*"

Hennessy might not have heard him – he still wore the plugs of fabric in his ears, seemed more frightened of what he might hear than of braving the swamp while deafened – but he clearly recognized the recitation all the same.

With a scream of fury, of guilt, of denial, but above all else of fear, he raised the shotgun toward the oncoming professor and fired.

Find LITANY OF DREAMS *in your local gamestore and everywhere books are sold.*

CONTRIBUTORS

By day, EVAN DICKEN studies old Japanese maps and crunches numbers for all manner of fascinating research at the Ohio State University. By night, he does neither of these things. His work has most recently appeared in *Analog, Beneath Ceaseless Skies,* and *Strange Horizons,* and he has stories forthcoming from Black Library and Rampant Loon Press.

evandicken.com
twitter.com/evandicken

GEORGINA KAMSIKA is a speculative fiction writer born in Yorkshire, England, to Anglo-Indian immigrant parents and has spent most of her life explaining her English first name, Polish surname and South Asian features. Georgina is a graduate of the Clarion West Writers Workshop where her first novel, *Goddess of the North,* started life as a short story.

kamsika.com
twitter.com/gkamsika

JOSH REYNOLDS is the author of over thirty novels and numerous short stories, including the wildly popular *Warhammer: Age of Sigmar* and *Warhammer 40,000*. He grew up in South Carolina and now lives in Sheffield, UK.

joshuamreynolds.co.uk
twitter.com/jmreynolds

THOMAS PARROTT lives in middle Georgia, US with his wife and three cats. He is the author of several short stories and novellas set in the *Warhammer 40,000* universe.

DAVIDE MANA was born and raised in Turin, Italy, with brief stints in London, Bonn and Urbino, where he studied paleontology (with a specialization in marine plankton) and geology. He currently lives in the wine hills of southern Piedmont, where he is a writer, translator and game designer. In his spare time, he cooks and listens to music, photographs the local feral cats, and collects old books. He co-hosts a podcast about horror movies, called Paura & Delirio.

karavansara.live
twitter.com/davide_mana

CATH LAURIA is a Colorado girl who loves snow and sunshine. She is a prolific author of science fiction, fantasy, suspense and romance fiction, and has a vast collection of beautiful edged weapons.

twitter.com/author_cariz

DAVID ANNANDALE is a lecturer at a Canadian university on subjects ranging from English literature to horror films and video games. He is the author of many novels in the *New York Times*-bestselling *Horus Heresy* and *Warhammer 40,000* universe, and a co-host of the Hugo Award-nominated podcast Skiffy and Fanty.

davidannandale.com
twitter.com/david_annandale

CHARLOTTE LLEWELYN-WELLS is a bibliophile who took a wrong turn in the wardrobe and ended up as an editor – luckily it was the best choice she ever made. She's a geek and fangirl with an addiction to unicorns, ice hockey and ice cream.

twitter.com/lottiellw

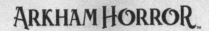

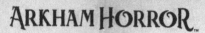

ARKHAM HORROR™

*Mysterious deaths herald the arrival of a
celebrated surrealist painter in Arkham, but
his illusions don't merely blur the boundary
between nightmare and reality – they
threaten to tear it apart.*

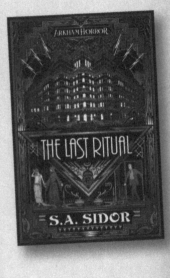

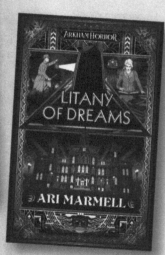

*Dark incantations infest the minds of
students at Miskatonic University, and
the only clue to the mystery of a missing
student is an ancient relic...*

ARKHAM HORROR™

The return of the Arkham Horror
Investigator novellas, collected together
for the first time! Seven explorations of
Arkham's dark side in omnibus editions.

ARKHAM HORROR
DARK ORIGINS
THE COLLECTED NOVELLAS VOLUME 1

DAVE GROSS · GRAEME DAVIS
RICHARD LEE BYERS
CHRIS A JACKSON

ARKHAM HORROR
GRIM INVESTIGATIONS
THE COLLECTED NOVELLAS VOLUME 2

JENNIFER BROZEK
RICHARD LEE BYERS
AMANDA DOWNUM

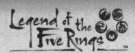

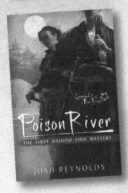

DESCENT
LEGENDS OF THE DARK™

Epic fantasy of heroes and monsters in the perilous realms of Terrinoth.

A reluctant trio are forced to investigate a mysterious city, but in doing so find themselves fighting a demonic atrocity, and a holy warrior is the only hope of salvation from a brutal demonic invasion...

Three legendary figures reunite to solve a mystery but instead uncover treachery and dark sorcery.

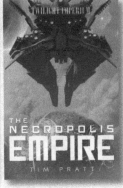

WORLD EXPANDING FICTION

Do you have them all?